NO VISIBLE
MEANS

A Stella Kirk Mystery #1

L. P. Suzanne Atkinson

lpsabooks
http://lpsabooks.wix.com/lpsabooks#

Copyright © 2017 by L. P. Suzanne Atkinson
First Edition — March, 2019

Cover Design by Majeau Designs
Editing by Lesley Carson

ISBN
978-0-9958-6964-6 (Paperback)
978-0-9958-6965-3 (eBook)

1. Fiction, Mystery/Detective-Cozy/General
2. Fiction, Mystery/Detective-Amateur Sleuth
3. Fiction, Mystery/Detective-Female Sleuths

Distributed to the trade by the Ingram Book Company

Table of Contents

...greed is a much more subtle vice than simply the desire to be rich.
Stanley Hauerwas

They say that abandonment is a wound that never heals. I say only that an abandoned child never forgets.
Mario Balotelli

Other works by L. P. Suzanne Atkinson

~Creative Non-Fiction~
Emily's Will Be Done

~Fiction~
Ties That Bind
Station Secrets: Regarding Hayworth Book I
Hexagon Dilemma: Regarding Hayworth Book II
Segue House Connection: Regarding Hayworth Book III
Diner Revelations: Regarding Hayworth Book IV

For David, always

Thank you to Pauline, Wyneth, Kat, Barb, Marguerite and Beverley
for your insights when I needed them most

**Dedicated to my fierce and fabulous friend
Joan E Langille (née Cannady)
1950–2018**
Who reminded me to
"live my life"

CHAPTER 1

She Might Be Sleeping

The pressures of mounting debt, insufficient electricity, and aging water pumps weigh on Stella's mind. Nick's puzzled expression, when he kissed her forehead and returned to the manager's cottage, troubles her as much as deteriorating RV park infrastructure. Reluctant to fall in love again, Stella reminds herself on a regular basis that Nick is nine years her junior and their relationship is likely a lark for him. When he finds a better job, he'll be gone. No need for their affair to be obvious in front of her employees.

Stella Kirk, co-owner of the Shale Cliffs RV Park, sits in the living room of her big house which serves as a staff meeting spot, office, and reception for the seasonal business. Dying embers in the old stone fireplace blink, reminding her of neon lights. She misses her life in the city and yearns for the safety of a regular pay cheque. Her goal was to become an investigative journalist. She has the university degree to prove it. Long before she found an opportunity to climb above the barriers of obituaries and local community events, into the complications of criminal behaviour, the call came from her father. Her mother died. He needed her in the business.

Summer camping season 1980 officially starts tomorrow.

****

The old woman heaves her hefty frame out of the lawn chair to add more split wood to the fire sputtering inside the confines of a rusted truck rim. Sparks jump up to meet her. She turns her face to avoid a sting, as Lorraine Young pulls her 1977 black Malibu in beside the neighbouring trailer. "Helloooo." Mildred attempts a flabby-armed wave when Lorraine slams the car door and walks over to her unit's entry stairs. The greeting goes unnoticed.

Mildred Fox squints through the haze of smoke produced by her smouldering campfire and the Craven A Menthol dangling from her pursed lips. A scarred plastic tumbler holds two inches of cheap scotch disguised as lemonade. It sits on a rusty patio table at her elbow.

Grunting with the effort, she bends to peer at her bare legs and feet, naked below the hem of her signature caftan. She wishes she could find a way to be rid of the purple varicose veins that crawl the length of both calves. She also regrets she didn't remember to make an appointment for a pedicure before her move to the RV park for the summer. Her yellowed toenails are gnarly, even considering her own minimal expectations.

Dusk moves in fast. It's still too early in the season for most people to live full-time out at the beach. They prefer a weekend or a few days at most. It gets cold at night in the middle of May, but Mildred doesn't care. Every year she's anxious to relocate from her subsidized seniors' apartment in town to her broken-down holiday trailer at Shale Cliffs RV Park.

Park owner, Stella Kirk, will be after her to clean up the yard and get her rotten deck fixed. There's not much money, and at eighty, little she is able to do for herself. She pays a guy to move her stuff in his truck, set up her water and power, flush her sewer tank, and check the place over to make sure it survived yet another winter. The trailer is a bright green and white 1956 Cardinal. It's only fifteen feet long and barely has the basics, but it belongs to her. Despite its age, at twenty-four years, her can-on-wheels has served her well. Back in the day, she drove a pickup and pulled it across the country by herself. She and the Cardinal are old friends.

Mildred knows Lorraine won't come out and join her. She's polite enough most of the time but avoids wood smoke so never comes near when Mildred has a fire. Mildred loves her fires and often builds one before noon.

The kitchen light blinks on and then goes out again in the trailer next door. Lorraine probably had a long day at the bank. It's after nine-thirty on the Friday before the Victoria Day weekend. Mildred hopes the young woman had supper with her boyfriend and wasn't at work until this hour.

Each time her thoughts linger on her athletic and petite park neighbour, she remembers her lot in life—old, alone, wrinkled, and spent. On the other hand, Lorraine is advancing her career. She takes good care of herself and, from the sounds of their limited casual conversations, is ready to make a commitment to her boyfriend. *What's his name? Rhymes with heaven—*

2

Kevin. Mildred finds it harder to remember names and places these days. Her mind isn't what it used to be.

Lorraine Young is well known in the park. She's a seasonal resident like Mildred. One major difference between the women, besides the fifty-year age gap, is Lorraine rents her little apartment to tourists or casual workers for the summer. She lives at Shale Cliffs and goes to town each day for work. When she has her two weeks of vacation, Mildred gets to see more of her. They become regular trailer neighbours for a short time.

Lorraine has a reputation. She is very particular. She's fashionable. All her outfits are paired with coordinated shoes and purses. Being security conscious, she keeps her doors and windows locked. Mildred is privy to this because Lorraine replaced the window in the bedroom of her almost new trailer with one designed to lock the second it closes. It has special buttons and can't be accessed from the outside. Mildred isn't sure why Lorraine's afraid someone might break in when she's asleep or away.

Mildred tosses the butt of her cigarette into the fire, readjusts her bottom within the confines of her chair, and reaches for the grubby comforter she wraps herself in when the air starts to turn chilly. She snuggles into her quilt and lights another menthol. Her scotch is gone, but she's done for the night. Sparks jump and sputter. She watches the smoke spiral straight up. There isn't a breath of wind, unusual for this time of year near the ocean. The waves lap on the beach. The tide is on the way out. She wonders why Lorraine didn't wave. She must be preoccupied. Busy girls usually are. The radio says the weekend will be perfect.

****

"Give me a minute."

Stella hears Nick rattle her big old coffee pot before he plays back her answering machine to check for reservations. Stella's upstairs apartment is a one-bedroom unit with a passable bathroom and a functional personalized kitchen. A door off her bedroom gives her access to a small deck from where she can peruse the entire property.

When her parents operated the park, the family lived in the whole house. She and her younger sister, Trixie, had the run of the place. When people registered to stay, they arrived at the front entry and her mother did the paperwork on a miniscule telephone table tucked behind the door. Stella prefers her privacy. Nick has become the exception.

Her empty cereal bowl rattles when it lands in the kitchenette's single stainless-steel sink. Nick will have coffee brewed by the time she gets downstairs. He always does. This weekend will be busy. Most of the seasonal residents are here, moved in, campfires ready to light, and barbecues cleaned. There are a few stragglers who don't manage to get their rigs settled until Victoria Day Monday, but everyone has paid their fees. Stella doesn't care when they decide to show. Although not at full capacity the first weekend of the season, the weather forecast holds promise, and she expects to be at seventy-five percent or better.

Despite her optimism regarding business this summer, money is Stella's biggest worry. She knows the time has come for her to stop resisting and apply for a loan. She wants to upgrade the power and water systems. Most of the fancier parks have full sewer systems installed, but Shale Cliffs RV Park still depends on the honey wagon turning up once a week to pump out the tanks of the seasonal trailers. There's a dumping station for travellers to empty tanks before they take off for parts unknown. The bigger honey wagon cleans out the park tank every few days. For right now, her operation isn't large enough to justify the cost of a built-in sewer system.

"Hey Nick? You're up at the crack of dawn. Can I run an idea by you?"

Nick Cochran is a bean pole at six feet three inches tall. He's American. He came up to Canada during the Vietnam War, worked odd jobs to get by, and stayed. He says he was fine with the draft until somebody handed him a rifle with live ammunition and then expected him to shoot it. He boarded a train to Winnipeg and never looked back. He received a pardon in 1977, and for the first time in years, he went to Florida to visit his parents this past winter. Stella wondered if he'd return. There are other opportunities for a guy with his skills. She has no expectations.

"Have you eaten?"

"Yeah. I had cereal upstairs. Don't worry, Nick. I eat."

"What did you want to discuss?" He pauses for a second and then proceeds with a schedule rundown. "Alice and Paul will be here anytime. I need Paul to help me trim trees and clear out any fallen branches. When Eve arrives, she can mow. I imagine Alice will be ready to man the phone and the front desk. We have our caravan of twelve big rigs expected this afternoon. I want to be ready for them."

"Once Alice gets here, I thought I might walk to Lorraine Young's and talk with her regarding my loan prospects; see what she imagines my chances are. We need to do the power and water upgrades this year."

"Is Lorraine the right person? I understand she wants to be promoted, but currently she's just a teller at the Savings and Loan." Nick sounds doubtful.

"I thought she could give me a few tips—you know—how to deal with the bank manager. You remember, I met with Ruby Wilson once before, but I was undecided and never followed through. My impression was that she's tough." She swallows as she reflects on that initial encounter. "She made me uncomfortable, as if the bank's money was hers." She sighs. "There's one more problem. Trixie will have to sign the papers, too."

"Borrow enough money to buy Trixie out." Nick grins and peers over at Stella. "If I buy her out you'd be rid of her. I have that money from Dad's sister."

"Right…and you're prepared to never get another pay cheque?"

"Not forever but give the idea some thought." He winks and raises one brow. "Your silent investor."

As he pauses and runs his fingers through his hair, Stella struggles with the extent of Nick's commitment and whether accepting his offer is a viable option.

"Now, not to change the subject, but there are three new reservation requests for the weekend. I took the messages off the machine for Alice. One unit arrives today. They have four dogs, but they say they're small."

Her grunt speaks volumes. Small is in the eye of the beholder. The park rule is three small dogs or two big ones. Pets are to be kept on leashes and under control. Many campers are cooperative; others, not so much.

Nick continues. "There are two more units expected Sunday and both want to stay for a week. Alice will need to assign the sites and do the paperwork. I thought you'd want to know. And, as a matter of fact, a loan to upgrade the park systems is a good idea, despite the thirteen percent interest rates. People can't afford to stay in hotels and eat out. Camping is the one option folks have to take their kids on a holiday." He leans over to pat her hand. "You'll be fine. Talk to Lorraine if you think it will help, but don't forget to keep Trixie in the loop."

His hand lingers for a moment and Stella reacts to his touch with a flush on her cheeks she's unable to disguise. "As long as Trixie gets her cut every month, she doesn't care. I don't want her to pitch in around here, but I wish she visited Dad more often." Stella meets Nick's eyes, but then checks her watch. "The staff will be here any minute. We might as well get started."

****

Alice and Paul Morgan tumble in the front door of the main house. They chatter and laugh as they push each other to arrive first. Both are redheads. Alice is twenty and Paul is a year younger although they resemble twins. Alice has worked for Stella every summer since she graduated from high school. She is very organized. She can have two people on hold on the phone, remember their concerns or questions, and check somebody in to the park at the same time. Stella never pretends to be as good in reception as Alice. She's happy to be Alice's back-up, but Eve Trembly is also becoming comfortable at the front desk.

Paul came on board a year ago when he decided he wanted steadier work than mowing lawns for the neighbours. He likes handyman chores and completes tasks for residents and travellers when they need help—a deflated tire, a broken window seal, a leaky faucet, or an awning that doesn't roll as expected. Stella wants her seasonals and overnight guests to be comfortable and realize her employees are there to assist. Paul is great with people.

Eve is Stella's newest hire. She's eighteen and starts university in the fall. She wants to become an accountant and can handle any piece of machinery she's given. Eve is short, compact, and tough. The tallest part of her is the raven black and wavy hair piled in a big and tangled topknot. She never stops. If not assigned a specific task, she scours the lawns for garbage or cleans out abandoned fire pits where campers have deposited cardboard instead of using the bins provided. She's a keeper.

The employees gather in the kitchen to grab a cup of coffee and discuss expectations for the day. Nick takes the lead. He and Paul will trim tree branches and Eve will mow. There is always an area requiring the services of the mower. Alice takes her post in reception. Everyone is excited because of the dozen units from Ontario expected mid-afternoon.

****

Once the staff is directed, Stella pours yet another cup of coffee and begins her trek toward Lorraine Young's rig, and the cliffs overlooking the water.

Stella knows Lorraine is always up with the birds on the weekend. Since she is one of those seasonal residents who commute into town to work each day, she doesn't waste a minute when she has days off.

Stella lifts her nose and sniffs the air. Late spring has its own scent. It settles between fresh earth recently turned in the flower beds, and Forsythia bursting on to the scene. Despite how annoyed she gets with the struggles to keep the business afloat, and the occasional wishful imaginings about her previous life, she begrudgingly admits there aren't many other places she'd rather be.

Shale Cliffs RV Park, and the nearby town of Shale Harbour, are the only real destinations on this little spit of land connected to the mainland of Nova Scotia by a natural causeway. The isthmus is one lane of sand and dunes held together by sea grasses. On most days, cars can travel to and from with no problem, but there are occasions when high tide and bad weather conspire to cover the road and render the area a true island. Stella remembers an occasion when she was a kid and they were stuck on the Shale Harbour side for a week.

Part of the quaint character of the community, and the RV park, is the possibility you might get marooned if a storm comes up. This atmosphere is fine for charm and tourism but can be a challenge if a resident needs a hospital. They have one doctor in town, but even doctors want a vacation. He tries to hire a physician to cover for him. It doesn't always happen.

Lorraine's trailer is a 1978 version of a Rambler. She bought it from a Savings and Loan client who defaulted on their payments. She took over the loan. It stands to reason, since she works at the bank and interest rates are atrocious, but the story is pure gossip. No one knows for sure. It's big, at twenty-seven feet long, and is neat as a pin. She has a flower bed on either side of the front window that faces the cliffs and out to sea.

A glance over toward Mildred Fox's place reminds Stella she wishes her regulars were more like Lorraine. Stella notices how the black Malibu isn't snuggled in beside the trailer as is most often the case but parked at a slight angle. Lorraine's boyfriend might have driven home with her and handled the parking.

Coffee cup in hand, she climbs the wooden steps built for Lorraine by Paul last year and knocks on the outside door. No answer. She raps louder and manages to get a rise out of Mildred, who lumbers out of her trailer to check and see what's making the noise.

"I saw her come home last night. It was late. Maybe she's sleepin' in."

If her boyfriend is there, then the old lady could be right, but Stella's doubtful.

"Should I tell her you're wantin' to talk to her, if she shows her face to the sun today?"

"Thanks, Mildred. You're right. She might be sleeping."

****

Each staff member arrives at the main house for lunch around the same time. The downstairs kitchen is well stocked. The employees make sandwiches, have soup if it's cold outside, drink tea or coffee, and have a piece of fruit and a cookie. Stella wants them to be comfortable and relaxed. Most often, each person works alone on an assigned task. This way, they take their break times together. The whole point of turning the main floor of the house into an accessible area for her staff was this comradery.

Ham and cheese sandwiches will be the option for everyone. There's lots of lemonade and oatmeal cookies. She has a bowl of strawberries in the fridge. Stella and Alice have lunch ready to serve when Nick, Paul, and Eve turn up.

Everyone chatters. She sits back and watches as the kids and Nick hoe into the grub. Someone turns on the little clock radio she keeps in the kitchen and The Beach Boys belt out their latest hit. Other than the immediate need for an influx of cash to secure those improvements, the status of the park and her employees is better than ever. She hopes Mildred sees Lorraine before the day's over. Maybe she has, in fact, slept in.

CHAPTER 2

People Have Started to Worry

She drags on her signature park work attire of blue jeans, a T-shirt, and an oversized blouse left unbuttoned. Today, Stella has chosen pink and white stripes to flatter her complexion and brighten her mood. She examines her form in the mirror, self-conscious as usual of her pencil-like figure now compromised by advancing age. Her waist and hips show little differentiation. The flowing top serves to camouflage this fault with which she has been saddled for her entire adult life. Her form is more masculine with long legs as her most valuable asset. She slides bare feet into leather sandals and clatters down the worn wooden stairs to the promise of coffee and Nick's morning company.

"Too early to talk work?" Nick chuckles when he hands her a steaming mug of java brewed to perfection and doctored just the way she prefers.

"You're back here in a hurry. At least I'm showered and dressed."

"No matter if you weren't," he teases as he holds up a loaf of homemade multi-grain bread picked up at the Farmers' Market the day before. "Toast?"

"Sure." Stella blushes. They rarely discuss their relationship and today will be no exception. "What's on your mind? It's Sunday. Our fleet of Class A rigs are settled in for the week. My family is coming for a barbecue at lunch. You promised to help." Her tone accuses and teases. "What's on your mind this morning?"

"I need to change each of the filters on the water system, Stella. I thought we could put the job off because we're gonna upgrade this summer if you find the money, but it won't wait. I noticed iron deposits on the fixtures in the public washrooms. I left Eve a special cleanser to clean them when she goes through the bathrooms today, but those filters are in bad shape."

She understands he's worried because of spending cash she doesn't have, so Stella's voice exudes patience. "No problem, Nick. There are a few new filters in the back room. If you change them this week, it'll take the pressure off me before my appointment at the bank. Buys me time." She sighs. "I wonder if Lorraine is home. I want to talk with her. See if she might be able to provide any helpful hints as to how I should play nice with Ruby." She reaches for the toast Nick hands her from across the table. "Thanks, big guy. You're the best." She grins. Her expression is soft.

"I'll start at five tomorrow morning and change them before anybody needs the water."

"Okay. Great. Now, I expect the staff soon. Everybody has their work cut out for them. The place will be busy by ten. My family should be here around eleven. Lots to do. You'll still man the cooker?"

"No problem. Has your sister planned to pick up Norbert, or do you want me to taxi your dad?"

Sadness washes, unchecked, across Stella's face. "Nick, I'm not sure he'd recognize you anymore. I hope Dad will go in the car with Trixie." She sighs. "The manor staff will remind him Trixie's his daughter. He can be sharp as a tack in certain matters and then he'll forget the point of a conversation completely."

Norbert Kirk's dementia came on like a freight train following the death of his wife five years ago. If one's mind consists of rooms with many areas for different uses, Norbert's rooms suddenly became inaccessible. Doors and windows are locked now. He doesn't recall recent events. His long-term memory isn't much better. In an unusual turn, his ability to think critically has not been impaired. This serves to make for eventful discussions. He's happy enough at the care home. On any occasion when an event upsets him, he forgets it right away. Stella and Trixie trust the caregivers to provide for his needs.

****

The park hums with activity. Alice arrives sharply at nine, her brother Paul in tow. They chose to dress in matching bright green Shale Cliffs RV Park T-shirts today. Cute. Alice immediately opens the office and checks the answering machine. Paul and Nick decide to paint the outside walls of the public bathrooms. Instead of waiting for a repair man, Nick says he will attempt to fix a temperamental washer in the laundromat. When Eve rolls in on her Honda 50 scooter, she grabs her cleaning supplies and marches her way to the bathrooms without having to be asked.

Later in the morning, before Stella finds an uninterrupted path toward the documents she expects to require for a potential banking appointment, Trixie's 1970 Volkswagen Microbus trundles into the driveway on the private side of the house.

Stella watches her family disembark from the red and cream vehicle parked askew with one wheel wedged unceremoniously up on the lawn. Trixie represents the image Stella used to think she wanted to be—short and curvy with long blond hair—the quintessential girly-girl. She dresses in coordinated outfits with cute high-heeled sandals and big jewellery.

Trixie was married to Brigitte's father for a couple of months before her daughter was born. When she left him, she returned to her parents' home here at the park until after she gave birth to her baby when she was twenty. At the time, Stella had graduated from journalism school and was deep in the process of trying to advance her career in a challengingly male-dominated field.

Brigitte and her two-year-old toddler, Mia, clamour out of the back seat while Trixie holds the door for Norbert. Their father is relatively spry but has to be supervised or he will put his hand on a hinge at the wrong time or not notice where he's placed his feet. Stella smiles when she sees Mia; such an angelic little girl. She might have risked parenthood if guaranteed a child with Mia's temperament and personality.

Names tell a story. When Mia was born two years ago, Brigitte made sure everyone was aware she planned to name her daughter after the movie star, Mia Farrow. The name is suitable until you understand Trixie named Brigitte after Brigitte Bardot. Mothers and daughters closely resemble one another. Stella looks very different. A person might assume one or the other sister, or even both, were adopted. Knowing Dorothy Kirk would clarify the mystery. Trixie, Brigitte, and Mia are each reflections of their mother in some way. As Stella observes their arrival, she wonders how she ended up related to this bunch. Stella drew the short straw, in her mind, and resembles her father rather than the beautiful and very dramatic Dorothy Kirk.

While they get organized, Stella requests Alice contact Nick on the walkie-talkie and ask him to come up to the house. Paul will continue to paint until lunch is ready. Food and drinks are assembled. Fresh buns cool on the counter and salads are made. There is a vegetable tray and fruit with dip. There's ice cream. Steaks are marinating. Wine and soda sit chilled in the big downstairs fridge.

Everyone makes for the veranda and then they collapse into the Victorian wicker scattered randomly toward the side and Stella's private entrance.

"You got him here." She touches Trixie's arm to signal her thanks for picking up their father.

"Not easy." Trixie removes a pair of hundred-dollar sun glasses and tosses them on the wobbly coffee table. "Dad forgot who I was, but an attendant convinced him to climb into the van." She leans closer to Stella. "He whispered to the orderly he was being kidnapped by scruffy, drug-crazed hippies. I reminded him the one quality I do not possess is scruffiness!" She pokes Stella in the ribs and giggles.

There are occasions when Stella wishes they were friends. She examines the sunglasses again. Trixie has yet another new man. She works as a part-time receptionist at the local fish plant. There is no way, between her employment and the twelve thousand a year Stella pays her to reflect her share of the business after expenses, for her to afford such luxuries.

"I'm glad you brought him, Trixie. We likely won't be able to do this for much longer. Each time we take him out somewhere, his memory is worse. We should visit him at the manor more, instead."

"Well, you know how reliable I am. I'd send Brigitte and Mia, but he doesn't recognize them from rocks in a bag. They are strangers to him even if he sees them on a daily basis."

"Let's talk before we start lunch, okay? It's business."

"Remember what I told you, Stella. Pay me my thousand a month and do whatever you think best." She grunts. "I don't need to tell you I hate this place. Not interested, and never will be."

"I understand, but I may ask you to sign papers and I wanted to give you a head's up. Let's fix everybody a drink and then talk."

"Let me help." Nick emerges from around the corner and climbs the stairs to the veranda. "Hi, Norbert. You look especially fit today. How ya doin'?"

"Well, hello there, Nick Cochran, my old friend. Are you camping here this weekend?"

Nick steals a glance at Stella and winks. "No, I work for your daughter, Norbert. Been here a couple of years, now." He pats Norbert's shoulder as he turns toward Brigitte. "Hi. Can I fetch you or the baby a drink? I'm gonna search for a cola for myself."

As usual, he has the situation well in hand. Stella nudges Trixie and they proceed to the office.

"You two act cozy, Stella. What's up? He's way younger than you." A giggle tumbles out of her pink and pouty mouth. "Don't get your hopes up, old girl. That fella's more Brigitte's type."

"He's nine years younger." She knows her response unintentionally reveals her sensitivity.

"What? You and Nick? No!" She gushes, as only Trixie can. She throws the back of her hand against her forehead in a simulated swoon. "Say it isn't so! Enjoy him while he sticks around. I'm dating a new man, too, but he's my age and boring compared to this, for God's sake!"

More will not be revealed to her overly dramatic sister as Stella anxiously changes the subject. "I am off to the bank on Tuesday to try to wangle a loan for power and water system upgrades, Trixie. I'll need your signature on the paperwork."

****

Nick manages the barbecue. Norbert eats with hearty abandon as he thanks his family at regular intervals and reports how he is delighted "you strangers" came to Nick's for lunch and invited him to join in.

"Learning to live with the issue is the hardest part," Stella reminds Trixie, who more easily becomes frustrated with their father's condition.

"You are hereby declared our go-to person from now on regarding Dad, Nick. He remembers you more than anybody else." Trixie conveniently removes herself from the hook that is her filial responsibility.

Park duties resume. Eve finished her clean-up of the public bathrooms and has gone on to weed flower beds. Paul continues to paint. Nick offers to drive Norbert home.

"Do you want to walk with me to Lorraine Young's trailer, Trixie? I made one attempt to reach her yesterday. Mildred Fox said she would tell Lorraine to find me if she ever showed her face. I guess she didn't."

"She might be away for the weekend."

"I can't figure out where she'd go. She rents her apartment out for the summer. We're in the middle of a holiday. The park is where she wants to spend her time. I wonder what she's up to?"

"Does she have a boyfriend?"

"Yes. Kevin Flores. He works at the lumberyard. Besides, Lorraine's car is in the yard. Will you walk with me?"

"Sure. Do I need flat shoes?" Trixie looks at her fussy heeled sandals with the rhinestone trim.

"You'll be fine. The road is paved on the way." Stella expels a small gust of air and fails to hide her impatience with Trixie's fashion preoccupation—and she knows the damned road is paved!

As always, the walk through the RV park takes significantly longer than one might predict. Users, both seasonal and temporary, are anxious for a few words with the owner.

"Can I make a flower bed in front of my trailer?"

"Yes, you may make a flower bed. Stay on your lot only."

"My neighbours use my lot as their own personal shortcut. Their dog comes and sits on my deck."

"I'll tell the people next door that their dog has to be on a leash and they need to walk on the road."

"We want to camp here one more week."

"Go to the office and talk to Alice for a stay extension. You may have to move to another site if she has a reservation where the people arriving specified this one."

"My picnic table needs replacing."

"Report your table to Alice and she'll tell Nick or Paul to deliver a new one."

"I admire your patience. Honest to God, I wouldn't be able to avoid punching one of these happy campers by the time I walked from one end of the park to the other." Trixie sputters her annoyance.

Her sister's assessment is correct, and Stella laughs out loud. Trixie does not possess the temperament to be part of the park's operations. "I try to take a walk around every day. Might as well face the music. There are always complaints and anxieties, but compliments, too. I meet great people."

"It's all yours."

As they approach Lorraine's lot, Mildred Fox emerges from her trailer. The picture presented reminds Stella of a pet confined to a cage that's way too small. She fills the little doorway of the Cardinal. Her turquoise caftan threatens to become tangled in the stairs as she holds the casing during her less than graceful exit. "She ain't around, Stella. I been keepin' an eye out."

"Do you think her car was moved, Mildred?"

"Nope. Haven't seen Lorraine, the boyfriend, or anybody since I saw her come home late Friday night."

"You remember my sister, Trixie." Stella attempts to exercise manners likely wasted on Mildred.

"Yeah, I recall from when you were kids. You were the bratty one."

"Thanks, Mildred. Nice to see you, too." Trixie turns to Stella and adds, "So where the hell's Lorraine? She came home Friday night and has been inside ever since?"

"There was no answer when I knocked yesterday." Stella is reluctant to bang on the door, but Lorraine could be unconscious, or worse.

Trixie marches over to the trailer, climbs the stairs, and bangs loud enough to be heard across the park. "Lorraine, open up! People have started to worry. Are you sick, or what?"

No response. She shields her eyes with a delicate hand, manicured to perfection, and tries to peek in the side window. Stella knows any attempt is fruitless. Lorraine always keeps her curtains tightly closed.

Mildred is plunked in her lounger. "You gals want a drink? It's after two. I guess I can open the refreshments." She winks at Trixie. Larger-than-necessary dentures protrude out from behind chapped lips. "I still think she left with her boyfriend. He coulda parked his car at the office and they walked up the road without me seein' 'em."

"I'll call Kevin after I return to the house. Something is making me uncomfortable. Does anybody keep a key to her place?"

"Maybe," Mildred frowns. "The boyfriend might." She heaves her body out of the chair and lumbers up the steps to her trailer.

"I guess she went to find that drink." Trixie turns toward the road.

"Well, so much for learning the inside scoop on Ruby Wilson. I hoped Lorraine would give me a few tips on how to impress her. Apparently, she's a hard nut to crack, and although I've met her before, I haven't done any serious business with the woman."

Trixie waves off Stella's concerns. "You'll be fine. I'll sign whatever papers they want. You could borrow a couple extra thousand for me. What d'ya think?" She wobbles slightly on her heels as she says this and catches Stella by the elbow.

Stella hopes her sister's remarks are in jest, and she doesn't expect more money out of the park. She keeps her worries to herself.

****

Trixie and her troop leave for home. Nick returns from the manor. He delivered her father and is now in the pump house ensuring he has the supplies required to change the filters in the morning. Stella retreats to her office to call Lorraine Young's boyfriend, Kevin Flores.

"Hi. Is Kevin there?" She's never met the guy, but the phone is, thankfully, listed in his name. There could be a roommate or two though.

"This is Kevin. Who's this?"

"Hi, Kevin. This is Stella Kirk, at the Shale Cliffs RV Park, where Lorraine Young has her trailer for the summer."

"Is Lorraine okay? I haven't seen her this weekend." His voice sounds concerned, but hesitant, too.

"We were wondering if she's with you, Kevin. Her car's in the yard. Her neighbour saw her arrive home late Friday night, but her place is locked up with the curtains closed, and we can't get a rise out of her."

His breath comes in short gasps. "She ain't here. She worked on Friday, but said she'd visit me yesterday. She never showed. I was gonna drive to the park, but I figured she must be dating another guy—Mark Bell at the bank. He's real smart, like her. They work lots together."

Stella forces her voice to remain calm and asks, "Do you hold a key for her, Kevin?"

"God, no! Lorraine has never given me a key to her place! I might put a cup in the wrong spot when she's not there." He pauses and catches his breath. "Sorry, I don't want to sound mean, but everybody knows Lorraine is crazy fussy. I try not to take it personal."

Mounting anxiety hides beneath her words. "She's certainly particular, Kevin. She must have been preoccupied when she arrived home because her car is parked crooked. Not her way, for sure."

"Should I come to the park? What can I do to help?"

"To be honest, Kevin, I don't know." Stella sighs. "I think one of her neighbours has a key and I need to find out who. There's a plausible explanation for this." She tries to sound certain, for his sake.

CHAPTER 3

Facts, Not Conjecture

By Tuesday morning, with the busy long weekend behind her, Stella waits to schedule a meeting with Ruby Wilson at the Savings and Loan. Her elbows are planted on the wooden kitchen table in her upstairs apartment. She watches with impatience as the wall clock above the refrigerator clicks steadily toward ten.

She could have opted to take Norbert's old Jeep and driven to town. She could have angle parked in front of the bank and waited until the assigned employee unlocked the plate glass entry door. She could have been on the step, but she doesn't want to look anxious. Ruby Wilson may not even be working today. She might be on vacation. It's stupid to sit in the car, or worse yet, stand in the cement alcove beside the entrance, wait, and then discover Ruby is away. Better to call and not appear desperate.

Ever pragmatic and independent, Stella resents the concept of a loan. The added responsibility, and the anticipated pressure of payments create an uncomfortable sensation in the pit of her stomach. If she knew Ruby, the nausea might disappear.

Did Lorraine go to work? When she drove around the park at seven this morning, to check on the status of garbage cans and fire pits, the Malibu was still parked in the same spot. There has been no sign of her since Mildred saw her arrive home Friday evening. No sign and no explanation. A conversation with Lorraine, focused on bank business with Ruby, is no longer her number one priority. Locating Lorraine has become the focus.

If she wasn't forced to pay Trixie a thousand dollars every month, her financial stress would evaporate. With a five-month season, she needs to realize twenty-four hundred dollars in each of those months to make their arrangement work. She sighs. At the time she took over the park from her father, the monthly cheques were the lesser of two evils. She was in no position to buy Trixie out, especially with interest rates both then and now.

"Click, click." The sound of the second hand on her mother's old kitchen clock creeps into her consciousness and alerts her to the time.

"Shale Harbour Savings and Loan. How may I help you?"

"I want to make an appointment with Ruby Wilson if she's available to discuss loan options."

"No problem! Please hold while I check her book." The singsong voice disappears, and the line sounds dead. "Hi, I'm back. Ruby says she can see you at eleven. Your name?"

"Sure. This is Stella Kirk from the Shale Cliffs RV Park. I'll be there. Tell me, is Lorraine Young at work today? May I speak to her for a moment?"

"Sorry. Lorraine isn't in yet. She's not on holiday, but she's not here. Sorry," she repeats.

"Thanks for the appointment. See you in an hour."

Stella wanders downstairs. "Alice," she calls to the young woman parked behind the reception desk. "I'm off downtown in a few minutes. Are there items on the supplies list I can pick up?"

Alice, her red curls fanned out around her face creating an Elizabethan collar effect, pokes her head out of the tiny front office with a list on yellow foolscap clutched between her fingers. "We need more registration cards. The printer said they'd be ready today. I ordered them a week ago because I figured we'd run out." She beams at her boss. "We also need a few groceries for the downstairs kitchen because we managed to go through a pile of food this weekend."

"Every detail organized as usual, Alice. I could not manage without you."

Before Alice answers the ringing phone, she first replies to Stella, "You'd have no grub and no reservation records, for sure." She giggles. "Shale Cliffs RV Park. This is Alice. How can I help you?"

The screen bangs behind Stella as she emerges on to the veranda. The day has warmed considerably. She rethinks the jeans she dragged on earlier.

****

"Got a minute?"

As Stella hoists her butt in the direction of the cracked leather seat of the old Jeep, Duke Powell trundles into the space between the open vehicle door and her extended leg. His yappy little Pomeranian planks a pair of dusty paws, with aggressive firmness, on her calf. "What's on your mind, Duke? I'm on my way to town for an appointment. Can Alice help you today? Hi, Kiki." She addresses the dog to see if a measure of attention will shut the mutt up.

Obviously distracted from the task at hand, Duke tugs on the leash and hisses at her to be quiet. In a bizarre turn, Kiki obeys. "Easy weekend. Everybody behaved themselves. I thought those folks in the big rigs might make noise after eleven, but they settled."

Duke Powell handles after-hours security for Stella. He gets his site for free and in exchange, he drives around the park on a golf cart. He closes and locks the gate around ten o'clock each evening and reopens it at six-thirty in the morning. He manages any noise complaints, reminds people not to leave their lots with open liquor, corrals visitors still in the park after ten PM and escorts them to the main gate, notes if fires are unattended, and ensures there's quiet after eleven.

John is his given name, but he prefers Duke, as in John Wayne. Unlike John Wayne, Duke is short and stocky. He puffs his chest out to appear authoritative, but his fashion sense of Madras plaid shirts and stripped Bermuda shorts, along with his fluffy little dog, serve to undermine his attempts. His slicked-back hair and stubble-covered cheeks do not enhance the picture. Eve and Alice have mentioned more than once how creepy he is, but he does his job every day for five months, and the cost to the business is a site with a view.

"Here's the question, Stella. What's up with Lorraine Young? Has she gone away, or what? I saw her Friday. I was on my way out to lock the gate when she drove in, but I've seen neither hide nor hair of her since then. I spoke with her neighbour, Mildred. Well, Mildred saw her Friday night and hasn't seen her again, either. Do you know where she's at?"

"Duke, thanks for the good job over the long weekend. No, I haven't seen Lorraine. She's a big girl and has a private life. I'm sure she's fine." Stella will not share her worries with Duke. She has accused Duke, on occasion, of hanging around near Lorraine's trailer too often.

"I might go to her site and knock on her door. She could be sick."

She nods and starts the engine, unsure how to respond. "Talk to you later, Duke. I'm certain Lorraine is fine." *She has to be fine.*

****

The short drive into Shale Harbour allows Stella time to review her pitch for a loan from the bank. Interest rates are high. She can afford no more than a few hundred dollars in monthly payments so will not borrow a large amount. Her hands are sweaty as she clutches the wheel.

When Stella turns the corner and follows the two-lane highway as it parallels the ocean, the hometown she has always loved emerges. The first image is of the wide commercial dock where more than twenty fishing boats are tied in neat rows. There are people here she has known forever. She waves. They yell greetings. The water twinkles in the way a calm ocean does when blankets of diamonds are created by the mid-morning sun.

Her signal light clicks in a familiar rhythm as she navigates the Jeep onto the main thoroughfare of the tourist town. There are no brick buildings here. There are no asphalt parking lots or street lights. The bank, a Federal style and former eight-bedroom residence built in 1820, is located halfway along the narrow roadway. The building has been the Shale Harbour Savings and Loan since she was a child. Painted a bright salmon colour, the square two-story affair, with its four windows and front door across the lower level and five symmetrical windows across the top floor, is a stunning and aristocratic element in the community's tiny downtown. A deteriorated widow's walk sits on the roof. Although she has never been up there, Stella imagines a full view of the harbour entrance from the top.

There are no parking spaces. Cars are pulled off to the side, between driveways. She parks the Jeep further past the bank. Most drivers try to avoid blocking front walks, but tourists are another story. On numerous occasions, Stella has seen a vehicle parked halfway up on the lawn of one of the little businesses situated on the street.

She climbs out and glances at her watch. Enough time to stroll back to the bank. The first retail shop she passes is the weaver's house, a pale blue Victorian with white trim. Mrs. Carlyle is older than Stella. After her husband died, she renovated the downstairs, except for the kitchen, into her weaving studio and she has her private rooms above, similar to Stella's home in the RV park.

Then she approaches "Cocoa and Café", the converted carriage factory. A young couple from Toronto turned the property into a café last winter. Stella doesn't know them well, but hopes to stop by soon with park brochures, which she will exchange for any of their advertising she can display in her reception.

This is how they work together in Shale Harbour. Each business—the jewellery shop where exquisite pieces are created from sea glass found at the bottom of the cliffs, the library which is tucked inside the yellow farmhouse further up the street, the local community hall and playhouse situated around the corner, the hotel anchored at the end, or the pub plunked out on the wharf— shares local information with tourists who fill their streets throughout the summer. When winter closes in, many pack up and move south, but there are the faithful and stalwart few who remain. Stella considers herself among this number; those who face the icy elements in Shale Harbour. They are the residents who risk the ocean's wrath and take the chance the isthmus remains accessible to the mainland.

The clock on the centre chimes eleven. She senses her heart thump an anxious rhythm and admonishes herself on the way in the door. *The worst result is you don't get the loan. If that happens, you can use savings to do the water this year and power the next. There's always Nick's offer to invest. You have options. Relax!*

****

Of course, as the bank's exterior reflects the historical significance of such a majestic home, the inside resembles banks everywhere. The floors are stone. There are three wickets on the left, a row of seating by the windows at the front on the right, and the manager's office further away. Shale Harbour is a small town. The Shale Harbour Savings and Loan mirrors the size. The manager handles business loans—and Ruby Wilson is the manager.

As Stella sets foot on the cool slate, she catches a glimpse of Ruby, standing at her office entrance. She is leaning up against the door frame, eyes fixed on Stella. They both nod.

For a second, her teeth grind, but Stella lifts her chin and squares her shoulders. She approaches Ruby and extends her hand. "Good morning. I think I saw you at the last play in the community centre. I believe we spoke for a moment there, right?"

"Correct, but that was weeks ago. You never come into the bank, Stella."

The remark sounds accusatory. "Oh, I wander in on occasion, but often I send my assistant to make deposits." The reference to Alice as an assistant gives her an instant promotion. "I always have other tasks on my 'to do' list." *There. Do I sound busy and important?*

"Take a seat. What can we do for you today?" Ruby Wilson navigates around her office toward the chair behind her desk. She balances one palm on the corner and limps as she makes her way. The chair is leather—expensive, but with obvious mileage. The desk is a fake wood contraption that's seen better days, too. Ruby, on the other hand, is dressed to the nines in a navy business suit consisting of a tight skirt and a jacket with a bottom flare—just enough to accent her tiny waist. Pale pink manicured nails brush across a professionally coiffed hairdo that does not require a check.

"First off, Ruby, is Lorraine Young here today?"

"No. Why do you ask?"

"Well, she came home Friday. Her neighbour saw her. My security guy spotted her on the camp road quite late that evening. In any event, no one has laid eyes on her since." Stella wants Ruby to understand there may be an issue. "Her boyfriend had no contact over the weekend. We thought she went off with a friend for a few days, but expected her to be here for work today."

Ruby starts to fiddle with a pen on her desk. "Oh, my! She hasn't shown up yet. I assumed she was sick. If she didn't get here by noon, I planned to call your place and ask you or one of your staff to go and check on her. What do you suppose has happened?"

"Her car's in the yard—parked crooked for Lorraine—but there, nonetheless. If she doesn't come to the bank soon, we'll ask each of her neighbours if anybody has a key."

"I will call the police at noon if she isn't here by then."

"Okay. Good idea, Ruby. I'm so worried, I forgot the reason for my appointment. I came to see if there's any possibility I might apply for a business loan. Our water and power systems desperately require upgrading." Anxiety compels an explanation. "We get a higher number of big RVs each year. They need space and consume lots of power with their air conditioners and microwaves. There's a multi-unit caravan in the park right now. Anybody else with a Class A unit must be refused if they appear without a reservation. My power won't handle any more." Stella stops to take a breath.

"What are your expenditures, Stella? How much will the projects cost?"

"My park manager has estimates completed, and I brought them with me. We calculated that ten thousand might get us where we need to be." She leans back into the wooden office chair placed in front of Ruby's desk. Mental exhaustion overwhelms her.

"Let me examine your figures. In the meantime, take home the application and answer the questions." Her voice becomes robotic as she spouts the rehearsed requirements. "We need a copy of your latest financial statements and a report of your anticipated expenses and payroll over the next five months. In addition, I want to assess your reservation numbers and see an estimate of what kind of year you expect this will be. Drop the paperwork off to me when it's completed. Once I do a review and speak with my regional manager, I'll schedule another appointment for you to stop by and we'll finalize the details. If my understanding is correct, you are not a sole owner."

"No. My sister owns half the park but does not get involved with operations."

"Trixie must co-sign if your loan is approved."

"Yes, we understand. She said she will agree to the loan."

"Good." Ruby glances at the clock. "Why don't I call the police while you're here? This way, we can both tell them what we know, or in this case don't know, regarding Lorraine's whereabouts." She eyes Stella. Her expression is conspiratorial, and her voice becomes a whisper. "The police should talk with Mark Bell, too. I have been observing Mark and Lorraine. They are quite cozy. I bet he has an idea where she is."

"I thought she was involved with Kevin Flores." Stella doesn't let on she has talked to Kevin, or that he referenced a guy at the bank. Facts, not conjecture. She can't remember who gave her this advice. "As far as the loan, I will endeavour to get the paperwork to you as soon as I can. Let's focus on Lorraine."

While Stella remains rigid in the uncomfortable chair, Ruby calls the local detachment of the RCMP. Stella listens to Ruby's side of the conversation, where she explains what they assume are the facts. She says Lorraine left the bank on Friday at five in the afternoon. Lorraine's departure at the end of the work day comes as a surprise to Stella. Ruby goes on to say how Lorraine didn't return to Shale Cliffs RV Park until shortly before ten that night. Everyone assumed she was at work until late because she wasn't out with her boyfriend. As Ruby talks, she confirms observations with Stella, who prefers to tell her own story. She abdicates the role of the informer to Ruby since they are seated in the woman's office.

"The owner of the RV park assumes one of her neighbours has a key. She will determine who this person might be once she leaves town and returns home. Correct, Stella?"

Stella nods.

"Yes, she will try to find out right away. Okay, I will tell her your instructions. If you need any more information from me, I am here at the branch for the day. Thank you, Sergeant."

Ruby turns her attention back to Stella. "Sergeant Moyer says once you determine whether there is a key to her property, you are to call him. You are not to enter her home without the RCMP on site. Due to the fact she has not been seen since Friday evening, they can enter the premises by force if no one has a spare key. Is this clear, Stella?"

Feeling like an admonished fifth grader, Stella nods once again, and rises as she prepares to leave. She stuffs the loan application form into her purse, thanks Ruby for her time, and escapes into the bank foyer and out to the street. To hell with paperwork. Her first task, when she returns to the park, is to knock on every trailer door until she discovers if anyone has a key to Lorraine Young's place. Stationary and groceries have to wait.

CHAPTER 4

An Emergency on Our Hands

Stella wastes no time on the return trip to Shale Cliffs. Fabulous views of the Atlantic, always guaranteed to mesmerize, slide past without a sideways glance. She speeds in the entrance and follows the drive straight home.

At the front door, she shouts for Alice. "Get the staff together. I want everyone to knock on doors. Talk to as many seasonals as you can and find out if anyone has a key to Lorraine Young's trailer."

Alice appears at the kitchen door, a bowl of egg salad in her hand, and provides feedback via a blank stare. "Now, Alice. Whatever they're doing can wait." Eve is in the office and Stella hears Alice instruct her to take the golf cart and round up Paul and Nick.

Returning to her Jeep, Stella barrels toward the front row of trailers. She slams the vehicle into neutral and yanks on the emergency break. Lorraine's trailer conjures an image of a silver coffin perched on the bluff overlooking the sea. Stella experiences a chill, the kind she gets when she suspects something isn't right.

She jumps up to the top step and bangs on the door.

"Lorraine! Lorraine! Are you hurt? I will call the police if we can't get inside. Lorraine!" Her imagination has placed Lorraine in a coma or dead under the kitchen table but out of view if one could see through the windows.

Mildred Fox sits in her deck chair with an unobstructed line of sight to Lorraine's entry stairs. She sips a glass of what is no doubt supposed to appear to be pink lemonade. It's near noon. Stella is sure there's rum in the lemonade.

"Lots a people want to find Lorraine." She slurps with the aid of one of those straws they give you in the hospital with the bendable part in the middle.

Stella clumps back down the stairs. "Who's been around, Mildred?"

Mildred smirks and takes her time. Stella realizes the old lady relishes being in the driver's seat—know-it-all—purveyor of information. "Well, her young fella named Kevin was here. Sally and Rob Black came by. Turns out she has a key, but she couldn't open the door. She told me it's bolted from the inside."

"And no one thought to tell me this?" As her exasperation with Mildred starts to bubble over, Sally and Rob Black meander across an empty lot. They wave at Stella as they approach.

"Any sign of our lovely neighbour?" Rob is first to ask. He's heavy set with dyed straight hair combed back in a style reminiscent of The Everly Brothers or Elvis Presley. One might assume Sally has never provided the necessary feedback he requires to fully comprehend the year is 1980. He must be sixty-five, and the impression he creates isn't sexy—especially paired with his Hawaiian shirts and sandals with socks.

"No. She wasn't at work. We may have an emergency on our hands."

At this moment, Paul rounds the corner. "I've asked, Stella. Everybody says the people who might have a key are these folks."

"Well, they're right. Tell the staff. Rob and Sally have a key, but we can't access the unit."

"I installed the bolt for her," Paul explains. "She said she always wanted to be sure, when she was asleep, nobody could get inside." His quick glance at Rob does not escape Stella's notice. "If the bolt is on, then she must be in there. Are we gonna break the door?"

"Anybody want a drink? It's lunch time." Mildred has managed to climb off her deck and insert herself into the middle of their little discussion group.

"No drinks, thanks, Mildred. We won't break in, Paul. Our strict instructions are to contact Sergeant Moyer once we find a key. We are not to access on our own. You get the rest of the staff and go back to the office. Alice was making sandwiches. I'll be along in a minute to make the call."

Mildred saw Lorraine come home Friday night. Duke corroborated her story. Her car is here, and the trailer is locked. Stella expects Lorraine has experienced what is described in medical circles as a catastrophic health occurrence.

"Rob, you and Sally go on back to your site and I will come get you when the police arrive. Mildred, don't gossip with your neighbours. We need to find out what's happened and not start to speculate."

Sally Black, who has said little until this point, smiles up at Stella. "You are a calm and controlled person. I admire you, Stella. Me, on the other hand, I'm rattled beyond words."

"Come on, old girl. Let's take you home." Rob looks over her blond curls at Stella. "Lorraine's a pretty one. I expect she's in there with another guy havin' her fun." He wraps his arm around his wife's shoulder and lets his fingers drop so he grazes her breast. He turns back toward Stella and winks.

Her hard swallow prevents a retch.

"I'll return when Sergeant Moyer arrives, Mildred." Stella walks toward the Jeep.

"I ain't goin' far. Hope they don't find what I suspect they're gonna find—and I'm not talkin' two rabbits havin' a time."

"Let's hope you're wrong, Mildred. Sally's key might be bent. Lorraine could be off with friends. I'll go back to my office for now."

As she points the Jeep toward the house, an image of Lorraine, dead on the kitchen floor, becomes more pronounced. Stella is scared.

****

She tucks her vehicle into a spot by the door and enters the kitchen as the staff finish up their delayed lunch. "I need to contact the RCMP, Alice. Any news?"

The red curls vibrate. "No. Other than a complaint from one of the caravan group who said our water pressure is too low, the office has been quiet."

"I guess you realize I didn't do those errands. Take my vehicle and leave Eve in reception. She's ready. Should be good experience for her." Alice hands her an egg salad sandwich as she turns toward the office. "Thanks. I'll eat after I talk to Sergeant Moyer."

Her anxiety is hard to control as emotion creeps into her tone. "Sergeant Moyer, please. This is Stella Kirk at the Shale Cliffs RV Park. He expects my call."

After a couple of clicks, a young voice fills her ear. "Sergeant Moyer here. Miss Kirk?"

"Yes. Stella, please. As you requested through Ruby Wilson, we managed to locate a neighbour with an emergency key to Lorraine Young's trailer. The key will not work and Sally Black, the neighbour, expects the bolt is latched inside. Lorraine is security conscious. When she returned home Friday night,

I am sure she locked the door before she went to bed." After her conversation with Rob Black, Stella is positive Lorraine performed this task before retiring. The guy's a creep.

"We will be there within the hour. I called an investigator from Port Ephron and I expect him any time. Once he arrives, we'll be along."

"Why did you need to request an investigator, Sergeant Moyer? We have no idea what's happened to her yet. She may be fine."

"Investigative support is protocol in these cases. There's no one in the detachment in Shale Harbour, so we make the call. Please meet me at the scene in an hour."

Still defensive, she responds, "Let's not refer to her trailer as a scene, Sergeant, but I will meet you at Lorraine's. Shall I gather the other people involved—her neighbours, my security man?"

"Not now."

"Okay, but they will no doubt turn up, anyway. Her trailer is Number 16, the one on the far right in the front row of units nearest the cliffs."

"Thanks. See you in an hour."

Stella checks her watch and wanders out to reception. "Did Nick go to work, Alice?"

"Yes. He and Paul gobbled their lunch and are painting again. Since you're around, I'll go get Eve to come in to cover the office. What did the cop say?"

"He wants me to meet him at Lorraine's trailer. If the door is, in fact, secured from the inside, this story may not end well. You stay put. I'll go get Nick and find Eve." She realizes she still has her sandwich in her hand.

After jumping on the golf cart, she purrs toward the public bathrooms. Sure enough, both Nick and Paul are there painting up a storm. What's Eve doing? Why, weeding flower beds at the entry to the women's side of the building. What a kid. She never, ever, stands idle or asks for direction. She gets out there and works. A stint inside will be good for her.

"Hey, Eve. Lookin' great. I came to fetch you. Want to cover reception for an hour? I need Alice to run into town and do the errands I neglected this morning. You won't be alone. I'll hang around until I meet the police at Lorraine's."

Eve's face lights up as she listens to Stella. Her piles of dark hair are scrunched into a ball cap sporting the park logo. She has on overalls and a bright orange T-shirt. "Stella, I'm happy to cover for Alice, but look at me!"

She points to her muddy pants.

"No problem. Most of us end up grubby, don't we Nick?" He's approached the cart and put his hand on the back of the seat. "Nick, will you come to the office, too? I want to fill you in on details before I meet Sergeant Moyer at Lorraine's. They'll need to break in. He's showing up with an investigator from Port Ephron."

Nick nods and returns to tell Paul.

"Come on, Eve. Hop on."

At the house, Alice is packed up and ready to take a quick trip into town. Stella leaves her to give Eve basic instructions and takes the stairs to her apartment. Nick will be back in a minute.

The door bangs when Alice leaves. Stella yells down the stairs. "Eve, if you need me, give a shout. Nick and I will have a short meeting when he arrives. Send him up, please."

"No problem, Stella. Alice asked me to go through the reservations and make sure they're in order by date. There might be overlap with smaller sites and we'll have to move people. I'll try to sort out the mix-up, as long as no one comes into the office."

"Good, Eve." The back door squeaks when Nick enters. "I'm upstairs, Nick." She hears his tread on the old and worn wooden stairs.

His presence calms her.

"Sounds bad, Stella. I hope she hasn't been locked inside her trailer all weekend bleeding to death or having a stroke or heart attack. God, we yelled and yelled." This time he touches her shoulder. "Want me to come with you?"

"Yeah, I do. The sergeant said they don't want other witnesses around right now, but Mildred will be on her deck. Sally and Rob will show up if they managed to finish whatever they were up to, and Duke won't be able to keep his nose out. So, yes, I want you to come with me."

"Good, because I told Paul to finish up the paint job on his own. Now, there's a few minutes before you meet the cops. How was your appointment at the bank?"

"I almost forgot. She gave me an application to fill out to go with a bunch of other documents—financial statement, anticipated reservations, and a payroll report. She took your estimates. She seemed optimistic enough, but our meeting was secondary to the whole Lorraine question."

"She called the RCMP, correct?"

"Right. She suggested there's a relationship between Lorraine and Mark Bell, another of her employees, too. I mentioned how Kevin Flores is her boyfriend. I never repeated that Kevin told me he thought she might be stepping out with someone at the bank, perhaps Mark Bell."

****

Walking along the sloping road to the cliff's edge and Lorraine Young's site might serve as the highlight of the day under different circumstances. Stella is in the company of a man she regards with the utmost respect; a man she depends on more than she could ever rely on family to help her run the business. The air is crisp while sunny and warm—a perfect spring day that promises to be summer soon. The grass has turned green and the early flowers are popping up in the beds around people's permanent sites. She shades her eyes with one hand and surveys the property.

The park consists of three streets parallel to the cliffs. Each is divided by this central paved roadway running from her home to the street closest to the water. There are additional sites up nearer the house and various unserviced spots for tenters interspersed around the edges. There are public bathrooms, showers, and a laundry tucked into a cinder block building located in the centre of the development. This is hers. As difficult as many days may be, she has made her peace with the decision to move back and run the place when her father could no longer handle the burden.

Today will be a challenge…when they find Lorraine dead in her trailer.

They sit, hips barely touching, on Lorraine's step and stare out at the water. "Do you think she's inside, Nick?"

"Yup."

"What makes you sure? Maybe she climbed out a window. Maybe the key Sally has doesn't work." She clings to hope which is faint at best.

"Lorraine couldn't climb out a window, Stella. The new one in the bedroom slams when you lift the unit enough to be able to squeeze out. Remember, Paul and I helped her complete the installation the end of last year. It's specifically designed to lock in the up position. Then, you push out the screen to escape. If you don't engage the lock mechanism, the whole damned unit slams…hard enough we thought we broke it the first time we tried to follow emergency procedures. Of course, if the place is on fire, it's not important if the glass breaks when you jump out. The window is locked. I checked."

"Why did she want a special emergency escape window instead of the standard one you push on, to make it fall out?"

"A friend of hers was attacked, she told me, when a guy pulled the window from the outside and climbed into her room. I thought she was crazy. I expect the person was unaware they had a broken latch. Specifics didn't matter to Lorraine. We replaced the unit which locks in three open positions, but the locking buttons can't be accessed from the outside. Pricey, if I recall."

"And the other windows?"

"These trailers use jalousie windows with glass awning slats you crank open and closed. The screens are on the inside and you couldn't get out without breaking the glass slats as well as removing the screen. Old eagle-ears Mildred would hear the escape window slam or a jalousie window break. I'm positive Lorraine's in there."

Duke speeds across the front lawn on the golf cart. She hopes he won't notice they're there. No such luck.

"Hey, Duke. Hey, Kiki."

"Kiki, shut up! Saw you two sittin' here on the step and thought I'd come see what the story is on Lorraine."

"No story. We reported what we know to the cops and Moyer is on his way. He will no doubt want to talk to you. I gave him your name."

"I should hang around."

A ketchup stain decorates the front of his plaid shirt. She expects he decided the mark blended in with the pattern. He has the short sleeves rolled up to his shoulders, exposing flabby and hairy upper arms. His sunglasses are tucked under the re-invented cuff.

"No need. I'll tell them where you are."

"I'll go sit with old Mildred. I bet she could use my company."

Lorraine's neighbour wiggles the fingers of one hand and raises her plastic tumbler with the other. Duke's eyes are locked with hers.

There are bits of information a park owner should not know. "Well, I can't stop you from visiting with Mildred Fox, Duke, but neither one of you are to interfere. The police will talk to you in due course, I expect, after they find out the status inside the trailer."

Nick stands. "I'll pop over to the Black's and get the spare key. We don't want them hangin' around on Mildred's deck, too. I'll be right back. There's the cop car on the road now."

Duke rumbles over to Mildred's and Nick disappears around the side of the trailer to make his way to Rob and Sally's. Stella stands up as well. She sighs. It's barely two-thirty, and this day is never ending. She's not prepared for what they'll find.

Sergeant Moyer, she assumes, is driving. There's another man, in a business suit, occupying the passenger seat. She approaches the car. "Sergeant Moyer? I'm Stella Kirk. My manager, Nick Cochran, has gone across the way to get the spare key from Sally Black. Nice to meet you." He's a big man. It takes him time to disengage himself from behind the wheel. Stella absently wonders how a foot chase might play out.

The other door opens, and Stella is startled by the changed but familiar face observing her. "Stella, let me introduce...."

"I'll save you the trouble, Sergeant. Miss Kirk and I know one another. Hi, Stella. I heard you took over the park from your father. How's his health these days?"

"He's as you might expect, Aiden, if you consider he can't remember family half the time. He's contented." Her heart thumps. "I wasn't aware you were in the area." She turns to address the sergeant. "Aiden North and I were in high school together. We were friends years ago." Her smile is unwillingly sad.

CHAPTER 5

There's No Sign of a Struggle

"Who has the key to Miss Young's trailer?" Sergeant Moyer is all business. No more small talk.

"Here." Nick steps up and produces the one provided to him by Sally Black.

"A neighbour keeps a spare key?"

"Yes," Stella answers. "Sally Black." She points toward Mildred's deck where Duke, Mildred, Rob, and Sally sip pink lemonade and watch the show. Mildred's mouldy and worn red and white striped awning flaps in the breeze reminding Stella of a wet sheet on her mother's clothesline. How the canvas remains intact is a mystery.

"Okay. We can talk with everyone later. I'll try the key." Moyer climbs the stairs to Lorraine's door. Aiden North moves into position beside Stella, as she and Nick watch. The key turns in the lock but the door doesn't budge.

Nick speaks first. "Lorraine hired one of our staff, Paul Morgan, to install a deadbolt for her. Lorraine is security conscious. I imagine, if she's inside, the bolt is set. I expect the slide latch on the inside screen door is locked, too. You'll need a crowbar."

"Agreed. Detective North, I'll get a bar out of the trunk and we'll proceed."

They sound formal. At least, Sergeant Moyer sounds formal. He no doubt dreads what he might discover

Access to the trailer isn't easy. As expected, Paul's well-installed deadbolt causes the difficulties. The screen door poses less challenge. "Stay outside." Moyer directs his command toward Nick and Stella. He gives Aiden a perfunctory nod.

Both men enter. Aiden goes first. They are inside for a long time. Aiden emerges in the doorway. "She's not here, Stella. Her coat is on a chair in the living room and her purse has been tossed on the table. She's not here," he repeats.

"May I come in, Aiden?"

"Not right now. I want to talk to the witnesses and your staff. I'll request that a team arrive as soon as possible to take pictures, check out her car, and dust for prints. There's no sign of a struggle. The whole place has been secured."

"Aiden, she came home." Stella's heart thumps in her chest. "Mildred saw her get out of her car and go in the trailer as always. She sure as hell didn't vaporize!"

"Lots to figure out. Are you able to make time to be my liaison and introduce me to residents and employees? You were always good with people. I might get more information if you provide introductions. I'll have a quick interview with the folks next door and then go from there."

Stella glances at Nick when she addresses Aiden. "Do you need Nick in the vicinity?"

"No, but I require a lesson later, on how trailer windows work. The one way out of here besides the door is through a window. She didn't climb out a tiny roof vent, but the skylight in the bathroom is big enough." His tone contains a mixture of sarcasm and annoyance.

"I'll return to the painting and check on the staff, Stella. Come find me if you need me." She senses his light touch on her elbow, a behaviour he has never exhibited in front of others before. When she glances toward the peanut gallery perched on Mildred's deck, Stella imagines the rumours.

****

"Detective North, let me introduce you to Mildred Fox. This is her trailer, and she's a long time seasonal resident." Aiden leans across the old deck to shake Mildred's wrinkled and, Stella expects, sticky hand. "Please meet Duke Powell. Duke is my security guard for the park. He follows a procedure I'm sure he will explain." Kiki growls while Duke nods. Stella supposes Duke sees their encounter as one law enforcer to another. "Sally and Rob Black, here, are the couple who were in possession of Lorraine's emergency key. They live in a unit behind this row we're in now. Duke has a spot at the other end of the front row."

"Nice to meet you. Sergeant Moyer has radioed the office to request an identification team come out from Port Ephron. We are required to secure the scene. I need everyone's cooperation." He rustles in his inside jacket pocket and produces a notebook and pen.

"I can keep an eye out once your people leave, Detective." Duke puffs out his chest. The palm trees on his Hawaiian shirt flutter with the effort.

"Your offer of assistance is appreciated, but we will assign a car to the property if the identification team discovers any information of significance. I want to interview each of you individually. Shall we meet at your trailers, or...?" He glances toward Stella.

"Detective North, you are more than welcome to use my office."

"Not me," pipes up Mildred. "I ain't hobblin' up to Stella's house to be grilled by a cop. You got questions, you ask them here."

"Fine, Mrs. Fox." He surveys the group. "You folks may convene up at Stella's place any time and I will make my way right after I complete my visit with Mrs. Fox."

"*Miss* Fox," she simpers, "and I need more lemonade." She adjusts her caftan and uses the rickety arms of her lounger to hoist her ample person out of the chair. "Back in a flash."

"I'll do a run around the park and then be up to the office, Stella. The detective, here, can have a word with the Blacks first. Come on, Kiki."

The dog, firmly locked in the crook of Duke's arm, has few options.

Sally Black stands up and reaches for her husband's empty glass. "I'll put these in the sink for Mildred and then we'll make our way, right Rob?"

To see Sally assume the lead is unusual. Stella notices Rob's nervous expression as he nods and then waits on the grass for his wife to emerge from Mildred's trailer.

"Do you want me to stay?" Stella isn't sure of her role but will provide information when possible.

"Thanks, Stella. Miss Fox will be more cooperative," he grins, "with you here."

Although unconvinced Aiden's assessment is accurate, she agrees. "Tell Alice what's happened and make yourselves comfortable in the main lounge until we arrive." She directs her remarks toward Sally and Rob.

****

Perched on a corner of Mildred's rotten deck, she examines Lorraine's trailer as it twinkles in the afternoon sunshine. She is desperate to examine the inside; to absorb the space; to understand.

Mildred is seated in her lounger once again, pink lemonade on the metal table beside her. "Okay, Detective. What's your name again?"

"North. I'm Detective North, Miss Fox."

"Okay, Detective North. Call me Mildred. The cute guys call me Mildred." She winks at Stella, but her attempt resembles a twitch. "Ask away."

"Tell me what you saw. Let's start there and I'll decide if I need clarification."

The old lady glances toward Stella again. "He's smooth, Stella. Butter wouldn't melt in his mouth. Are you two friends, or what?"

"Mildred, try to pay attention to the detective. Don't make the afternoon longer than necessary." Stella suspects Mildred has a load on. She's been into the lemonade for a while.

"Okay, okay. I was sittin' here by my fire on Friday night, havin' a drink, and enjoyin' finally bein' settled out here and then Lorraine comes home. I bet you're gonna ask, so I'll tell you it was goin' on ten. Seemed late for workin' at the bank. I hope she had a date with her boyfriend—what's his name? Rhymes with heaven—Kevin."

"What is Kevin's last name?"

"No idea, but she's sweet on him. She said so when we were both settin' up our trailers. He came out to help her."

Aiden turns to Stella and lifts a brow.

"Kevin Flores. He works at the lumberyard."

"Thanks. Okay, Mildred, anything else?"

"Nope. Kevin came over yesterday to find Lorraine. Then Sally and Rob showed up and tried to use their key."

Aiden scribbles in his notebook. "Did Kevin know where Lorraine might be?"

"Nope," she repeats. "He said Stella, here, called and asked if Lorraine was with him."

North raises an eyebrow at Stella for the second time.

"Are you in cahoots or what? I may be old, but I can tell when people are talkin' without words. You two musta been *really* good friends." She wriggles further into her chair and reaches for her drink.

"Now Mildred, is your lemonade doing the talking?" Stella is unnerved by her emotions. She's desperate to maintain a blank expression and keep her memories in check. Yes, Aiden was her first, but certainly not her last. Her current relationship suits her sensibilities. Aiden is married, she's sure. *You're flustered! It shows! Stop!*

Aiden summarizes Mildred's information and then adds, "Do you have any other observations?"

"Her car is parked crooked. No one else drove. Nobody touched the car after Friday night. I think she had somethin' on her mind—or she drank lemonade before she came home." Mildred hoists her drink in a wobbly salute.

North ignores the alcohol reference. "She was preoccupied?"

Mildred sighs and refrains from additional humour. "She didn't wave. I figure she was bothered, for sure."

"Thanks for your help today, Mildred." Aiden, still standing at the edge of the deck, reaches across, and for the second time, shakes her sticky hand. "If I need more information, I'll visit again, okay?"

"Stop by any time, Detective. You don't have to drag Stella, here, along with you." She turns and winks again, but toward Stella. She has difficulty coordinating which eye should be closed.

They walk up the roadway. Stella is compelled to fill the void of silence with conversation. "So...tell me what you've been up to for the last, what, twenty-five years?" She tries to make her voice sound light.

"I joined the RCMP right out of high school if you remember. I married after I was in for four years. Her name is Rosemary. I'm the one soul who gets away with calling her Rosie." He studies Stella. He cocks his head to the side as if he constantly listens to silent questions; a robin sensing a worm. His eyes have a sad cast.

"You and Rosemary, I suppose, were posted across the country? What brought you back here?"

"Family connections, for the most part. We don't have kids. Rosemary isn't well—depression—and I thought a return to Port Ephron, so we could be near her sisters, was best. This is my last post. I'll be retiring soon."

Snow white hair flutters over his forehead in the breeze. Time has not been kind to Aiden. "How long have you been in Port Ephron?"

"Six months. The move from out west hasn't helped Rosemary as I hoped. Toni and Mary Jo try, at various times, to convince her to go into a treatment centre for a few weeks to get the depression under control. She's resistant. It's understandable, I guess. Her illness is a mystery to me, and I can't fix her." He sounds discouraged and shares with a measure of candour as if they had maintained a friendship over the years.

A police van pulls up beside them as they trudge toward the house. The driver leans out the open window. "We left a car for you in the camp's parking lot. Where's the scene?"

Stella responds to the request. "Drive straight along this road and turn right at the stop. Lorraine's trailer is Number 16, the one on the far end. You'll be able to see the patrol car from the turn."

Her glance toward Aiden is apologetic. "Sorry. Force of habit. I'm always directing someone somewhere."

They arrive at the house to find Alice keeping the Blacks company. Duke and Kiki are on the veranda.

"Do you want me to sit in with you?"

"If you don't mind." He lowers his voice and bends closer to her ear. "I need a second set of eyes; an interpreter, I guess."

"Happy to help." She leads the way to her office, clears the loan application off the top of her desk, and points to her chair. "This one's for you." She shouts out to Alice, "Please get me another chair."

Sally Black is first to be interviewed. She sits in the wooden straight-backed chair in her capris and yellow polka dot blouse. Her hair is an unmanaged array of cowlicks, whipped up by the wind into a mess of spikes and sprigs. She fidgets as she tells them Lorraine requested she keep a key for emergencies. She sniffs, in apparent annoyance, as she recalls when Paul installed the deadbolt. "There isn't much point in a neighbour with a key for emergencies if they're locked out. I asked her, what did she expect? Was she worried I'd creep into her trailer in the middle of the night? She's weird; fussy."

They saw Kevin at Lorraine's trailer and when he talked to Mildred, she and Rob wandered over to find out if there was a problem. She attempted to get in, but the stupid deadbolt was engaged.

Rob Black fills the chair with his enormous behind. He corroborates Sally's story. "Lorraine's a classy woman. She wanted Sally to have her key but has never invited us inside her place. I've often walked past in case she might need help, but she's not open to company. I try to be nice to her, but she isn't friendly, if I'm bein' honest."

Stella appreciates Lorraine's behaviour, as she attempts to control the crawling sensation that creeps across her skin.

When Duke lumbers into the office, he is without the dog. "Where's Kiki?" Stella does not relish the idea of Kiki unattended in her house, regardless of what areas are open to the public.

"Oh, she's with Alice. She adores Alice. We both adore Alice." He leers at Aiden.

Duke's attitude is as unacceptable as Rob's, but she assumes they're harmless, albeit annoying.

"You saw Lorraine Friday night, Duke?"

"Yup. She drove into the park near ten. I went out to the road to secure the gate and passed her on the way home. Haven't talked to her in ages although I do drive-bys everywhere on a regular basis. Stella, here, keeps track of my routine."

"Duke is observant, Detective. He would have noticed if there was any activity around Lorraine's place."

"Any other information you might care to add, Duke?"

"I asked her to go on a date two different times. She wasn't interested. Said she was 'involved' with Kevin." He makes air quotes with the index fingers of both hands. "Kevin Flores ain't the right fella for her."

"Why not?"

"Lorraine needs a strong man; a guy of my calibre, with a few miles on him." He sits up straighter in the chair. "I'd stay around to protect her."

"I see. But she isn't interested, correct?"

"Well, right now she's not." His face lights up. "But people change. Kevin isn't here for the long haul. I'm committed."

After Duke retrieves Kiki and makes his exit, Stella turns to Aiden. "Tea? I'll fill you in on any details."

"Okay, but first I have to take a trip to Lorraine's trailer and check in with Moyer. I'll return as soon as possible. Are you able to provide me with a list of your other employees and anybody else involved? Lorraine works at the Savings and Loan, right?"

****

With Aiden North away for a few minutes, Stella rallies her staff. She jumps on a golf cart and roars over to the pump shed where Nick is busy checking filters. "Please come to the house for a while. Aiden has gone to Lorraine's to check on the identification team's progress, and then he plans to talk with everyone. I'd appreciate your input."

Nick wipes his hands on a rag he's dug out of his back pocket and breaks into a sly grin. "Sure you don't want to spend time with Detective North alone—reminiscing?"

"Cut it out. He and I dated in high school, Nick—more than twenty-five years ago. Quit teasing me."

An arm slides around her shoulders and he leans into her for a moment. There's mischief in his eyes.

"Are you done? Will you come to the office? He wants to talk to the staff." She's desperate to refocus away from her old relationship with Aiden and back on the matter at hand.

She adds, "Paul has the most information. He helped her with odd jobs. Nevertheless, I expect one of us should be present for each of them when they're interviewed. Aiden wants me to join him. I assume you're included." With a small pang of disappointment, she senses his arm slide away.

"I'll round up Paul and Eve. We'll be up in a minute. What the hell's happened to Lorraine? She went home, climbed inside her trailer, bolted the door, and disappeared. We need to check for a trap door in the floor."

"None of this is right, Nick. I have a bad feeling."

In their common room, as they often refer to the big living room on the main floor of her house, Stella sets out a tray of sodas and puts the kettle on for tea. Alice expects two different family groups of campers to arrive any time, therefore she will participate from the reception doorway until she meets with Aiden. Eve will cover for her.

The afternoon is never-ending. Stella listens to North ask the same questions over and over. Her staff are polite and cooperative. Eve has no information. She could barely describe the location of Lorraine's lot. Alice knows Lorraine because Alice runs the office and is in contact with everybody from time to time. No surprises there. Paul describes Lorraine with an anxious fondness. He has helped her set up her services. He built her steps last year and installed her now infamous and destroyed deadbolt. He references her attention to detail and how she prefers tasks done in her own particular way. He tells them he never goes inside her trailer with his shoes on. He says she's the kind of person who makes him want to be better when he's around her.

By six o'clock, the staff are ready to go home. The reception office remains open until eight, but Stella always takes her turn at the end of the day.

"Do you plan to stay in Shale Harbour, Aiden? You don't have to drive to Port Ephron tonight, right?" Nick gathers up pop cans and makes conversation while he works.

"No, I have a room at the Harbour Hotel. The place is a reject from the 1940s but serves my purpose." His grin is sheepish. "They have a breakfast room, so there's food, and one of my sisters-in-law will stay with my wife. There's no timeline on this investigation, since we still have no idea what we're investigating."

"Speaking of food—Stella? Shall we invite your high school chum, here, for pizza tonight? I'll run into town, if you order."

"Sure. I think I've seen the last of the reservations. Pizza will work."

"If I stay," Aiden begins, "will you help me fill in any blanks with my notes? Are you up for more work? I still need to get a handle on what makes this Lorraine Young tick, but I expect a visit to the bank tomorrow might be wise at this point."

CHAPTER 6

It's What I Feel

The three of them sit in the lounge of the main house. They eat pepperoni pizza and beer brewed by a buddy of Nick's from Port Ephron. There's a small fire in the grate. A single lamp, in the shape of a ship—a fixture on the end table for as long as Stella can remember—casts a shadowed glow throughout the big space. She and her old home are much the same. They appear more attractive in the dim lighting, which serves to camouflage the worn furniture, tattered carpet, and chipped coffee table.

Nick has stretched out in an over-stuffed armchair. A relic from the 1940s, it's positioned next to the stone hearth—yet another permanent fixture. Nick is relaxed; pink in the reflection of the fire and the consumption of the beer.

Aiden sits on the edge of the couch cushions. He sips his drink and checks his notebook. He's still in a suit but has removed the jacket and stuffed his tie in the pocket. He's aged. Stella realizes the image of her first love has always been stuck in 1954. His sudden arrival here at the park has shocked her into the reality of time's passage.

"More pizza?" She directs her question toward both men. Nick raises his hand and simultaneously shakes his head.

"No thanks, Stella. If there's any left, I'll eat cold pizza for lunch tomorrow."

"God! The thought of cold pizza! Aiden? Any more for you?"

"No, thanks. I'm surprised Shale Harbour has such a good pizza joint. I'll have their food anytime." He turns his attention to Nick, "but I'm with Stella. You eat the cold stuff. Not for me."

"Okay, I'll stick the rest of this in the fridge and plug in the kettle. Tea?" She peers at the small mantle clock above the fireplace. Nine o'clock, but still lots of time to review Aiden's notes. They spent the last hour acquainting, reacquainting, and catching up on each other's lives. Topics ranged from Aiden's career to Nick's relocation from the US, to Stella's decision to return to take over the park from her father. The conversation switches to the main issue at hand—the disappearance of Lorraine Young.

"Our identification team finished. They report the scene appeared normal. You can go inside now and have a peek."

"Thanks." Stella is sure she'll be able to sense Lorraine's status once she surrounds herself in the woman's space. They relax with their tea.

"Hard to determine if a suspicious incident happened in the yard. Staff mow on a regular basis?"

Stella nods. "If she has no other task, and the weather isn't rainy, Eve will mow. Short grass helps keep the mosquito population at bay and makes the place look much neater. If I had suspected an issue…well, who knew?"

"I know. I know. Tell me who you talked to and what they said, Stella."

"Mildred Fox told me the same information she told you. Duke Powell, ditto. I believe them. Mildred drinks most of the time and Duke is conceited, but despite how they present themselves, their statements regarding when they saw Lorraine match. What they report is the truth."

She sips her tea. "We'll discuss the bank employees after your visit there tomorrow. I'm only acquainted with Mark Bell and Terri Price as tellers, not personally, but I've met Ruby Wilson on different occasions. When I was in there this morning for a loan application, she told me Lorraine left work at the normal time on Friday but hadn't shown up yet today. When I spoke with Kevin Flores earlier and discovered she wasn't with him overnight, and wasn't currently with him, I assumed she was at work Friday night until she came home to the park. Never assume."

Nick has been quiet throughout the discussion. "She could have gone to visit a sick friend, been out to dinner with a girlfriend, or handled a problem with her tenant at her apartment. I suspect she was on a date with a guy other than Kevin. There's little information, not even regarding her family."

She can't read his mood. Nick's blasé attitude is unsettling. "Lorraine has no family now," Stella responds. "Her parents died when she was a kid—one right after the other, if I recall the story details. She was shipped here to Shale Harbour and her father's maiden aunt provided a home for her. Her father's people were from outside Port Ephron and Lorraine's aunt taught piano for years. She's been dead since the early 1970s." She notices how Aiden writes furiously as they talk.

Aiden catches up with his notes before she continues. "She might well have been out with another man. Kevin told me he was suspicious of Mark Bell, from the bank. Then Ruby hinted how she thought Lorraine and Mark are involved."

"Okay. The best course of action is a conversation with Ruby Wilson, Mark Bell, and who was the other one?" He fiddles with his note book. "Ah, yes, Terri Price, correct?"

"Right, Aiden. Do you want company tomorrow? Alice has managed to compile the documentation I need for my loan application. I have to go to the bank, anyway."

"Your presence is helpful and appreciated. Another set of eyes will assist me, Stella. Thanks." He pauses for a second as if his thoughts are ahead of his words. "In the meantime, I should be on my way. Shall we meet at Lorraine's, say nine o'clock, and then visit the Savings and Loan afterward?"

"Perfect." Stella accompanies Aiden to the veranda and stands on the top step until he navigates the car up the drive to the main road. The light on Duke's golf cart approaches the bend nearest the house. This will be his final circle before he locks the gate. It must be ten-thirty, so he's running late. She turns her attention to her living room and Nick, who is in the process of picking up mugs.

"More tea?"

"No. I need to go to my place and sleep. Long day." He doesn't meet her eyes when he says this.

"Are you okay?"

"Sure. Just tired. I'll see you tomorrow, Stella." His voice is flat.

There's a dampness in the night air as she watches him saunter over to the cottage assigned for the manager; the one he hasn't used much lately.

****

"Where are you, Nick?" The lower floor of her house is quiet. The smell of coffee floats up the stairs. It's seven-thirty. She wants to take the time necessary to ensure the paperwork is together for the loan application. She'll relax once she reviews the forms with Nick before leaving to go to the Savings and Loan. A call to Trixie later today will be necessary if she's required to run in and sign. Trixie lives two streets over from the bank and around the corner from the community center and theatre.

Her papers are held together with a black binder clip and wedged into her armpit as she scurries down the worn wooden stairs. "Nick? Nick? Are you here yet?"

"Out on the veranda, Stella."

She shivers for no reason. "Let me get a coffee. What are you doin' out there?"

No answer. She pours her coffee, splashes milk into the mug, and turns toward the screen door. The day promises to be stunning. She needs time with Nick. Her mental chill won't ease.

"Good morning." She sets her mug on the rattan side table and places the pile of papers nearby. "You're quiet. I wondered if you were even here."

"I'm here, Stella. You haven't noticed?"

"What the hell? Nick, spill it. What's the problem? You and I don't keep secrets."

"Were you and North a serious item?"

"You mean twenty-five, or was it twenty-six, years ago when we graduated from high school? Yes. He was my first real boyfriend, but we were in *high school*. He attended the RCMP Training Academy out west. I tried to study journalism at night and sold advertising for a newspaper as my day job." Most of this old history is familiar to him. "I wanted to be an investigative journalist. Too many men; not enough male bosses who appreciated what a woman could do. This is not new information, Nick." Her pulse pounds in her ears.

"We drifted apart after the first Christmas he was home. I lost touch with most of my high school friends one way or the other. He was a good guy though. He met someone, Rosemary, but I was never friends with her. She was from the port. Port Ephron was far away in those days." She smiles, remembering how worldly they thought they were. She places her hand on the sleeve of Nick's plaid cotton shirt.

He doesn't move and directs his gaze out toward the drive. "You two are close."

"*Were* close, Nick. I was shocked to see him. I'm excited to help him try to solve the puzzle of Lorraine." She softens her tone. "We were good friends a long time ago. We thought alike. He has a full plate because his personal life is a strain. We aren't the same people anymore, Nick." She squeezes his arm and glances around to ensure none of the staff have arrived to work yet. She leans in near his ear. "Don't be upset. We're a team." Shock comes with the realization of how much she cares. She's overwhelmed by the sensation.

His hand drifts across her cheek. "Let's have a bite to eat. Will we review the bank forms before you leave?"

"Yeah." Relief floods through her. "I need your help to make sure I didn't miss any detail. Toast? By the way, will you come with me to Lorraine's trailer when Aiden gets here? He gave me permission to look inside her unit, but I want you there, too. You'll get an opportunity to explain the security window while I nose around."

****

Aiden North, no different from when they were in high school, makes an appearance on the veranda precisely five minutes before their nine o'clock rendezvous.

"Hi, Aiden. Come on in. There's not much formality around here when the office is open. Good night at the hotel?"

"Not bad. I miss my own bed though." He doesn't dwell on the personal. "When they left yesterday, the team said they were able to lock the door despite the damage from the broken deadbolt. I have the spare key. We'll go inside but you are not to handle her possessions, Stella. Wear gloves. I can't imagine what you expect to see."

"It's not what I see, it's what I feel, Aiden." Stella pours him a cup of fresh coffee. Nick should be over from the pump house any minute. The guest count is high for mid-week and he wanted to check on water pressure and make sure the new filters are doing their job. "Have you ever walked into a room and known someone was there even though they weren't there anymore?"

"You mean a ghost? Come on, Stella. You don't seriously expect a ghost abducted Lorraine Young and dispatched her through the walls?"

No one understands, except for her father when he was in his right mind. Her confidence requires a boost. "No, Aiden. I want to try to 'sense' what happened. Humour me, okay?"

"Sure. Remember we're due at the bank between ten and eleven. I contacted the lumberyard and Kevin Flores is available shortly before noon."

She swallows the sensation of being dismissed. "Do you still expect me to be your Dr. Watson?"

"If you're up for the challenge. Pressure to solve the mystery of Miss Young's disappearance is mounting."

"Nick will go to the trailer with us." She makes a statement rather than asks a question.

"Fine with me. Here he comes, now."

The screen door opens and Nick breezes in. His face reads "back to normal", at least for company. Stella hopes her domestic crisis has blown over. She does not want their relationship to be disrupted, despite attempts to think of it as casual.

****

They walk toward the front row of trailers strung out along the cliff's edge. The view is second to none, but the wind can whip up a gale with a moment's notice. Stella is one who prefers her digs further away from the ocean's potential rage. Not every day is as benign as today.

Yellow tape, affixed to stakes wedged into the clay soil—crime scene tape without any evidence of a crime—surrounds the trailer. The door is splintered but secure. Stella imagines Lorraine's reaction if she wandered home after a jaunt with girlfriends, to find her trailer had been broken into by the police. *Lorraine will not wander in. Lorraine is dead.*

Aiden unlocks the unit, and she enters. It's stifling; so warm she smells panelling and plastics—the essences of trailers. She stands still and listens to her surroundings. Stella absorbs the idea of Lorraine's death as emotion washes over her. She hears Aiden and Nick walk around the rig and discuss the mechanics of different forms of windows. They go up the ladder at the rear to access the roof.

Lorraine's coat is slung, with unceremonious abandon, over a chair in the living area to the left, as Aiden reported. Her purse is on the booth table to the right, across from the tiny kitchen, and her car keys are beside it. Stella is mystified. *This is not the behaviour of the Lorraine Young I know.* She has a hook for her keys near the door. She never leaves her purse in plain sight. She places it in a drawer in her bedroom. As for her coat tossed across a piece of furniture, Stella is surprised by this act of disregard from such a finicky woman. She parked her car crooked. Stella understands it could happen, but the sum of these issues illustrates how Lorraine must have been under severe duress when she came home Friday night. Was there an issue with Mark Bell, or Kevin Flores?

How did she get out? Stella, although aware the windows are locked from the inside, examines them regardless. At the end of the trailer is Lorraine's bedroom. She notices a small water stain on the sill of the new window, which faces the cliffs and away from the park. It proves a leak occurred at some point—another illogical observation, since a leaky window would be intolerable for Lorraine and, furthermore, there has been no rain in a few days.

She stands in the bathroom which is small but serviceable and separates the dining booth from the bedroom. Lorraine's shower is minuscule and has a clear plastic dome in the roof to provide light along with the illusion of spaciousness. The dome frame is screwed into the ceiling and untouched in any way.

The bedroom resembles most trailers. There's a double bed with storage underneath, end tables affixed to the wall, and a closet. She gently pushes the sliding door on the right and admires Lorraine's attention to detail as her clothes are arranged according to colour and use. Her shoes are lined up on the floor, toes out. There are empty spots for two pairs. *Did she take a pair to her apartment in town*? She notices there are no runners or walkers. *She might take walking shoes with her everywhere. Could Mildred have noticed if she was wearing dress shoes when she got home?* Another conversation with the neighbour is in order.

With her emotions steeled, Stella lifts the mattress as well as the plywood top on which it rests. She expects the extra storage under the bed houses the water tank needed by campers who park where access to water is not available. The other half of the space stores items seldom used. Lorraine is not crammed under her own bed, much to Stella's relief. She examines the layout of the storage compartment but sees no readily accessible route to the ground where you could take the box apart and then easily rebuild the unit once outside. Her relief is mixed with disappointment. She hoped Lorraine wanted to disappear and this was her exit.

What she senses, after her experience in the trailer for the better part of thirty minutes, is that Lorraine's disappearance will not end well. Lorraine is gone; most likely dead.

She opens the door and lets her eyes adjust to the bright sun. Aiden and Nick are off the roof and waiting for her with expectant expressions. She

L. P. Suzanne Atkinson

gazes past their shoulders and out at the water. "Did your people search the shore? I assume they did."

"Oh yes. They walked a mile in either direction. The tide comes right up to the cliffs, so foot prints weren't expected. We didn't find a scrap, not so much as a button or a shoelace, Stella. What's your assessment since you've been inside?"

"There is no sense of her presence here if you're asking for my impressions. I even looked in the storage space under the bed and took a gander at the skylight, but no luck. She entered and never came out, Aiden, the way old Mildred Fox said." She turns to Nick. "Is there any possible option where the new bedroom window was manipulated? I see it leaked, so it isn't as fool-proof as everybody assumed."

"Leaked! No way! Well, once this whole issue with Lorraine is settled, I'll have to check the seals." He sounds disgusted. "That damned window was supposed to be the very best money could buy. A person could never exit through the window and relock it. But a leak!" He raises both hands, palms exposed. "There you go."

Aiden secures the door and they start to walk. "Are you able to come with me to the bank and the lumberyard, Stella?"

She steals a glance at Nick for confirmation, a behaviour foreign to her for the last many years.

"Good idea, Aiden. You take Stella with you. I might need the Jeep while you two are off asking questions."

Stella breathes a sigh of relief. This relationship wasn't supposed to be complicated. She did not expect to care what any man thought of her ever again. She and Nick are convenient, or so she assumed.

CHAPTER 7

There Must Be a Piece We Missed

Back at the house, Stella grabs her shoulder bag and the necessary bank forms from her office and returns to meet Aiden. As the screen door slams behind her, she can see him standing beside the white, late model Chevrolet Caprice surveying her property.

"Pretty place, Stella. Not much has changed since we were kids."

"If you saw my cheque book, you'd realize pretty comes with a price, I'm afraid." She climbs into the front seat of the big car without an invitation as she continues. "The main reason I made an appointment at the Savings and Loan was for money to update the water and electrical systems. As RVs get larger and have more equipment, we need better pressure and more power. We try our best, but that involves constant upgrades."

"You saw this Ruby Wilson person to negotiate financing." It isn't a question.

"Yeah. We had an appointment," she repeats. "I tried to find Lorraine beforehand, to see if she might be able to help me with a few pointers on how the woman works, and this whole mess happened." She pats the papers on her lap. "Still need the loan, and my last errand is to drop off this package today."

"Okay. We'll interview Ruby Wilson and the two other employees."

"Yes. Mark Bell and Terri Price. I have no information about Terri except she's a teller. Both Kevin, Lorraine's boyfriend, and Ruby, have indicated Mark and Lorraine might have a relationship. To be frank, Lorraine has never struck me as the type to carry on behind a boyfriend's back. Now, Trixie— she's another story." Stella guffaws. Aiden remembers Trixie. There's no need for a detailed explanation.

"I gather I can park wherever I want?"

"Not on people's lawns or in front of their driveways."

Aiden glances over at her from his position at the wheel. "I am a policeman, Stella. I understand avoiding the landscaping."

Stella brushes a stray strand of hair off her forehead and absently ponders the need for a haircut in the foreseeable future. She grins across at her friend. "You asked," she teases as she climbs out and slams the heavy door.

****

Ruby is standing with Terri behind the counter when they walk in. Although ten-thirty, the bank isn't busy. Mark is waiting on a customer, but Terri and Ruby are reviewing a stack of documents. Ruby waves and motions them both toward her office.

"There's Ruby. I'll introduce you when she joins us."

In a few minutes, after they make themselves comfortable, the uneven click of Ruby's dark green stilettos announces her arrival as she flutters in the door. Stella observes how her floral dress is more suitable for a cocktail party than as work attire even if Ruby had seen fit to wear a jacket which she didn't. The sleeves are capped and the neckline plunges. Stella doesn't consider herself a prude and isn't sure of Ruby's age. Regardless, the skirt is too short for a woman of Ruby's vintage. She examines her own ensemble of faded blue jeans and extra-large white blouse dragged on over a navy T-shirt. *Glass houses.*

"Ruby Wilson, please meet Aiden North. He is the detective from Port Ephron assigned to investigate Lorraine's disappearance. Aiden, this is Ruby Wilson, the manager here at the Savings and Loan."

Aiden rises to shake Ruby's hand before she takes her seat behind the desk. "Nice to meet you, Miss Wilson."

"Detective North." She sits, with an erectness to her posture which projects her command of the room. "We don't stand on much ceremony here at the bank. Please call me Ruby."

"Thank you." Aiden's head is tilted to the side as usual. He always appears to be peering out over the top of reading glasses, which he doesn't wear. This creates the illusion of serious and intent interest in the current conversation. Stella isn't convinced his body language indicates a direct message regarding his thoughts.

Ruby clasps her hands, manicured to perfection, in front of her on the desk. The surface is bereft of any potential paperwork except for the manila envelope Stella has placed with precision on the corner nearest her chair. "I gather you want to interview Terri and Mark, Detective?"

Stella notices he doesn't request to be called by his first name.

"Yes, as well as you, Ruby. We have no idea as to the whereabouts of Lorraine Young. My purpose, at this juncture, is to recreate her movements from the time she left the bank until she arrived home at her trailer in the Shale Cliffs RV Park."

"Have you checked with her boyfriend or her tenants? There are lots of possible places she might go after work."

Aiden North is skillful in his avoidance of a response to her question and asks one of his own. "You told Stella, here, how she left the bank around five. Correct?"

"Yes. Terri and Mark left for home a few minutes before her." She bends toward them and repeats, "Have you checked with her boyfriend?"

"We keep our investigations private until we have assembled the facts, Ruby. Is there additional information you're able to give me regarding Lorraine?"

"Well, I'm sure she's involved with Mark Bell." She leans forward further as if the three of them are co-conspirators. "I discourage employees from involvement with one another, but there is no firm rule as it relates to people who are on the same tier of the corporate ladder. Of course, managers cannot date their staff, a policy which is common practice."

"What makes you certain Mark and Lorraine are involved?"

"Because they spend a great deal of time together. They visit when the bank is quiet. They often leave at the same time. Each of my staff takes their lunch and coffee breaks on different schedules, but they socialize whenever they find a moment." Her smile is indulgent. "I ignore their interactions for the most part. As long as the work gets done...you understand. Young love."

Aiden switches gears so fast, Stella is caught off guard. "May I meet with Terri and Mark individually here in your office?"

Ruby's reaction is one of surprise, but she attempts graciousness. "Of course, Detective. I'll make sure Terri isn't busy and then send her in first?"

Aiden's face remains expressionless.

"Stella, is this your paperwork?"

Stella nods, picks up the envelope, and hands it to Ruby.

"I'll review your forms and forward the package on to head office before the day's over."

"Thanks, Ruby."

The door is ajar after she goes to collect Terri.

"Stella, I will be very interested in your observations once we get back to your place...or a lunch and debriefing in town?"

Stella blinks her agreement as Terri enters the manager's office. Terri Price is a nondescript little woman who appears to be thirty years old, but her petite stature renders it difficult for Stella to make an accurate assessment. Her attire calls to mind a school teacher in the 1950s. Her shoes are flats.

Aiden stands for introductions and indicates Terri take the chair behind her boss' desk. "Miss Price, I am given to understand you are the newest member of the Shale Harbour Saving and Loan staff?"

"Correct, Detective. I started my job here in January of this year after Mr. Phelps retired and Ruby took his place. I am very fond of the work." There is a ring of desperation in this last remark. Stella suspects she's afraid her circumstances will change.

"I'm sure you do, Miss Price. We want you to tell us whatever you can remember of Lorraine Young on Friday, as well as any other information you guess might be pertinent as it relates to her possible disappearance. Our sole role, here, is to find Miss Young." He then acknowledges Stella. "Stella Kirk is an old friend. She's here to aid me with introductions. I'm not a Shale Harbour resident and have been away from the area for many years."

"I won't be much help," she prefaces. "Lorraine came in to work on Friday as normal. We were busy right before the long weekend. We didn't have a chance to talk at all." She turns to Stella. "Lorraine loves her trailer. She says she's on a vacation except she works here at the bank. For days, she talked of nothing besides her new window and the deadbolt a guy at the park installed on her door. She is such a safety freak. She likes to be the last one out at night, so she can ensure the bank alarm is set. She doesn't trust Ruby to remember." This portion of the conversation is whispered even though the office door is closed.

Terri continues, "As usual, I left before her on Friday, at five to five. We are closed to the public at three. I was balanced, and my drawer was secured in the vault, so I was permitted to go. I stay to help if I'm needed, but I was sure Mark and Lorraine were both balanced as well. They were deep in conversation when I left. Ruby was alone in her office."

"Do you have any idea why Lorraine is nervous when it comes to security, Terri?"

"No, not for sure. I don't imagine she's always been nervous, but she's been skittish ever since I've known her. She surveys the bank all the time, too."

"What do you mean—surveys?"

"Well, she snoops. I've seen her go in Ruby's office. She says she wants to use the phone in private when Ruby's out, but I've seen her peek at papers on Ruby's desk. She goes in the vault when she isn't busy and digs around in there. She has a remarkable memory for numbers, which comes in handy I guess, but she's forever on the prowl. It's weird."

"Does Mark Bell discuss her behaviour with you?"

"No. I tried to ask him once. Lorraine was in Ruby's office. The bank was quiet, and I asked him what she was up to. He kind of snapped at me and told me to mind my own business."

"And Ruby?"

Terri's eyes expand to twice their size. "I would never say a word to Ruby, Detective. She runs a tight ship. Lorraine could get fired if Ruby expected she was meddling in bank business."

"Thanks for your time, Terri. I will call on you again if I have any other questions. Please don't share our conversation with your co-workers, and this includes Ruby, okay?"

"Of course, Detective. Nice to meet you. Bye, Stella." With social graces completed, she scuffs her way out of the office.

Stella studies Aiden as he continues to write in his notebook. She surmises, with an element of surprise, Lorraine must have been up to no good in one form or another. Perhaps she stole from the bank and then orchestrated her own disappearance. Lunch promises to be of particular interest.

Mark Bell's knock is soft. Aiden rises from his chair to meet him and introduce himself. Mark is a typical tall, dark, and handsome young man in his early thirties. He's dressed in a well-tailored suit Stella expects was expensive. His curls are cut short. It's obvious he is fit and takes pride in his looks. His smile is confident. Mark presents himself as likeable and not threatening in any way.

"Detective Aiden North, Port Ephron RCMP. Nice to meet you, Mr. Bell."

"Please, call me Mark, sir. What can I do to help you find Lorraine?"

He sits in Ruby's chair. He's very comfortable in the office, unlike Terri, who perched on the edge of the seat, and behaved as if she wanted to bolt any minute.

"Describe to me the last time you saw Lorraine, your relationship with her, and what you suppose might have happened."

"Sure. I saw Lorraine at work on Friday. We were busy, what with the long weekend. Terri left for home a few minutes before five. When I left at five, Lorraine was still here. I presume she wanted to meet with Ruby. Employees have not been told the whole story, but I've heard bank funds have gone missing. Head office has narrowed the possible branches to two—this one and another. Ruby has hinted how Lorraine might be suspected."

"Is her involvement possible?"

Stella cannot believe what she's hearing. Ruby did not mention an issue with bank funds although she clearly indicated a potential relationship between Mark and Lorraine.

"No, Detective. Lorraine has been convinced the culprit is a manager higher up in the bank. We've discussed the situation many times. Funny, I bet Kevin, her boyfriend, wonders if she's cheating on him with me because we talk together all the time." He directs a nod toward Aiden. "We are friends, and have no personal interest, despite rumours to the contrary. She has been exploring possibilities of who could be taking money. She did not reveal every detail, but she said if anything happened to her, for me to assume she figured the problem out."

"Did she uncover additional information?"

Mark leans back in the office chair and starts to rock. "Not sure. She was consumed by the bank investigation. She's got a remarkable memory for figures and has been trying to remember lists with discrepancies. I tried to tell her head office is responsible to figure out who was at fault and for her not to get involved."

"What do you conclude might have happened?"

"There's no telling. I hope she took off for a while. I expect she got too close and feared for her safety. Who knows? My best guess is she left town."

****

The interview with Kevin Flores at the lumberyard yielded much less than the interviews with the Savings and Loan employees. Kevin had a date with Lorraine on Saturday because she said she expected to stay late at the bank on Friday. She never showed, and he provided them with no additional information. His anxiety and obvious concern overwhelmed the conversation.

After their interview with Kevin, they return to Cocoa and Café for lunch. The young couple who run the place keep the wide pine floor boards gleaming and the hazelnut flavoured coffee hot and fresh. They choose a table which can support two cups and saucers but not much more, and order.

Stella assesses the patrons in the busy café. She muses about the ease with which she differentiates the locals, the summer residents, and the travellers. The clues are in the hair styles, the clothes, purses, and jewellery, as well as the makes and models of vehicles parked outside. She notices the designer outfits on certain children and the fancy camera gear.

Their order is for ham and cheese croissants. Items are homemade and produce often comes from the couple's own garden. The food is reported to taste better here than anywhere.

Aiden starts the conversation. "What's your conclusion, Stella? Any theories?"

"If I weren't acquainted with Lorraine, I'd say she embezzled money from the Savings and Loan and then took off, but even as I make the statement, the behaviour sounds preposterous."

Aiden slurps his coffee and replies, "There are those occasions when we can presume we understand a person, but we don't. I will have staff speak with the manager of the bank in Port Ephron and try to ascertain more details."

"Why not ask Ruby?"

He tilts his head to the side, even further than normal. "We shouldn't muddy the waters. Ruby is a witness, and not a forthcoming one. We'll talk to her superiors and determine the facts. Do you suppose Mark might be Lorraine's co-conspirator?"

"You mean, do I suspect he put on a show for us today? It's possible. He has the type of personality that can convince any audience he's telling the truth. There's an argument to be made for Kevin's involvement, but I don't expect Terri has a clue." She takes a moment to sip her coffee. "Ruby never revealed information regarding the bank investigation. I'm curious. Was her omission an attempt to maintain Lorraine's reputation? Did she not want to cast Lorraine in a negative light? Maybe she didn't want to cast the bank in that same light."

"Ruby concerns me. It was painfully obvious she tried to manipulate me, which is why I cut our interview short. I might ask you to return and talk to her again. I'm sure she'll be more open with you if you're alone. She spent too much time trying to distract me. Interviewing certain women can be a challenge."

Stella laughs out loud. His blush has not escaped her notice. "Trixie Kirk is my sister. Need I say more? I'll need to have another face to face with her because of my loan. I can use that as an excuse to get my foot in the door."

Lunch is finished in comfortable and thoughtful silence. Before they return to the park, Stella voices her biggest concern again, "Aiden, there is no visible means for Lorraine to leave her trailer after she arrived home. I've been over the lack of possibilities a hundred times. I need to try and figure out how in hell she left."

"Do you want to go through the place one more time and see what you 'feel'?" His smile is slight, but obvious, nonetheless.

"You are making fun of me, Aiden North. Seriously, there must be a piece we missed and yes, I want to go through the place again. It was almost ten when she arrived back home. Two people saw her. She entered her trailer and isn't there anymore. We still don't understand what happened."

"Alright. If you don't mind, I'll make a few calls from your office and get my staff involved. I need officers to interview Lorraine's tenants and inquire at the Port Ephron Savings and Loan. Then we can visit Lorraine's trailer and go over the place again."

CHAPTER 8

We Don't Even Know If She's Hurt

A walk down to Lorraine's rather than waiting at the office for Aiden is Stella's preference. As is her custom, she greets those seated on decks, chats with residents and visitors who approach her with questions or comments, and peruses the overall condition of the park. She makes a mental note to remind Eve to clean garbage out of fire pits once a lot becomes available. There is no reason for campers to stuff cardboard boxes and egg cartons in the fire pit, but they invariably do.

"Does anybody have an idea what happened to Lorraine?" Buddy McGarvey crawls out from under his tent trailer where he's been fiddling with the water connection, and approaches Stella.

"No, Buddy. I'm meeting Detective North over at her unit. I suppose Lorraine is the talk of the park, eh?"

Buddy's rig is minuscule, and it's hard to imagine there's enough room for a grown man to sleep inside. He ties up a few lights used for trim. They likely detached with a gust of wind—not an uncommon occurrence along the cliffs. There are so many rounded globes strung from one side of the trailer to the other, people have been known to come to the office and complain he needs to turn them off before he goes to bed. In addition, he has a pickup truck which is too big for his lot. It blocks traffic and Stella was obliged to find him a spot further up the road in the visitor parking section. Today, he has his vehicle beside his unit, yet again.

"Well, sorta. People are nervous because a young woman went missin'. Don't bother me none. She never talked to me. I tried bein' hospitable, but her type never heeds a guy like me."

He might be digging for a compliment. She can't find words without sarcasm, to allay his insecurities. "Please move your truck out, Buddy. Rigs scheduled to check in today will need to get past."

"No problem, Stella. I will." He turns on his heel and climbs into the trailer.

She isn't sure she's offended him or not. She notes there are several men in her RV park who appear to be interested in Lorraine Young. *They are normal guys who like to watch a single girl alone in the park. Could any of these residents harm Lorraine? No. Conceivably. Stop, Stella. We don't even know if she's hurt.*

Yellow tape snaps in the breeze before she sees it. Every element remains the same. The trailer twinkles in the afternoon sun. The black, 1977 Malibu is still parked askew. As she walks along the road on which Lot Number 16 is located, Aiden pulls up beside her in the ghost car.

"Lift?"

"No." She hears the sadness in her voice. "I need a clue, Aiden. I want to understand what happened to Lorraine. This is ridiculous." She sighs.

"Well, we'll go through her trailer again and identify what we can." His voice sounds patient. He cares but there's little more to be done.

She nods. "Park the car. I'm right behind you. We'll try to find something, Aiden. We have to."

****

"Examine the inside and tell me what you observe, Stella. You have personal knowledge of Lorraine. You understand what is normal and what isn't. We'll explore every inch of her place, from the cupboards to the closets. Will this process work for you?"

"I guess. You want a running commentary as I invade the privacy of my resident's rig?"

"Correct." The damaged lock wobbles with the insertion of the key, and they climb into the stuffy unit.

She's disturbed and surprised, as she was previously, by the coat and purse—tossed aside. "I'll start with her coat and purse. I told you before, this is not the Lorraine I know. Her coat thrown in a heap still unsettles me."

There aren't many kitchen cupboards. There's never enough storage in a trailer to suit their owners. Stella has never been a person who cares if the cans are put here or the baking supplies stored there. Lorraine, on the other hand, has placed her dry goods in alphabetical order on three shelves of one cupboard. Items purchased in a bag, oatmeal for example, are in plastic containers with identification labels. "Her cabinets are as neat as a pin and over-organized, Aiden. There are no surprises here."

He jots a few notes. "Open the fridge and freezer," he instructs. "They're tiny. You can't get much food ahead. I can see Rosemary with a big bucket of ice cream and then no room for a package of hamburger." His smile is wistful.

There is the usual assortment of condiments, orange juice in a glass pitcher, and a milk carton in the fridge. The cardboard spout is stained yellow and Stella expects the milk has soured. There are a few apples and a brownish lettuce in the vegetable drawer. "The fridge seems normal. I assume she planned to shop on her way home from work on Friday, but Mildred never mentioned any bags, and there're no other indications she shopped."

The freezer, which is big enough for a couple of metal ice cube trays, a few buns, and a steak or two, is a mess. "Did the identification people open the freezer, Aiden?"

"Of course. Are you able to detect black residue around the front of the door? They dusted for prints. Why? What's the matter?"

She turns to him and leaves the door wide open. "Lorraine would never let her freezer become this chaotic. The ice cube trays aren't on top of one another. There are ice cubes on the floor of the freezer. Others are topsy-turvy in the trays—as if someone came in here and grabbed ice cubes."

"That's not possible."

"I appreciate how silly this sounds." She can't prevent the irritation from creeping into her tone.

He raises a hand to settle her. "We took Sally Black's key. No one can get in." He turns back to his notepad.

"Okay." Stella is rattled, regardless. "Her cupboards and fridge are in the state I expect them to be—neat as a pin. Her freezer is a mess. I don't understand."

"Let's look under the dining booth benches. Did you inspect those when you were in before? You didn't mention them."

She opens them both, and finds one stuffed with extra linens, folded and in plastic bags. The other holds a few gardening tools as well as insect repellent, rain gear, and a fabric welcome sign attached to a black wrought iron post. "This is typical storage, Aiden. Could a person get out through here?"

They take the time to unload each bench storage box to examine the floor below. They can detect no signs of tampering. Lorraine did not remove the base of her dining booth and slip out under her trailer, any more than she escaped through a secret hatch under her bed. Nor did she depart through the bathroom sky light.

Stella sits with a thud on the couch. "I have no idea what to tell you, Aiden. So far, her freezer is a mess."

"It's hot in here, Stella. Let's see what there is to discover in Lorraine's bedroom. The screen door doesn't provide much in the way of ventilation alone, but I don't want to open any windows. Storage benches aside, we're here to observe and not disturb, if possible."

They enter the bedroom at the back of the trailer—Stella first. Her eyes dart to the new window and the stain on the sill. "Nick has decided, once we locate Lorraine, he will inspect this super secure window and determine why the hell it leaked."

"There must be an increase in acid rain this summer. The stain is rimmed in red. Think about the damage caused to vehicles and buildings if it can stain a window sill. Anything else appear out of place?" Aiden retreats to stand in the doorway.

Stella surveys the room. "It looks the same as it did the last time." The head of the bed is against the wall opposite the new window. This closet is considered generous by trailer standards. There are built-in lights installed in additional cupboards above the bed. "I'll do my best."

"You'll notice if her space isn't in order, in the same way you noted with the freezer."

She starts with the storage over the bed. This is where Lorraine keeps her sweaters and casual pants, her sweats, and jeans, stacked in neat piles. "The shelves are normal for Lorraine, Aiden. My cupboards are stuffed to the gunnels with no sense of order." She sneaks a glance over at him and grins.

The closet doors slide along a track so one covers the other. She has skirts and blouses hung in coordinated sets. They resemble a display rack at Eaton's. She slides the door back and opens the one on the other side. Here are her dress pants and dresses, each hung on individual hangers. Stella peers at Lorraine's shoes. Each pair is placed side by side, toes out, and the two empty spots she observed initially, remain. One could assume a space is for the shoes she wore to work, but why is there another empty area? "This is weird."

"What do you see?" Aiden leans against the door frame, notepad in hand.

"Her closet is in order. There are a couple of empty hangers which indicate clothes she wore to work on Friday, but there are two pairs of shoes gone. There are no sneakers. I assume one of the empty spots is for them and the other for the shoes she wore to work."

"Possibly she took her sneakers with her to walk over her lunch break."

"You might be right. Can we ask Mildred if Lorraine carried a shoe bag in her hands when she arrived home?"

"Sure. She was lounging on her deck when we came in, enjoying the sunshine, barefoot, and sipping lemonade. Her fire pit is lit up, too. She told us she observed a purse, and that was all."

"I am aware." Stella closes her eyes. The situation is complicated. She takes her time. "But if she took her sneakers to work, she would bring them home for the weekend, or else wear them and leave her shoes at the bank. A plausible option. I want to know for sure, though."

"Okay. What we can identify is a messy freezer and, since I didn't observe them in the car either, a pair of footwear unaccounted for. Correct?"

"Yes. Not much for an hour-long search."

"Every little bit helps. Let's go visit with my friend Mildred Fox, shall we?"

His expression is sheepish. She's reminded of when they were kids and thought they had a secret. He is fully aware Mildred will talk his leg off if he comes across to her as enthusiastic.

****

"Hey, Mildred! Are you in there?" Stella bellows through the screen into the darkness of the trailer made more subdued by the tired pink curtains hung over tiny windows.

She looms into the doorway and fills the space. "Hold yer horses, Stella. Can't an old woman take a piss without gettin' yelled at?" A serious edge creeps into her voice. "Did ya find her?"

"No, Mildred. There's no sign of her. May we ask a couple of questions, though?"

"Oh, hi, Officer." She offers Aiden a flirty bat of her eyes. "Let me dig out my slippers for these poor feet, and I'll be out in a sec. Happy to help."

"He's a detective, Mildred. Detective North."

"Okay. Okay." She lumbers through the door which seems to swell with the effort to permit her passage. "I heard you call him Aiden." She draws out the word to make the two syllables stretch to three, and snickers as she plunks into a pink plastic basket chair near the door and well under the awning. Flies gather where the canvas meets the wall of the trailer—trapped under the canopy and ready to fly straight into the unit the moment the old lady opens the screen. She keeps a swatter on the table beside the chair.

Aiden North waits until she's comfortable. "We need to know more, Mildred. I want you to take your time and provide as many details as you can remember, okay?"

Mildred nods. Stella thinks she's more interested than when they first arrived.

"Please be so kind as to describe exactly what Lorraine wore, and any particular objects she carried, when she came home on Friday night. You are a pivotal witness and your recollections are very important to the investigation."

Stella glares at Aiden. He's laid his charm on as thick as icing. He wants Mildred to be cooperative, but really?

"I thought I told you what I saw, but here goes. She got out of her car. She wore a coat and I couldn't make out what she had on underneath. You know the kind of summer coat you throw on in the morning when the air is misty, but you lug home because it's hot now? Well, it was late and cool, and she wore a coat. She carried a purse. She didn't have no groceries or packages I could make out."

"What did she wear on her feet, Mildred? Do you remember?"

Mildred beams up at Aiden. Her dental plate needs attention and clacks when she talks. "Shoes."

Aiden is the epitome of patience. "Are you able to describe her shoes, Mildred? Your observations are important."

"They were shoes, as far as I recall." She casts a glance at Stella for confirmation. "What are those low-heeled kind young women wear when they prefer sandals but aren't allowed to at work. What are they called?"

"Flats? Do you mean flats?" Stella opens her mouth for the first time. *Our primary witness can't identify a shoe with no heel.*

Mildred points an arthritis damaged finger toward Stella. "Right. Flats." She returns her attention to Aiden. "She wore flats."

"You're certain."

"Yes, I'm sure. I may not remember the name, but I can tell the difference between a flat and a heel. I think it's time I found another drink. You folks interested in lemonade?" She struggles to extricate herself from the basket chair that has no doubt imprinted its plastic pattern on her ample behind.

Stella catches Aiden's attention with a withered expression, and he poses the question she has wanted him to ask from the start. "Any chance she wore sneakers, Mildred; or carried her sneakers in her hand?"

"Or carried a shoe bag along with her purse?"

"Listen, you two. Lorraine came home around ten o'clock Friday night and parked her car over there as you see it now. She wore a light coat and flats. She carried her purse. No hat, no sneakers, no other person. She never looked over at me or my fire. She climbed her deck and went inside her trailer. In a couple of minutes, the lights were out. There's no more. I'm gonna get my drink now." She climbs up the steps and stumbles through the door. The flies take advantage and follow her in.

Aiden nods to Stella. He leans toward the screen. "Thanks, Mildred. We appreciate your help. Try not to gossip, okay?"

"Don't worry. Nobody ever wants to know what I think, anyway. See ya."

"Later, Mildred." Stella waves. "Easy on the lemonade, now."

As Stella and Aiden return to his vehicle over at Lorraine's, Duke purrs up beside them in the golf cart. Kiki is on the passenger side. She starts to growl the minute the machine comes to a stop. "Kiki, shut the hell up."

"Hi, Duke. You're out and around early, today. Problems? Time for you to catch up on your laundry?" Stella notes how Duke is dressed in his traditional tank top, but the plaid pyjama bottoms are a new fashion statement.

He ignores her observation. "Yes and no. Lorraine's been on my mind. Did you talk to her much since she moved out to the park last week?"

"No, Duke. This started because I tried to visit with her before the long weekend. Why?"

"Well, she acted like a scared rabbit all the time." His voice changes at this point. His tone drops its bravado and becomes more John—his given name—and less Duke. "I realize she thinks I'm a sleaze, and I can be, but she started to act frightened of me. I came right out and asked her, last week, if I bothered her 'cause I don't mean to, and you won't believe what she said."

Aiden has his notebook out. "What did she say, Duke?"

"She told me she wasn't afraid of me and she was sorry if she gave me the wrong impression. That was nice of her, right?"

He's anxious. Stella isn't sure why.

"Yes, but why didn't you tell us this before?"

"Seemed personal, I guess. Then, thinkin' she might be hurt—well, she was sure as hell scared of somethin', Detective."

While he talks, he pets his dog with a steady rhythm, and holds her collar so she remains calm. Stella glimpses the real John Powell through the overpowering act that has become Duke Powell, her security guard at the park. She likes him, even though she isn't privy to this version very often and frequently forgets John exists.

"Do you have any idea what she was afraid of, Duke?"

"Not a clue, but I was startin' to git worried. She avoided spendin' any time with her neighbours or stoppin' on the road to chat. She wasn't takin' walks. I only ever saw her comin' and goin' from work. She was hidin' in her trailer. Weird."

"Thanks for letting us in on your concerns, Duke." Aiden closes his notebook with a flick.

"No problem." He re-engages the cart and points the tiny nose up the road along the cliff's edge.

Stella searches Aiden's face for any indication of his thoughts.

"What is his motive for telling us he asked her on a date in the past, but wants us to understand how she's afraid, but not of him? I'm suspicious there might be more information he needs to share." Aiden gazes out across the expanse of open ocean.

"You met Duke first, when we did the staff interview. Since he's had a chance to mull over the issue, he's decided the time was right to introduce you to John."

CHAPTER 9

That's Not a Bad Theory

Stella is puzzled as to why her sister called. Trixie isn't usually enthusiastic if a task relates to the act of cooperation. She agreed to sign the papers, but Stella assumed getting her to the bank would be the challenge. "No, Ruby hasn't called from the bank, but it's only been a couple of days. Why don't we meet for lunch? We can take a few minutes to stop in and visit with Dad, at least."

"Okay, we can go to Cocoa and Café if you pay. I'm by myself, today. Brigitte and Mia are off to their mother and kid program at the community centre theatre."

"I'm your back-up entertainment?"

"I can kill two birds with one stone—enjoy a free lunch as well as go sign the loan papers."

Loneliness echoes in her sister's voice. She suspects Trixie and her new man parted ways. Trixie's world revolves around her daughter and granddaughter, despite the bravado she displays when discussing her lovers. The job at the fish plant is part-time and dead-end. She's no doubt down in the dumps because life isn't filled with glamour and excitement. "You can still kill two birds with one stone—we can go for lunch and then visit Dad."

"Okay. I'll meet you at the café around noon. Bring Nick."

Her chuckle accompanies the click of the phone as Trixie hangs up. *She should learn how to say good bye.*

"I thought I heard you come downstairs." Nick rounds the corner into Stella's office. He's showered and changed. He appears younger still, if that's even possible.

Stella's heart does a wee flip. "When the phone rang, I came into the

67

office. I hoped the call was work, but it was Trixie." She sighs. "We made a lunch date and we'll go to the manor afterward since the bank hasn't called. Want to come along? At least the old coot knows you." Her forced laugh has a tinge of sadness. She knows Nick understands.

He places a mug of coffee in front of her and then proceeds to lower his long frame into the wooden office chair that dates from before World War II. He studies her from across the cluttered desk. "Speaking of banks, you could put an end to your worries and let me invest, you know. We make a good team, right?"

She sighs again. Her voice holds an element of resolve. "I need to be able to manage this on my own, Nick. You understand."

Nick's nod confirms he is well aware of her determination. "Okay, but you can come to me for help. I'd love to go visit with Norbert, but not right now. The place is busy, and there's a work list as long as my arm. Paul and Eve are already assigned tasks for the day. My priority is to tangle with those two big old pine trees at the back of the tenting site. When I get the equipment in place to knock them over, Paul will help me."

His plans tumble out of him before he abruptly changes the subject. "Has Aiden given you an update? Any news?"

"Nope." She leans back in her chair. Her long fingers are wrapped around her pottery mug. "The way I view this mystery, there are three possible scenarios: she's dead, or a person we might well know took her and she isn't dead, or she disappeared of her own accord." She frowns at her coffee. "I hope the last one is the correct option, but if so, we've missed an obvious exit point. There is no reasonable explanation for how she managed to get the hell out of the trailer."

"I bet old Mildred drank one too many lemonades, Stella. Not uncommon. If Lorraine took off, she pulled her car up beside the trailer and didn't give a damn how straight she parked before she ran around to the other side. She could double back through the fields and be out to the road in fifteen minutes with a vehicle waiting for her."

"Mildred is positive Lorraine went up the steps and into the trailer. Besides, Nick, her coat and purse were in there."

"My theory is she planted those before she ever left for work on Friday. She had two coats and purses. Mildred thinks she entered, but she actually crept around to the back, grabbed her sneakers from under the trailer, and took off."

"That's not a bad theory, but it's necessary to assume Mildred was drunk and didn't realize Lorraine never went inside—despite the fact she swears she saw the lights come on."

At this point, Alice pokes her red halo of curls around the door casing. "A guy named Kevin Forbes is in reception, Stella. He says he needs to talk to you and it's personal."

"I'll be right there, Alice. Tell him I'm on my way." She turns her attention to Nick. "Will you stay for this?"

"No way! There are two trees calling my name. You can give me the details tonight at supper. You will eat supper with me, won't you? I'll provide a couple of steaks and a bottle of red wine. Are you in?"

She giggles. "I'm in. Now, get your ass to work, mister!"

He's still guffawing as he makes his way toward the screen door and the veranda.

Kevin Flores stands in reception. He shifts his weight from one foot to the other and fails to notice when Stella approaches. "Hi, Kevin. What brings you to the RV park on a Thursday morning? Day off?"

Kevin flinches. "Oh, Miss Kirk, you startled me. No, I'm goin' in to work but I said I'd be late 'cause I wanted to talk to you. No sign of Lorraine, right?"

"No sign, Kevin. The police are doing what they can."

A gust of anxiety puffs across the space between them. "Thank God. If there's no news, then there's a chance she might still be alive."

Stay calm. She lets no expression show on her face or in her voice. "Any reason she might not be alive, Kevin? She may have discovered a creative way to disappear."

Stella steers him into the big living room to give them more privacy. His accusations fall out of him in a rush. "Mark Bell and Lorraine were up to no good. They stole money from the bank and planned to take off together. Then he double-crossed her and killed her."

His words are paced in pants and jolts. Stella does not interrupt. She wants to hear what he has to say.

"Lorraine was messed up. She was afraid most of the time, as if people were after her or she was gonna get caught or hurt any minute. She got weird. I didn't know what to do to help her. She was spendin' day after day workin' late with Mark. She told me somethin' was goin' on, but she refused to say what."

Her voice remains steady and calm. "Do you want to tell this to Detective North, Kevin? I'll call him. You can make a statement. Every little bit helps."

****

By the time Kevin leaves the park to meet with Aiden North and give voice to his theory relating to Lorraine and Mark Bell, Stella has little time to get ready for her lunch with Trixie and their planned visit with Norbert Kirk. She hustles upstairs to her apartment, changes clothes, and slides her feet into canvas espadrilles. She clatters down the stairs, and shouts to Alice who is making sandwiches for the staff lunches, to say she will be gone for a couple of hours. The screen door slams as she trots to her Jeep.

She fights annoyance when she casts her eyes around Cocoa and Café. Trixie is nowhere to be seen, of course. God forbid she should be on time, for once. Stella chooses a small table near the window, in order to view the deck, resplendent with potted annuals. There are more people seated outside than inside, with most under festive umbrellas advertising various brands of beer. She rationalizes her choice. She sits outside most of the time at home.

Trixie appears at the door. She's perky. Her thick, long, and blond highlighted tresses are tied with contrived abandon. Tendrils frame her perfect complexion. She's wearing short shorts and a puffy top that falls off one shoulder. Her purse is white leather with studs and fringes. They move around her as she walks.

"Come on, Stella. Let's sit on the veranda."

"No. I spend most of my days outside, Trixie. Sit here. We'll drink iced tea and order."

Trixie does as she's told, but pouts regardless. They order croissant sandwiches. Stella watches Trixie, whose eyes dart around the café and squint out toward the sun-drenched deck. She is forever on the alert for someone she knows, or for an opportunity to impress. Trixie wants to be recognized.

"How's the new boyfriend?" Stella asks her sister the question with malice and forethought. If her new man is still in the picture, Trixie would not be so enthusiastic in her scanning of the restaurant.

"New man? Oh, Jimmy was a lark. Lots of money." She taps the sunglasses as her proof. "Buckets of money, but not a brain cell in his head. Spends too much time with his mummy if you get my drift." Trixie sits on the edge of her bistro chair and leans over the table so more of her cleavage than necessary is

NO VISIBLE MEANS: A Stella Kirk Mystery #1

revealed to the neighbouring lunch goers. Not sensing an immediate response, she wiggles back into her bistro chair. "How's Nick?"

"Great, thanks." Stella plays dumb. She refuses to acknowledge her discomfort with Trixie's behaviour. Furthermore, she will not share details related to her relationship. "Nick needs to cut down trees this morning and supervise the staff, so I can lunch with my sister and visit my demented father, guilt-free."

"You won't tell me the scoop, will you?"

"There's not much to tell, Trixie. I depend on Nick to manage the park. I couldn't do all the work alone. He's good at his job and a fine person. We get along, which is most important."

"Okay, okay. As long as he helps you, so you don't ask me." She is immediately distracted by two middle-aged men who come in to the café and choose a table near the back. "Do you know them? Do they work here in town?"

Stella, who never notices a new man in town, unless he owns a big fifth wheel he wants to park at Shale Cliffs, has no idea. She watches Trixie sit up straighter, fluff her hair, and plant a fixed smile on her beautiful, albeit aging, face.

"Maybe they're lawyers. Someone said there's so much property changing hands around here, they needed to hire more lawyers at Stephens and Stephens. Can you make out wedding rings from your angle?"

Trixie hisses when Stella turns to look. "No, don't be obvious!"

The remainder of their lunch is much the same. Trixie scans. Stella eats. They drive their separate vehicles to the local manor for a visit with their father.

The wide corridor stretches into the distance as they walk side by side to his room. He doesn't share because of his condition. He would never remember his roommate, which would cause continual problems for him, the staff, and any other resident unlucky enough to be lodged with Norbert. When they get to his door and crane to see inside, he isn't there. Stella always calls the facility to give them notice of when she plans to visit. Today was no exception.

As they turn toward the common room, a sunny voice reverberates down the hall. "Here we are. Here we are. Norbert, your daughters have arrived for a visit. Aren't you the lucky duck, with such nice family to come visit you?"

"Nice family? What? I gut no family."

Stella and Trixie exchange a glance. A few months ago, he recognized one or the other of them, but not now. "Hi, Dad," the two women say in unison.

Norbert takes his hand off the nurse's arm and extends it. "Norbert Kirk, here. And who might you be?"

Stella reaches out to shake her father's hand in an act of acceptance and compliance. Trixie, on the other hand, starts to argue. "Dad, you know us. We're your daughters. I'm Trixie and this is Stella."

He shakes Stella's hand. "Nice to meet you. What did you say your name was, again?"

Most of the visit is the same. Stella finds the easiest way to cope is to tell her father a story. He never remembers, but her words fill the stale air, devoid of any hints of a relationship. He responds with comments. On occasion, they might even make sense.

"Dad, a young woman, one of our seasonal residents, has disappeared from the park. Mildred watched her go into her trailer. The door was locked from the inside, but she is nowhere to be found. We're afraid she's been hurt or worse. People at the park are in a state. What do you think happened?"

Norbert is busy as he tries to tie his shoe. Trixie offers to help, but he refuses. He's bent at the waist and Stella isn't convinced he comprehended much of the story she told.

He glares up at her for a moment. "Anybody ever tell you seein' is believin'? Who are you people, for God's sake, and what're you doin' here?"

****

Trixie was apoplectic when they left the care home. Stella was happy they took separate cars to the manor. Her sister said this was her last visit and for Stella to not ask her again. She'll calm down. They need to support one another; there's no one else.

"Are you home, Stella?" Alice shouts from reception as the screen door slams to announce her boss' return to the house.

"Yeah, I'm here. Busy afternoon?" She heads straight for the office and Alice, who is seated behind the counter. She has two items in her lap—a novel and Kiki.

"Nope. Quiet for a Thursday. Ten new arrivals are booked but nobody yet. You'd wonder if there's water over the causeway." She giggles at her own joke. "The lady from the bank called. Ruby Wilson, right? She asked if you could come around four and it's almost four now. I told her I hoped you'd be back."

Stella grimaces at the idea of retracing her steps to town. "Okay. By the way, is Kiki your new assistant in reception?"

"No, but Duke needed to go on an errand and didn't want to leave her in his trailer. He said the place was too hot and his air conditioner is on the fritz."

Not an issue. Kiki can visit with Alice anytime…and Alice knows this. "I need you to call Ruby back and tell her I'm on my way. I also want you to radio Nick, wherever he is on the grounds, and tell him I needed to go to the bank, but supper is still on. Will you make those calls for me?"

Alice places Kiki gently on the floor beside her. She's on a tie and can't become a guard, running after visitors to protect Alice from vicious campers. "Of course, Boss." She grins. Stella figures Alice is aware of her relationship with Nick, but trusts she would never, in a million years, let on.

The bank is closed. Stella wishes she had called Ruby earlier in the day to confirm the loan papers are ready for signature. Now, she'll need to make another trip to accompany Trixie to sign off. This is a pile of work for a lousy ten thousand dollars.

Ruby's heels tap on the stone floor as she makes her way across the lobby to unlock the door. The bank has been closed for ninety minutes. She is dressed to perfection, as usual. Stella does a quick assessment of her linen capris to determine the wrinkle level. The expression "an unmade bed" springs to mind.

"Come in. Come in. Let me lock the door behind you. Don't need any more customers today. Terri and Mark left. The place is ours. Let's go into my office."

"You seem to be better, Ruby."

"What?"

"You aren't limping anymore."

"I had a little blister. Minor casualty. I wish I could wear sensible, clunky shoes the way you do, but I must keep up appearances. Now, I wanted to share information regarding my interviews with the staff."

"Interviews? I assumed I was here to sign loan papers, Ruby."

"Loan? Oh, yes, your loan. No. No. I haven't heard a word. I talked to both my staff earlier today. My assessment of the circumstances is clear and I'm sure I'm correct."

"Do tell." Stella is annoyed. Ruby needs to speak with Aiden. This little after-hours bank visit is unnecessary, and she has a business to run. She knows her annoyance has seeped through in her tone.

Ruby does not notice, or if she does, she doesn't appear offended. "Terri has no pertinent information. Mark, on the other hand, is convinced Lorraine has taken the money and vanished." She leans over her desk and shrinks the distance between them. Stella senses the back of her chair as she leans away. "I am suspicious Mark and Lorraine embezzled together. Lorraine has double-crossed Mark and now he's blamed the whole mess on her. What do you think?"

What does this conversation mean? Ruby is convinced Lorraine authored her own disappearance, which is what Nick hypothesized this morning. "You need to discuss this with Detective North, Ruby. He's the investigator, not me. I'm surprised the staff spoke with you because Aiden asked them to keep information to themselves until the situation is sorted out."

"You sat in on the first interviews. You should know my theory. Lorraine has taken off. As far as the staff is concerned, I am their manager. They will tell me what I need to know." Her frustration is barely hidden.

"Call Detective North, Ruby," she directs as she stands to take her leave. "I imagine he'll want to talk to you, as well as your staff."

CHAPTER 10

The Situation Is Chaotic

"Yes. There's room for a twenty-foot trailer. Have you been here before? Good. You'll be in the third row back, to the right of the intersection. Stop at the office when you arrive." Stella hangs up the phone and surveys the desk. She has managed to clutter Alice's order in less than three hours. Most of the check-outs are gone; there might be a couple of stragglers. The park will be almost full for the weekend which bodes well for summer if you consider June is not here yet.

"You sound busy." Nick rounds the corner with a late morning cup of coffee for Stella.

"Typical...give Alice a day off and I can't keep my head above water. She'll kick my ass tomorrow when she sees the mess I've made of her filing system."

"Will we be full for the weekend?"

Accepting the mug, she leans against the counter. "Still a dozen plus spaces, but we're in good shape for this time of the year, and there's lots of days left for the campers who can't be bothered to make reservations."

She peers across at him, sprawled on the bench under the window. "What are Eve and Paul up to today?"

"Oh, Paul's helping the Blacks fix their deck." He gives her an innocent wide-eyed look. "Sally was tickled pink to supervise Paul for the day. Eve's busy tidying lots after check-outs. Then she expects to mow. I'm sure she did the bathrooms before I even found my clothes this morning." He repeats the expression.

"Stop with the looks, mister!" She blushes despite a rigorous attempt to maintain her composure. "Are you here to make lunch for us, or are you off to shingle? If you need to go to work, then I'll do it."

"Nope, I'm good. I can help. I see enough for you to do." He leans back and holds his coffee with both hands. "Any more information about what's happened to Lorraine?"

"No word."

"I wish Aiden North would call with an idea as to their progress. People ask me, and there's no update. It's not as if we don't care."

"Even if we did get an update, we couldn't share it." Stella sips her coffee. *No need for rumours to start. An RV park is always ripe with rumours.*

"The other topic of conversation for our residents is whether we're gonna see any ash clouds from Mount St. Helens. My theory is the park's busy because Quebecers want to see the country before the next referendum and Americans are getting away from the pollution. Right?"

"The world is a crazy place. I'm glad Quebec voted to stay in Canada. If they separated, their decision would put the Maritimes in the same position as Alaska in the States—whole country between them and the rest of America. The news scares me sometimes."

They both sip their tepid coffee in silence while she sorts through the piles of paper bits on the counter. One puff of wind if door flies open and her organized chaos would be out of control. "As far as Lorraine is concerned, if she's in cahoots with Mark Bell, then every detail he shared was a lie." She looks across at Nick. "There's a distinct possibility she took off and he'll follow when the dust settles. Ruby Wilson agrees. She says they've stolen money. Aiden has never mentioned, yet, if a theft from the bank has been reported or if the embezzlement investigation is still internal."

"You may be right, but I'm convinced she managed this on her own. We aren't well acquainted with her at all. I've got a few theories. Her abusive husband, released from jail, wants to find her. Lorraine Young isn't her real name. She's a protected witness for the FBI. Who knows?"

"Too many Perry Mason reruns, Nick." As the phone jangles them both into reality, Stella picks up the receiver and Nick saunters back toward the kitchen to start lunch.

"Shale Cliffs RV Park. How may I help you? Aiden? Of course, you can come out. Nick and I are organizing lunch for the staff. No, I gave Alice the day off, which means I'm stuck here in reception, but you're welcome. If you want to talk windows again, Nick will be able to answer your questions. Great. See you soon."

As she replaces the receiver, two tent trailers, both pulled by station wagons, arrive in the front parking lot. Stella glances at her log book and finds the pair of reservations—a couple of brothers and their families who arrived right on time for the weekend. Before she has their paperwork sorted, an Airstream trailer, one of the longest ones she has ever seen, pulls in behind them. She can't immediately determine if they reserved, but she can put them further away from the shore and closer to the main house if they didn't plan.

By the time the office empties out, and she has drained the last of her cold coffee, Eve and Paul return from their work assignments, Aiden is parking his vehicle, and Nick has called out twice to announce lunch is ready. She expects he's placed a wedge of cheese along with a loaf of bread and a jar of peanut butter on the table, but whatever he serves up is fine with her.

"On my way! Hi, Aiden. Help yourself to what grub you can find. Nick! Check the fridge for lemonade. Alice said she made a batch yesterday before she left." She turns to the detective. "Today was supposed to be cool, but the air's warmer since you called."

Aiden, head tilted in his permanent quizzical expression, nods agreement regarding her weather report, but his focus must be elsewhere. "When the staff goes back to work, you, Nick, and I need a discussion."

****

"Eve, what are you up to this afternoon? Can you cover the office for an hour while I go to Lorraine's with Nick and Detective North?"

Piles of curls, tied into her signature loose and unruly bun, bounce around as she self-assesses her work attire. "Dressed in garden clothes? Are you sure I won't give you a bad reputation?"

Stella chuckles and pats her on the shoulder. "Don't ever take the time to notice what I wear from one day to the next. Campers only want you to find a spot for them. Folks are happy to get out of town. You look fine."

"I can mow again later this afternoon. I'll stay late, too, Stella, especially with Alice gone today." She grins at her boss.

"Thanks, Eve. Your flexibility is much appreciated right now."

Nick, Aiden, and Stella assemble on the back veranda. "Am I keeping you from your work, Nick? I don't want to interfere." Aiden's concern is misguided.

"Nope." He sneaks a glance at Stella. "I'm here most of the time. The utility shed can be roofed after supper if necessary. What's the story today? No news, eh?"

"Dead ends. There are issues I need to review. You two might be able to help."

Perched on the edge of a side chair, Stella props her elbows on her knees. "What issues, Aiden?"

The detective holds up the fingers on his right hand and turns each one in as he itemizes his concerns. "I need to understand more regarding the operation of the window you installed." He catches Nick's eye for confirmation. "A person could manage to get out that window, right?"

Nick raises his eyebrows and sighs. "Yes, in theory, but I still don't see how anyone could get out and avoid creating a significant slam behind them. Mildred would have heard it bang, or break, if it had been dropped."

"Okay. Next issue—Rob and Sally Black held a key. Is it possible he waited inside for her?"

"Mildred never mentioned seeing him that night, and I expect Sally notices anytime he's gone." Stella isn't convinced, despite Rob's sleazy personality, that the man is capable of such behaviour. "Do you surmise Rob hurt her, or scared her, and then she climbed out the window after he left?"

"Only conjecture, Stella."

Aiden's face has a grimace Stella finds disconcerting. *The police don't have a damned clue—literally.* "Nick is sure she ran away on her own; stole money from the bank and took off. Right, Nick?" She turns to her manager for confirmation.

Nick stretches long legs out under the old round wooden coffee table. "She never entered her trailer. She came home, Mildred saw her, but she sneaked around to the back of her rig and ran out through the field. Her runners were hidden underneath, out of sight. Bing, bang, boom, she's gone."

"It's a good theory, Nick, but Mildred insists the light came on in the trailer after Lorraine came home. The window holds the answers. Let's go do another examination." Aiden then turns to Stella. "There are two men who live here in the park I want to re-interview, if they're around—Rob Black and your security guy, Duke, is it?"

Stella nods. "Duke Powell." Her face is grim. She hates to implicate others, but expects she has no choice. "You would be wise to speak with Buddy McGarvey, too. I'll show you where his tent trailer is. He's a character and is another one who eyed Lorraine."

After standing, she changes her mind and sits again. "I planned to call you today to report on my visit to the bank yesterday. I assumed Ruby Wilson wanted to meet to complete my loan application, but it appeared she was anxious for me to hear how she's sure Mark Bell is Lorraine's accomplice. Her theory is they stole money together and then Lorraine double-crossed Mark and took off. She figures Lorraine is long gone. She interviewed Terri as well as Mark."

Aiden nods throughout her whole confession. "She called the station. I told her, in no uncertain terms, that it is inappropriate for her to interview her staff without police assistance, and she needs to share information and theories with me and not you." He grins. "I'm the one who shares with you, but she doesn't need to know."

"I said the same, except for the last part. I'm happy she called you, though."

They stand and prepare to walk the main park road to Lorraine's trailer. "The issue is that the Savings and Loan in Port Ephron told my investigators Ruby Wilson reported a discrepancy in the branch's figures, but the report was received early this week. I expect their assistant manager got the dates wrong. I need to double-check."

The three of them walk to the intersection near the cliffs. Stella points out Buddy's tent trailer. His truck is in front, for the umpteenth time. Stella notices he has installed a wooden post beside his unit and attached a sun umbrella to it with black duct tape. She makes a mental note for Nick to stop by later in the day to talk to him and determine if they can find a method to attach the umbrella with a goal to make it more aesthetically pleasing—a few metal cable fasteners might do the trick.

"Nick. Stella." His voice is solemn. "The time is right to call in a search team. Are you folks aware of a search and rescue organization on this side of the isthmus, or must I mobilize the one in Port Ephron?"

Stella glances first at Nick, eyes wide. "You presume she's dead, don't you Aiden?"

"Experience tells me, if she didn't fake her disappearance, then yes."

His voice is flat. Stella is unnerved. "To answer your question, yes, there is a small but mighty search and rescue group made up of locals from the immediate area. Ironically, it is led by none other than my own Duke Powell. Rob Black isn't involved, but Buddy McGarvey is. Paul attended meetings last summer although there were no issues for them except a lost dog found in two hours. Duke bragged for days, even though the mutt probably chased a rabbit, and would have been home for supper."

"Please get hold of Duke when you go back to the office. I'll interview Buddy, as well as Rob Black, if they're around, and then meet with Duke at the house." The visit to Lorraine's trailer is abandoned for the time being.

****

By early the next morning, Shale Harbour Volunteer Search and Rescue has assembled in the parking lot of the Shale Cliffs RV Park. Stella has consented to the use of the park as their headquarters—Operation Central, as Duke prefers it called. Six people, including Buddy McGarvey and Paul Morgan, dressed in bright orange and armed with walkie-talkies, mill around and attempt to get organized while Alice and Eve remain near the office with Stella. They rearrange the furniture in the common room and place two trestle tables in the middle. This is where the group will study aerial maps of the surrounding territory and gather for meals and updates. In addition to Sergeant Moyer, there are three other uniformed constables assigned to assist Search and Rescue.

Lorraine's boyfriend turns up unannounced. "Can I help? Word in town is Search and Rescue has been asked to look for Lorraine." He's approached Stella, who is out on the veranda with a mug of coffee, eyeing the action in her parking lot.

"Kevin. Great of you to offer. Duke Powell, my security guy, manages the search and rescue team. You must talk to him. I don't know if they want additional volunteers yet, but you can ask. Off work today?"

"I took vacation days. I'm at a loss, Stella. May I stay here and help?"

Stella peers at him as he stands at the foot of her veranda stairs, one hand on the railing. He's the picture of forlorn; an abandoned puppy. She could not be convinced he has hurt Lorraine, but she understands any circumstance is possible. "Go talk to Duke, over there on the golf cart."

"Stella?"

"Yeah?"

"Why didn't they start a search for her until now? She could be dying." The muscles of his pudgy face begin to collapse.

"I guess, because there's no sign of a struggle at her place. It's plausible she took off, Kevin. We'll hope that's what happened. You go find Duke, if you want to get involved, okay?"

Kevin turns toward the assembled group behind him.

As Stella watches him approach Duke, who is busy barking instructions, she opens the screen door and peers through the darkened indoor gloom. "Alice, are you dog-sitting Kiki? I don't see her."

Alice appears around the corner from reception. "Of course." Kiki is wedged under her arm. "You don't mind, do you? I didn't ask permission."

"No problem. Duke is running the show out here and I couldn't fathom how managing the dog, too, might work. No matter. There's Aiden—Detective North. I guess the time's come to get organized." She meets Aiden at the top of the stairs. "What's the bottom line? Do these guys have a plan?"

Aiden trudges up the steps and settles into a bentwood chair beside her. "Yes. My people will accompany each group as they fan out. If she's on this side of the isthmus, they should find her today."

"You mean if she's dead and her body is out there, they should find her today, right?"

"I didn't want to be too graphic, but yes, if she's dead, Stella."

Members of the search team spread out. Nick and Kevin Flores are included. Aiden stays at the park to handle one of the radios and be near a telephone. Alice and Eve start to make sandwiches.

The phone bleats and Stella races inside. "Trixie! What's up?" Stella is breathless and surprised to hear her sister's voice.

"Hi. I'm off for the weekend. Did you get the loan or what? We've waited for days."

"No idea, Trixie. The situation is chaotic out here right now. The police brought in Search and Rescue. This is 'Operation Central' as Duke refers to my living room. The money hasn't crossed my mind."

"Will you give her a ring on Monday? I work every day next week, but if you telephone me at the office, I'll do my best to get away. Need help?"

"No, thanks. My staff assumed control." She smiles into the receiver. "I'm on the porch with Aiden North and a cup of hot coffee." She knows the very last item on Trixie's wish list is to come out to Shale Cliffs and cook for a crew. "Listen. I'll contact Ruby and try to encourage her to move our request along. The park is busy, and Nick said he loves the idea of investing. Maybe I won't need bank money."

"Sounds serious. He's wanting to be an investor now? Do tell."

The teasing tone in Trixie's voice is overdone, to say the least, so Stella chooses to ignore her. "Enjoy your weekend. Hi to Brigitte and hug Mia for me." She returns to the veranda.

"You look done in, Aiden. Not sleeping well at the hotel?"

"Had to spend a few nights at home, Stella." He takes a sip of coffee. "Rosie isn't good. Her sisters said they needed me around, so I travelled back and forth for a few days."

His face is expressionless. Stella is unsure how to proceed. She refuses to pry. "I'm sorry, Aiden. I hope she can navigate a way through her troubles."

He nods but doesn't meet her eyes. His gaze is fixed on the flower beds at the far side of the parking lot, weeded with care by Eve. He clutches a police radio in his left hand. "This sort of case rarely ends well, Stella. I've been through enough of them. Right now, I hope they don't locate her; that she ran off with the bank's money. Nick's theory is enticing." He turns to stare at her full in the face. "And plausible, I might add."

"If you say so. We can't figure out how she left the trailer. Maybe she never went in and poor old Mildred imagined she saw the light go on in the kitchen."

"It's still unclear how the situation transpired, Stella, although I'm convinced Mildred saw the light come on. We just don't know how she left, yet. As for today, I hope I'm wrong, but if Lorraine Young's body is located, there's a good chance it will be her murderer who finds it."

CHAPTER 11

One Dressy Shoe with No Heel

Her house is in complete disarray. They've opened the antique pocket doors to double the size of the living room. Stella keeps them closed most of the time, to maintain a modicum of privacy, even though the downstairs of her home is available to staff, for the most part. There are two couches able to be converted into beds, arranged in the extra space. Both may be needed tonight for Search and Rescue crew members from Port Ephron, if they can't get home because there's a heavy storm on the way. If the causeway closes, they could end up with a full house.

Eve and Alice put sheets on the trestle tables. The party-sized coffee percolator is plugged in. Alice drove to town for necessities—bread, cold-cuts, juices, and salads. Stella heaves a sigh.

Seated on a Victorian rattan lounger, Stella's taken a break from the whirl of preparations downstairs to be alone on her upstairs balcony; to gaze out at the sea. The water is grey and the waves churn. Her distance views rarely enable her to see more than the odd white cap. The ocean rumbles. Its force is palpable. This will no doubt impede the search. The air, laden with moisture, scrapes across her cheeks. Her linen trousers brush dampness around her legs.

"Are you up here?"

Nick's voice floats from the apartment doorway. "Out here, Nick." He crosses the upstairs foyer in a couple of strides and steps over the threshold and out on the veranda. The wind catches his hair as the screen door slams behind him. "I needed a break for a minute. Aiden is convinced this won't end well."

He rests one heavy hand on her shoulder before he perches on a wicker armchair beside her. "The searchers began to wander in for a bite to eat. I expect their turnaround time to be quick because the storm will prevent any search after supper." He glances out toward the ocean. Wind gusts rattle the eaves. "Looks to be sooner rather than later. You'll host a houseful tonight."

On the rare occasion when the forecast is challenging, Stella permits tenters, and those housed in more flimsy trailers, to bunk on the common room floor. The issue doesn't arise often, but there have been times. Back nine years ago, her father had half the campground up here at the house when Hurricane Beth sped over Nova Scotia in August and dumped a couple hundred millimetres of rain. He said the main road through the camp became a river. Bigger rigs sank up to their axles in the soft earth of their lots.

"Well, this will be no Beth, not even of the sub-tropical variety, but if guests want to come up for the night, they'll be more than welcome. Let's take a ride around this afternoon and tell people." She pats his arm. "The over-nighters won't know we provide an option. Folks Mildred's age might be afraid to be alone."

"Okay. Ready to go downstairs?"

"Almost." She tosses her legs over the side of the lounger and stands. "I need to move these cushions inside, first. I think the rain could start any time, Nick."

A lunch buffet is in full swing in the common room. There are more volunteers than expected, and half of them show up to eat.

"These folks will get themselves fed, and then go out again for a couple of hours." Duke lays out their plan to Stella. "High tide isn't until around nine tonight. We'll use the daylight left and then send the volunteers home. For anybody who must cross the causeway, they could be forced to remain in Shale Harbour."

"Searchers are more than welcome to the floor, Duke, but I expect there are hotel rooms still available."

"Thanks, Stella. I can't predict the weather, but it stands to reason it's gonna get worse yet."

He sounds anxious; rattled. Stella knows the storm puts their plans in jeopardy. She casts her gaze around the main floor in search of Aiden.

Duke watches her and responds. "Detective North accompanied one of the crews. He said he couldn't sit here and wait for word. You were inside while he was talkin' to a constable, and then he left. He had gear in the car. He musta planned on helpin' out. Good man."

Stella smiles at her security guy. "Yes, Aiden is a fine person. I hope he's wrong and you don't find her, though. I want to think she disappeared for her own reasons."

"Me, too, Stella. Me, too."

Alice and Eve run back and forth between the kitchen and the trestle tables. Stella beams. They are two of the best staffers she's ever employed. She hopes they'll return next summer, and she'll be able to offer them more money. She grabs a sandwich and trots into reception to answer the phone.

"No, your cancellation is not a problem. I don't blame you. Nobody wants to be in an RV park in the middle of a storm as treacherous as this. Yes, I can reserve you a spot for next week instead. Let me get my book. Here we go." She grins as she speaks. The act makes her voice sound less stressed. "I'll put you up one row, but there's a lovely view from your new location. Will the alternate space work? Great. See you Saturday. We'll hope the weather improves."

The fewer people here the better tonight. A couple of trailer owners checked out earlier. If folks aren't too far from home, it's easier to pack up than stay huddled inside a swaying unit. Alice has issued credits—always a smart idea to encourage guests to make a return visit.

"I've processed five credit nights, Stella. Okay?" Alice wiggles into the tiny space behind the counter to stand near her boss.

"Better to let people rebook. We don't want them here in inclement weather if they're not up for the challenge. How goes the food situation?"

"Oh, Duke gave me a cheque to cover most of our costs. They raise funds to pay for times when private outfits provide for their base camp as he calls our contribution." She giggles. "I know this is no laughing matter, but Duke sure likes to be in charge. You'd better watch your back." She gives Stella's arm a gentle nudge.

****

After the food is cleared away, the tables washed, and a fresh urn of coffee set to perk, Nick and Stella jump on the golf cart and start their drive around the park. Wind gusts are stronger than she expected when they emerge from behind the protection of the utility shed. As they trundle down the main road, they shout to communicate. Their course is straight into the weather as it rolls off the water. "We'll check in with anybody in a tent or pop-up. Then we'll stop at Mildred's before we go back." Stella has to yell to Nick as she guides the bouncing vehicle along.

Nick jumps out at the first spot, but the residents of the tiny unit are anticipating the storm with relish. "Come up to the big house if the storm gets to be too much for you." Nick's instructions to the couple blow back to her on the wind.

They stop at six little pop-ups and four tents. Then they pause to see if old Mildred Fox will be alright alone in her trailer. She fills her doorway. Dishevelled strands of hair flap on her cheeks as she yells her response while she points skyward. "Leaky vent. Want to stay around in case I need to mop up. Rob came over and tied my awning. I should be fine. They said I could come over there if the storm gets vicious." She brushes damp strands out of her mouth. "Guess I'll havta take my lemonade if I go." Her cackling guffaw breaks in a splatter of rain.

When Nick climbs on the golf cart, Stella turns the machine toward home. They've made the offer. She expects the night to be a long one, but the old house has been through worse.

By six o'clock, the wind and fog cause enough problems for the volunteer teams to return and put an end to the day. Stella is secretly pleased there's nothing to show for their efforts. Many members of the Search and Rescue crew leave. Two men from Port Ephron decide to take Stella up on her offer and overnight at the park. They unpack sleeping bags from their trucks. Paul and Alice will remain, but Eve's mother has called and requested she come home. Alice sets out bowls and French bread to go along with the pots of chili Sally Black made. Nick secures equipment with Duke.

"Has anybody seen Detective North?" Stella asks to the room at large. Police personnel returned to their respective bases. She suspects Aiden has gone, too.

"Stella, Detective North is in your office. He asked if he could make a few calls and I told him okay." Stella notices how Alice's deep blue eyes question the decision and search for confirmation.

"Of course, Aiden can use the phone. He can make as many calls as he wants. I assume he's returning to the hotel." She searches Alice's face for answers. "The tide will be high and fast tonight. If he wanted to get home to Port Ephron, he should be on his way by now."

"He told me he'd stay for supper and then leave." Alice leans over and peers out the window into the descending gloom. "As long as he's not worried flying branches and falling trees will make his trip impossible."

"Well, he can bed down here if needs be. There are the pull-outs and lots of floor space."

"I never worry 'cause my trusty air mattress is always in the car...Paul's, too."

"You look forward to these nights." She laughs out loud but is then momentarily distracted from teasing her staff. "My God, I don't believe my eyes. A motor home has pulled into the parking lot, Alice. I thought we were done for the day."

"We were. Lots of reservations cancelled."

"Tell them to plug in over near the house, by the back veranda, and snuggle in there for the night. They can get settled in a real space tomorrow." She watches as the 1977 American Clipper rolls to a stop. Alice tears into reception to greet them.

Supper goes off without a hitch. In addition to Aiden, Nick, Paul, Alice, and Stella, the two guys from Port Ephron, Kevin Flores, three families of tenters, and a cyclist travelling by herself join them. Alice invites the couples, on vacation from Minnesota in the American Clipper, to come in. The four new visitors are a noisy and rambunctious bunch to start. They have no idea the primary reason for such a large group to be together is because of a search mission, not merely to avoid the storm. They settle soon enough.

From what Stella can ascertain, the Clipper was the last vehicle allowed across the causeway before closure. They said a policeman named Moyer let them go, directed them here, and then put up the barricades.

Of course, it doesn't take long for the group to start to talk. The woman tenting alone and preferring to wait out the storm at the house with her bicycle on the veranda, asks if the rumour is true.

"Another camper I met in the bathrooms told me Search and Rescue was here to try to find a resident who disappeared from her trailer. Were they correct?" She gazes around the room.

Stella checks Aiden's expression before she answers. "Yes, they were. And you are?"

"Gracie, from New York. She's in, or was in, the end site on Level Three," Alice pipes up with expected efficiency.

"Oh, I packed up all my gear for tonight. I didn't want to take the chance it would blow away. I'm here for another couple of days."

Nodding her thanks to Alice, Stella responds, "Well, Gracie. The rumour is correct. We don't know for sure what's happened to our friend, Lorraine. No one has seen her since last Friday night. Detective North, here," she indicates Aiden by lifting her hand in his direction, "decided to start a search."

"Do you think she ran away?"

Gracie is both inquisitive and persistent. Kevin Flores jumps in. "Lorraine didn't run away without telling me first. I'm sure she's been kidnapped."

"Let's not speculate." Aiden's voice is clear and calm. "Tomorrow is expected to be sunny and we will restart the search. Duke and his volunteers have done a fine job, thus far."

Duke sits up straighter. He leans over to pat Kiki, although the little dog is snuggled cozy and comfortable, locked in Alice's arms.

The night is long. Aiden returns to his hotel. The wind howls without mercy and two more groups of tenters fall in the door well after midnight. Room is made. Everyone finds a place to crash—on the floor or on the couches. The people in the Clipper drift out to bed. She watches Nick fight the storm as he struggles toward his cottage. Duke rides over to his own trailer, while Kiki stays with Alice.

When she finally wanders upstairs to her flat, it's one in the morning. The rain beats on the roof with the intensity of a water faucet turned on full force. She needs Nick here with her. She wants his opinion, but more importantly, she craves his company. Obviously, there's no way for him to sneak up the stairs unnoticed in front of the whole crew.

Go through what you know again. Could she orchestrate her own disappearance? Could someone want to hurt her? How did she leave the trailer? Why didn't she use the door? None of the story makes any sense.

By three o'clock in the morning, the wind has started to ease. The tide is receding, and the noise of the ocean's anger subsides. Sleep is inevitable.

****

Stella listens before she opens her eyes. The welcome Sunday sun twinkles through the curtains that hang limp against the closed windows. She senses Nick's presence. She smells the coffee.

"I came up to wake you. People are stirring downstairs. You must have been dead to the world not to notice when the campers left." He brushes a stray strand of hair off her forehead.

"What? Everyone's up?"

"A few, specifically Alice, never bothered to go to bed. She had coffee made and stacks of toast in your warming oven before I came in."

"I hear the noise now. What's going on?"

"Paul and Kevin are moving furniture. Aiden drove out from town, none the worse for wear, although there are tree branches everywhere. Duke has come in for a bite to eat while we wait for the rest of the crew to turn up. He wants to go at it fast and hard today, whatever that means in 'Duke-speak'."

"Has this been your report?" She teases. Stella, by now, is out of bed, back from the bathroom, and dressed in cotton pants and a sweat shirt. The air holds the expectation of warmth but has a distinctive after-the-storm chill this morning. She takes a sip of coffee and peeks at him over the rim. "Will you work with them today?"

"Nah, they don't need me. As a matter of fact, Mark Bell turned up a few minutes ago, and I overheard him when he talked to Duke. I guess he wants to pitch in, the same as Kevin."

"Aiden said, before the search even started, how he thought the murderer would be the person who finds the body. Since all the suspects are now here, his theory remains to be seen."

"What made him say that?"

"He says, in missing person cases, contrived discovery happens more often than you might think. If a murderer wants a body to be found, and they're involved in the search, they can move the process along."

She and Nick clomp downstairs together. She hopes a few people saw him go up first, or their secret will be in jeopardy despite recent efforts. She surveys the room as Nick approaches the coffee urn for refills. The campers went back to assess any damage and try to dry out their possessions. Gracie was the smart one when she dragged her stuff up to the house.

Stella smells bacon and hears eggs crackle in the frying pans. She is able to distinguish Eve's voice, so the kid obviously arrived a while ago. Although still early, tables are set up once more. The floor is cleared of any sleeping paraphernalia. The convertible sofas are couches again.

Duke approaches her. "Crews are off in a half hour. Anybody who wants to eat can get a bite before they leave. On behalf of Shale Harbour Volunteer Search and Rescue, I want to thank you for the use of the premises, Stella."

"You sound formal, my friend."

"If she's out there to be found, we'll find her today, Stella. Part of my role is to show appreciation to the community. I'm thankin' you now."

Stella pats him on the arm. "You've done a fine job, Duke. I had no idea you were such an organizational genius. I may put your skills to work in the future."

"Well, Stella. Organized for Search and Rescue, maybe, but the rest of my life is still a mess. You know I'm right." He nods and turns toward a couple of new arrivals.

****

Aiden North reclaimed his post on the veranda with the two-way radio and has been there for most of the morning.

"Detective North, are you there?"

"Here, Sergeant."

"Kevin Flores discovered her body, Sir, face down in a farmer's drainage ditch."

Stella's hand flies to her mouth to stifle a gasp.

He continues. "No coat or purse was spotted nearby. If not for the rain, it might have been late in the year, when the tall grasses die off, before we found her. The water lifted her up and gave the body visibility it needed to be seen."

Stella points to her shoes when she catches Aiden's eye.

"What is she wearing on her feet, Moyer?"

"One dressy shoe with no heel."

"Maintain the scene, Sergeant. I will contact forensics and am on my way. Give me your exact location."

CHAPTER 12

I Am Not Surprised Anymore

Her downstairs common room, the managed chaos of Duke's organization for the last twenty-four hours, falls into an eerie silence. The bubbling sound of the coffee perking floats into her office, but no one waits for a refresher or a refill. Alice is on the phone with a traveller who wants to make a reservation. Paul isn't back with the search party, yet. Eve is busy in the kitchen. *Where is Nick?* She aches to talk to Nick; to experience the sense of comfort she gets when he's nearby. As if on cue, he meanders in the door.

"Hi. Are you okay?"

"I guess. I was ready to pour a cup of coffee to drink with Aiden on the veranda when Moyer called through on the radio. Where were you?"

"At the pump house—my favourite spot. The heavy rain caused problems, but we're fine again."

She is aware he does not want to burden her with the details right now. As is Nick's habit, he has taken care of the problem with little or no fanfare.

"By the way," he continues, "I spoke with Aiden and he told me to ask you to stick around. He wants to interview Kevin up here after the dust settles. Said he wanted to talk to a couple of people, if it's okay with you, before he goes back to Port Ephron. An ongoing issue with his wife, I understand."

"Poor Aiden. Rosemary isn't well. Her sisters must be anxious for him to get home." Nick nods as Stella continues. "I guess the medical examiner and forensics are the main characters on stage right now. I assume Aiden wants to use my office?"

"Yeah. He said his assigned space in the detachment is too small and he doesn't want to transport witnesses back to the port."

"Who are the witnesses?"

"He expects to interview both Kevin and Mark. I'm not aware of anybody else. The coffee sure smells good. I'll get us each a cup and we'll take a break before people start to show up."

They are no sooner comfortable on the veranda, mugs in hand and feet propped on the over-sized hassock, when Aiden's car pulls in the lot. Kevin Flores is slumped in the back seat.

Stella watches Aiden move with methodical slowness as he climbs out of the front and opens the door for Kevin. The two men ascend the stairs. She is struck by Aiden's sadness, which surrounds him, impairing his ability to walk. He has become an old man.

Kevin's face is pinched. He is both stricken and anxious. His eyes dart toward Aiden every few seconds. She's reminded of a border collie when it studies its owner; not sure what to do next; waiting for the master's lead.

"I hoped to use your office once again, Stella. If our presence is an imposition, tell me. Can you sit in?" He glances in Nick's direction. "A second set of eyes and ears is helpful. Moyer is back at the scene." Kevin remains at the foot of the stairs.

"Of course." Stella rises and turns toward the interior of the house. "I'll let Alice know we're in my office."

She nods to Nick. He jumps up and clambers down the veranda steps, almost side-swiping Kevin on the way. "I'm off to finish the roof on the shed. Check with you later."

Stella is struck by everyone's awkwardness. No one is sure what the appropriate protocols are when a body has just been discovered.

They reassemble in her office. Aiden sits behind her desk. Kevin is hunched in a chair directly across from him while Stella takes her place in the blue floral wingback. Stella observes Kevin Flores. It's obvious to her the young man is devastated, but his expression is open and forthright. She hopes he's been asked in for an interview because he spotted Lorraine, and not because Aiden considers him a suspect.

Aiden leans across the desk. His elbows support his chin. "Kevin. This has been a horrible morning...for all of us. I understand your grief."

Kevin's eyes puddle up once more and his open expression crumbles.

"Please tell me how you found Lorraine."

Stella is confident Kevin wants to cooperate. He meets Aiden's gaze and sputters, "We were assigned to walk the drainage ditch line. Another guy named Buddy—he said he lives here in the summer—was walkin' on the other side. I saw her leg in the grass. I yelled over to Buddy and he seen it, too. Both of us called out. Duke and two more guys came from across the field. Alls I did was stand there starin' at her."

"Tell me the details."

"Her face was in the water. She wasn't wearin' no coat and only the one shoe. I felt bad. I wanted to crawl in the ditch and drag her out." His voice starts to elevate at this point. Stella notices his speech patterns become more heavily accented as his anxiety increases.

"Calm down, Kevin. We understand how difficult this is for you."

"Mark Bell killed her, Detective North."

Aiden's expression never changes. "What makes you sure?"

"He was jealous; jealous of Lorraine and me. We were gonna get married, and it made him crazy. She was unhappy at work. He was buggin' her at every turn and even called her at home once before she moved out here."

"Was she out in the field because she tried to run away from Mark?"

"No. He put her there. He waited for her at her trailer and he killed her and then dropped her in the ditch figurin' the grass would hide her."

Aiden's voice is quiet. "Well, you found her, Kevin."

His response was quicker than Stella expected. "Buddy found her, too. Can I go now?"

"Yes, we're done here for today, but stay around town. I may need to talk with you again."

As Kevin leaves to retrieve his car and return to Shale Harbour, Stella faces her old friend. "He didn't do this, Aiden."

"I agree, but his Mark Bell theory doesn't work, either. It's not possible Mark waited for her in the trailer. Mildred did not see or hear another person besides Lorraine. She was out on her deck most of the evening." He stands and stretches—an old cat woken from a sound sleep. "I want to talk with Mark again when he gets back, Stella."

****

The search and rescue volunteers begin to arrive at the Shale Cliffs RV Park in dribs and drabs. Aiden continues to avail himself of Stella's office to make phone calls. She trudges the path to the utility shed only to discover Nick up on the still-slippery roof alone. After only a moment or two, she recognizes the rumble of a search vehicle when it turns into her parking lot. "I guess I'll be needed, Nick. Shall I send Paul to help you?"

"Good, thanks. I want to finish today. I was surprised the roof didn't leak when the rains came last night. We might not be as lucky next time."

Following the path back to the house, her legs brush over-sized hostas, advantaged by the previous night's dampness. On her walk, she pauses to instruct Paul and then stops to exchange a few words with Duke. "I'm sorry circumstances turned out this way, Duke. Everyone hoped to find her alive."

Duke is all business. "At least we found her. The crew did a great job. I need to debrief with the volunteers. Where's Kevin?"

"Kevin went home after his interview with Detective North. Did you expect him to stay?"

"The debriefing is for every volunteer, Stella, even the ones who were out here for this specific incident. I'll call him to come back. Is Mark Bell inside? He's another one who needs to be included."

"Mark Bell is supposed to talk to the detective, too. I'll send him to your meeting when we're finished."

"Okay. We'll be in the lot for a while. We need to check and catalogue the equipment. Mounds of paperwork." His professional demeanour starts to crumble. "I'm gonna miss her, Stella. She was a nice girl."

"And a good tenant, Duke." Her touch is light as she pats him on the shoulder. *God forbid he should get the wrong idea.* She then turns toward the veranda steps and ultimately, her office.

Aiden is perched on the arm of a sofa in the big living room. Stella sees him as her eyes pierce the gloom created by the dark interior. "Mark's in the can." He lowers his voice. "The guy's anxious to talk; maybe too anxious. Everybody has a theory."

"Me, too. Aiden."

"Fair enough. We'll cover the options later before I go home for a couple of days. I hate to leave, but I'm forced to wait for forensics, anyway. We need hard evidence, Stella. Theories are only good for so long."

She watches her old flame chew on his lower lip as he flips through his notebook. He has no better idea than she does, even after this length of time. Stella is sure Kevin Flores did not hurt Lorraine. She is unsure of Mark Bell. Right now, Nick's theory has merit. Lorraine designed her return to appear as if she went in her trailer, but she didn't. Stella wonders if the plan was for

Mark to meet her by the road in another car, and instead, he killed her and dumped her body in the drainage ditch. There are loose ends. Where are her sneakers? If she left a duplicate coat and purse inside in order to fake her disappearance, where were the coat and purse Mildred reported she wore when she returned Friday night?

"Hey, Mark! Ready for a chat?" Aiden stands as the bank employee returns from the bathroom.

"Sure, Sir. I want to share my theory with you." He casts his gaze around in search of a place to sit.

"I am continuing to take advantage of Stella's hospitality and using her office, Mark." He extends his arm in the general direction. "Stella will join us, if you're okay with her in the room."

Mark nods to Stella. "Of course, Detective."

Once settled, Stella is struck with how Mark tries to assume control of the interview. "I'll get right to the point. I'm certain Lorraine discovered a problem at the bank. Funds are likely missing, and she figured out who was involved. Ruby Wilson should provide you with current information."

Stella worries her face has the same shocked expression as Aiden's, but Mark carries on regardless. "She told me she developed a theory. Now, Ruby might not be a thief, but I bet she knows stuff. She has access to files and documents the rest of us don't see. Lorraine *knew.* Perhaps she didn't have every detail, but she sure as hell connected a couple of the dots."

Aiden reviews his notes. "Mark, you said when we talked before, how Lorraine told you once if anything happened to her, it would mean she had discovered the truth. Correct?"

"Correct, Detective. I am positive whoever was up to no good at the bank hurt Lorraine. No question. I tried to find out the status of the investigation from a colleague over in Port Ephron. He reported there is money gone from either there or here and the managers are working on the discrepancy."

"Did your friend say why the police were never notified?"

"Banks always do their own investigations first. In many cases, sloppy paperwork proves to be the culprit— not people at the root of the problem." The sun streams through Stella's big office window and makes Mark's teeth twinkle when he smiles.

****

Later in the day, Nick, Stella, and Aiden assemble in the living room. The staff are gone, there's an abundance of food in the kitchen for supper, and both Nick and Stella enjoy an ice-cold beer. Aiden opts for a soda. He still must make the return trip home.

"Who killed her, Aiden?" Nick is stretched out in an overstuffed armchair with his feet on a hassock trimmed in cowhide.

Aiden, head tilted to the side, and eyes narrowed, assesses Nick's remark. "I hope you're kidding. If I had the answer to your question, we'd be set. Tell me your thoughts."

"She staged her disappearance. She was supposed to meet Mark, and he double-crossed her. Her help was no longer required, so he killed her in the field."

Stella gulps a mouthful of her beer and raises her hand like a stop sign. "Your theory sounds good, but where are her coat and purse? Where are her sneakers? How come Mildred saw her kitchen light?"

"I will request a search of both Mark Bell's and Kevin Flores' cars and apartments. They are cooperative. I don't anticipate a problem."

"Aiden, if one of them killed her and took her coat and purse, wouldn't they be at the dump by now? And then there's Lorraine's car?"

"Her vehicle was towed to the lab today, right after we found her, Stella."

"Good. We were at the other side of the house. I never noticed."

Nick refocuses the discussion back to the problem at hand. "Say, for argument, I'm wrong and Lorraine didn't intend to disappear with a truckload of cash from the Savings and Loan, and Mark Bell as her accomplice. Assume she wasn't betrayed by the guy; then what happened?" Nick sets his beer glass on the end table and sits up straighter. "Let's figure out the series of events."

"Mark claims she possessed evidence of a scam at the bank." Aiden avoids both Stella and Nick. He focuses on a watercolour of Shale Harbour as he talks. "Did the person involved in the fraud scheme kill her?"

"Well, if we decide we believe Mark, then other suspects include Ruby Wilson and Terri Price. Honestly, Aiden, neither one of them has the ability to murder Lorraine and then dispose of her body in a field." Stella remains unconvinced.

"The ditch is at the side of the road, Stella. It's possible to roll a body out of a car trunk." Nick sighs. "Sounds plausible, but maybe not for a woman."

"I've been amazed by women on many occasions, Nick, either by the feats they accomplished in order to commit a murder or to prevent one. I am not surprised anymore."

"Who killed her?"

"It's not impossible she fell into the ditch, Stella. All theories are probable until I get the report back. Despite my lack of hard evidence, Mark has convinced me her death has to do with theft and has no relationship to jealousy and another lover." He hasn't looked up from his notes. "I want to talk to the area manager of the Savings and Loan—a person in authority above the managers in Shale Harbour and Port Ephron. I expect their information will support Mark's theory. Other than the bank, I need to review forensics reports on both Lorraine and her car."

"Are we ready to plow through these leftovers before you take off for the port, Aiden?" Nick makes his way to the kitchen.

"Yes, a bite or two before my drive is a good idea."

Stella does not feel it's right to ignore the elephant in the room, and is compelled to ask, "How's Rosemary, Aiden?"

He responds with a slow reluctance. "Rosemary has caused my sisters-in-law considerable grief. I received their call to inform me they need a break. I told them once we moved forward in this case, I would stay at home for more than an afternoon or one night. I won't be in Shale Harbour again until sometime Tuesday."

"What do you mean by considerable grief?" Stella knows she's pushing.

Aiden glances at her before he turns to the sandwiches and sweets assembled on the kitchen table. "She threatened to kill herself if I don't come home. Her sisters coped for a while, but they're scared she might follow through."

"Oh, Aiden, how horrible for everyone. You must be under tremendous pressure." She's now ashamed she mentioned Rosemary. She can sense how difficult the subject is for him.

"You asked."

He sounds defeated and it makes Stella anxious.

"Time to go." Aiden stands. " I'll call if I need you to check on a piece of information for me, in her unit or with a witness. Between you and Moyer, I expect you will manage."

He may be teasing. She isn't sure.

Later that night, stretched out in her big bed, as Nick's soft snores rumble beside her, she tries once again to review the scenarios. She can't get the question about exiting the trailer out of her mind.

The cool evening breeze, crisp and fresh off the ocean after the heavy storm, floats through the curtains and flows across her skin like a silk scarf. *Lorraine, how did you leave, once you were inside? What happened to you? When did you die? How were you killed, Lorraine?*

CHAPTER 13

What's Your Theory?

"Alice!" Stella clatters down her stairs and strides into reception where Alice sorts reservations on the front counter.

"Hi, Stella. There were lots of check-outs yesterday. Now the paperwork needs organizing. The office has been crazy."

"I know. I know. Listen. Do we expect the whole gang in for lunch? I want to meet with the staff."

"Yes. Eve is on bathroom duty." She wrinkles her nose. "No sign of Duke yet, but he's never early. Paul and Nick are busy with one of the mowers. The small ride-on quit last week." She raises her eyebrows when she glances up from her reservation slips. "Eve's favourite mower is on the fritz and they don't want any excuses to prevent her from mowing."

Stella throws her head back and expels a hearty hoot. "Now, Alice. You think men prefer not to cut lawns, or what?"

"Bigger equipment is more fun. Paul drives around to pick up garbage out of the fire pits in the tractor with the bucket. What do you call that?"

"Efficiency, I guess. In any event, round everyone up and make sure they come in for a bite at the same time."

"To talk over what's happened?" Alice's expression is quizzical.

"Yes. No one has any idea how she ended up in the drainage ditch. We can try to find a fresh theory. Call lunch a brain storming session, okay?"

"I'll get everybody here for noon, Stella. What are you up to today?"

"I plan to stay on site, do clean-up, and there are a couple of people in the park I want to talk with later."

Stella takes an hour to vacuum the living room, sweep the veranda, and tidy her office. She knows the first bathroom Eve tackles is the one downstairs.

The old house absorbed a great deal of traffic over the weekend, but after a good scrub, appears to be none the worse for wear.

Her initial visit has no relation to Lorraine Young's death. There are complaints regarding a dog allowed to run loose. The owner booked into the park for a couple of weeks and still has six days on his reservation.

The golf cart hums to a stop in front of a fifteen-foot unit parked on a slight slope and not levelled. Stella absently wonders if the doors inside the trailer fall open or slam closed. Levelling is one of those basic tasks necessary when a rig sits on a lot for any length of time. There is a frayed mat below the door and a huge German shepherd stretched out in the sun. The striped blue and grey awning is set at an angle to enable the rain water to run off. The tilt causes the assembly to appear broken.

Since the trailer door is open, and the screen exposed, Stella shouts from the golf cart to the occupant. The idea of disembarking from her transportation to risk a confrontation with the dog makes her decidedly uncomfortable. "Good morning! Anybody home?"

In an instant, the doorway of the rig is filled with the figure of an overweight and unkempt gentleman in his mid-fifties. "I'm here. Who are you?" His voice is gruff but not antagonistic. Stella is always cautious with campers she has never met. The past week has been busy. As a result, Alice has made most of the arrangements with travellers.

Alice said this man is Rupert Donovan, from Illinois. He reports he likes to visit Canada in the summer to escape the heat. He spends his winters in the south.

"Mr. Donovan, I'm Stella Kirk, the park owner. Could we chat?"

"Sure. You want to come in?"

"That won't be necessary. Let's talk out here."

At this point, he lumbers down the two metal stairs and stands, thumbs looped in his belt, beside his dog. "Problem?"

She attempts to keep the conversation calm. "What's your dog's name? May I pat him?"

"He's friendly enough. Stella, right? His name is Murphy."

"Perfect name." Stella slides off the golf cart and extends her hand to the dog. "Hi, Murphy. Aren't you a good dog?"

He sniffs her fingers and then wags his tail. Stella heaves a sigh. She isn't great with animals, but she tries. As she continues to pat Murphy, she explains the problem to Rupert. "Mr. Donovan, there have been complaints regarding how Murphy, here, runs around other campsites. People reported you do not clean up after Murphy. Are these reports accurate?"

"The dog likes to sit out here on the mat. He don't wander very much."

Stella meets Rupert's eyes. "I think he takes a walk when he wants to do his business away from your trailer, sir. The rules in the park are for everyone. Pet owners must pick up after their animals."

Keeping one eye on the man, she continues to pay attention to the dog. At this point, Murphy has leaned his solid frame against her leg and has his snout firmly planted in her outstretched hand. Rupert Donovan's expression is thoughtful and not upset.

"To be honest, those kinda rules are for posh places. We don't often stay in fancy parks."

"My place isn't posh enough to pick up dog poop? Is this what you think of Shale Cliffs RV Park, Mr. Donovan?" She laughs as she concludes there will be no further worries from this campsite.

He looks sheepish. "I'll keep a better eye on Murphy, here. He'll cry if he's tied, but I'll watch him when he's outside. I don't got no bags though."

"Come up to the office. Alice keeps rolls of plastic bags under the counter." She extends her hand. "Thanks for your cooperation, Mr. Donovan. We want you to enjoy your stay."

"Nice to meet you, Stella. Murphy and me will take a walk to your place later on. You can call me Rup. Everybody does."

Next stop is Mildred Fox's trailer. There she is, wedged into her lounger on the dilapidated deck. Stella eyes the mug in her hand and hopes the old woman might offer a cup of coffee. She expects Mildred's cup is filled with her famous lemonade.

"Morning, Mildred. Time for a chin wag?" She slows the cart to a stop beside the property.

Mildred, in a flannelette nightie and cotton house coat, frowns as she peers up at Stella. "Nah, I'm busy. Can't you tell?" She cackles. "There's a pot of coffee inside and a wee bottle on the counter you can add for flavour if you have a mind." She cackles again.

"I'd love a cup, Mildred. No need for the extras though since I'm driving." She waves a hand toward her transportation. "Don't get up. I'll help myself." She ducks to avoid the door frame when she climbs into the miniscule trailer.

Space is tight. The gloom has a pink tinge created by the old curtains hung on the windows. There is the faint smell of garbage mixed with stale liquor. She spies a relatively clean mug, wipes the chipped pottery with a fresh tissue from her pocket, and pours the inky black liquid into the cup. She decides to forego any milk, and returns to the deck where she drops into a plastic basket chair.

"Thanks, Mildred. I missed my mid-morning java."

"Somethin' on your mind, Stella? Our girl's been found. We survived the storm. What else is goin' on?"

"Yes, they found her, Mildred, but I still want to understand how she ended up there. We can't figure out what happened in the field, if we can't find out what happened first. Will you go through what you saw again?"

"Sure, but what's the problem?"

"If I ask you a couple of questions, will you give your answers serious consideration, Mildred? You are an important witness." She wants the old girl's cooperation, so tries as best she can to butter her up.

"Ask away, Stella. I may be old, but I'm able to tell you what happened Friday night."

"Did Lorraine go into her trailer?"

"Of course! The door opened, and the kitchen light came on. The place was locked from the inside, too. Your detective friend said as much."

"There is no possibility she climbed out of her car, walked around out of sight, and headed toward the field?"

"No. Whoever drove her car went inside the trailer, for sure."

"What do you mean, whoever?"

"The car was parked crooked, Stella. Lorraine never parks on an angle, but everybody says she was upset or in a hurry." She meets Stella's gaze. "She always checks if I'm out here, too, and she never gave me a sideways glance. The person I watched might notta been her." She shifts in her chair and takes a sip of her doctored coffee. "But she wore her coat and carried her purse, so…?"

As Stella tries to formulate another question, Sally and Rob Black suddenly appear at the corner of Mildred's trailer. "We spied the golf cart over here, Stella, but we figured Duke and Kiki stopped for a visit. Nice to see you." Sally's gushing is enthusiastic, as she gives Stella a tiny wave.

Rob squats on the edge of the deck. The seams of his khaki shorts strain with the effort. Stella hears the old boards creak their complaint. "They found Lorraine. What's next?"

Stella is reluctant to say too much in front of Rob. He's not ruled out as a suspect in her opinion, even though she can't create a scenario in her mind where he killed Lorraine after she returned to the trailer. "I guess we still need to figure out who murdered her, Rob."

"What's your theory? You and Detective North are friends. You must have a theory."

"Theories aren't worth a helluva lot. Right now, Detective North is waiting for forensics on both Lorraine and her car. We hope they find answers."

"Thanks for your hospitality this morning, my dear. I'll put my cup in the sink and then be on my way." She does not want to share any information with Rob and Sally. Hopefully, Mildred can keep her mouth shut.

****

She rounds the corner to the veranda and the golf cart purrs to a stop. She spies Duke and Kiki approaching the house via the back path most often used by the staff as a shortcut to the opposite side of the park. Kiki is decked out in a sequined collar and leash to match. Stella observes Duke's attire doesn't meet Kiki's standard, as he swaggers toward the porch in his wrinkled blue denim shorts and yellow Hawaiian sports shirt. He waves. Kiki barks.

"Hi, you two. Up for lunch?"

"More wonderin' where the cart was, but I guess you were usin' my ride."

Stella thinks Duke might be miffed she took the golf cart while he was still in his trailer. *Duke needs to learn to share—in particular, those items which belong to me and not to him.* "I imagine you must be worn out after the last couple of days. I thought we could get together for lunch and discuss Lorraine. Are you up for a quick meeting?"

"Sure. And, yeah, I'm tired but I didn't sleep much. Too worked up, I guess. Do you want me to take the dog back to my place?"

"No need. Let's go inside to find out if Alice and Eve had any time to make sandwiches."

The screen flies open as Stella reaches the top step. Nick, the consummate host, holds the door for them—the maître d' at a fancy restaurant. "This way, folks. Lunch is served."

Duke paddles through ahead of Stella, with Kiki well in the lead. Nick pats Stella on the arm and winks.

In the kitchen, the big harvest table dominates the centre of the room. Nick has assembled leftovers, once again, from the day before. There are buns, cold-cuts, muffins, and slices of brown bread. There is a pitcher of lemonade and a fresh pot of coffee. There is a tray of cookies and squares.

"Help yourself, Duke. I'll go find everybody else."

Stella catches Alice for a moment and whispers in her ear. "Rupert Donovan will come up to the office to get poop bags for Murphy. He's okay. We can call him Rup. I guess we're friends, now." She winks at Alice.

Once everyone has milled around the table to load their plates with their preferences, Stella asks for their attention.

"I want to discuss Lorraine and what's happened. There are lots of rumours out there. I thought we could brainstorm together and try to come up with a plausible theory before Aiden gets back tomorrow night."

"Did they take her car to the RCMP lab? I heard they did."

"Have the cops figured out how she died?"

Duke pipes up. "Paul and I were out there, too, but Kevin Flores and Buddy, from here in the park, found her. She was in her work clothes and one shoe was gone. I'm not aware the police located it." His speech is more John than Duke. "We were told to leave when the forensics crew arrived. She was face down in a drainage ditch." His voice softens and his expression crumbles around the edges. "It was awful," he barely whispers.

"Funny, I thought, when I volunteered for Shale Harbour Search and Rescue, the job was more to do with the rescue part. Everyone was sad to find her in the field. Nobody deserves to be face first in a drainage ditch." Paul munches on his bunwich, loaded with ham and chicken, a slice of cheese, and chopped tomato. Poised to take a swig of lemonade, he stops long enough to add, "I think I overheard one of the cops say they found her other shoe."

His detached analysis speaks volumes about the impact of Lorraine's death.

"The police came with a tow truck for her car a couple of hours after the search and rescue folks had their briefing in the parking lot. When they said she was found dead, I thought I understood, but when her black Malibu was towed away, the whole nightmare became very real." Alice holds Kiki in her lap and strokes her with steady gentleness while she sips on lemonade. She has a sandwich on her plate but has yet to take a bite.

"I took the lawn mower to cut the grass where the vehicle sat, but the cop told me no. He said the scene needs to be released by Detective North before I mow." Eve looks over at Nick. "Tell me when it's okay, and I'll get the job done. What happens to her trailer?"

"Hard to say." Stella decides to err on the side of caution. "Lorraine did not have close relatives I'm aware of, but I assume she had a lawyer. The police go through papers and do proper notifications." She pauses to study her staff for a moment. Everyone is calm enough, but a thread of traumatization bubbles below the surface. Additional sensitivity will be required if she digs deeper into the topic of Lorraine's murder. Thus far, she has focused the discussion on the discovery of her body.

"Paul, when you helped Lorraine install the deadbolt on her outside door and the slide lock on her screen door, and when you and Nick replaced her window, what kinds of remarks did she make relating to why she wanted those jobs done? Were her security fears more specific than the general ones any one of us has when we live alone—doors need to be locked, etcetera?"

"Lorraine said over and over she didn't want anybody able to walk in on her, which is the reason she asked for the slide bolt on her screen. It wasn't to prevent a break-in, but she said people shout 'hello' and then barge right in if the outside door is open. She hated to be startled. The deadbolt was for when she was asleep. If someone had a key to her trailer, they still couldn't get in if she was inside. Her extra key was only for the person to use if she wasn't in the park and access was needed—I suppose for a fire or somethin." He takes another swallow of his drink and continues.

"As for the bedroom escape window, there was a break-in at her friend's place. I think Nick told the story before." He stops to take a breath and glances toward Nick for confirmation, encouraged by a nod from his boss. "Her friend left her window unlocked, but there was no way to convince Lorraine. She wanted a new window to be fool-proof from the outside." He looks around the room. "Unless the escape window was broken, which didn't happen, there is no way anybody crawled in there from the outside. No way," he repeats.

"I agree with Paul, Stella. Even if a person tried to climb out her new window, the unit slams the minute you let go. Mildred can hear a noise like that from her place. I'm confounded how the damned contraption leaked, though." Nick's voice is thoughtful.

Paul gasps. "Since when did the window leak? In the storm Saturday night? There is no way her new window allowed water to seep inside. The mouldings are perfect. You said so yourself when we finished the installation."

Nick shrugs. "I don't understand either, Paul. Stella said she saw the water stains when she and Aiden examined the place, days before the storm. Once we get inside again, I want to complete a thorough inspection."

"Me, too." Paul swigs the last of his lemonade as he downs a chocolate chip cookie the size of a saucer. "Time to go back to work." He turns toward Eve. "Your favourite mower will be repaired and running before the afternoon is over."

"Great."

Stella picks up on Paul's lead. "Okay, everyone. If no one has more to add, you can each return to the tasks at hand. If you remember an event or a conversation related to Lorraine, or a particular circumstance about her, tell me. Detective North is expected back tomorrow before day's end, and I hope the forensic reports will reveal what happened to our friend."

CHAPTER 14

I Have Little to Share

"Hi! No. No word from Ruby and I haven't found a moment to call. We've been crazy around here the last few days. How are you?"

"Fine. Fine."

Her voice is anxious. Stella's put off. "What's the problem, Trixie? The park won't go bankrupt if we wait a week or two to sign loan papers. Work on the power and water needs to be completed before the snow comes though."

"Long shifts are scheduled for me right now. Summer hours started. To be honest, Stella, I don't want to disappoint you, but I might not be able to get away in the middle of the day."

"Okay, Trixie. It's good you're scheduled for more work. No need to dither over the loan. Maybe Ruby will see us later in the day. I'll call and explain the situation. No one knows the right way to behave when a person is murdered in your own backyard. Did you notice if the bank was closed when you drove through town yesterday?"

"No, Stella. I cruise past before eight in the morning. The place is never open at that hour."

Stella wants to show how she appreciates Trixie's concern although she can't help but think her sister is more worried her monthly cheque will not arrive if their business enterprise doesn't receive the required improvements. "Come to the park this weekend. Let's get the family together. The last few days have been awful."

"I'll talk to Brigitte and see if she has plans. Ring me if you hear from the bank. Gotta run."

With this remark, the phone goes dead.

****

Once the clock reads ten, Stella takes a moment from her paperwork to call Ruby Wilson.

"Shale Harbour Savings and Loan. We will be closed the week of May 26 due to unforeseen circumstances. If you require immediate service, please contact Port Ephron Savings and Loan for further assistance."

The crackle of the answering machine sputters to a halt with no opportunity to leave a message. Stella replaces the telephone receiver into its cradle with unnecessary care. In a sudden force she finds disturbing, the whole ordeal becomes overwhelmingly real. *This is more than an exercise; more than a puzzle.*

"Are you busy, Stella?"

"In here, Alice. What's up?"

"There are a couple of people out in reception who asked to see you. One is Mark Bell. The other might be Terri Price, but I'm not sure. Shouldn't they be at the bank?"

"The bank's closed for the week. I'll meet them in the living room. I imagine they want to discuss Lorraine's death." She reluctantly moves from behind her desk. "I doubt Ruby has encouraged her staff to visit her home to debrief."

Alice returns to the front office and Stella enters the kitchen. She prepares a pot of coffee while she stares out the window at the tangle of overgrown rose bushes which tickle the panes above the sink. She must remind Nick to assign Paul or Eve the task of wrestling the overabundance of growth into some semblance of order.

"Good morning, you two. Please take a seat. I've made coffee and it'll be ready in a minute. Then we can go out to the veranda." She assesses her company while she talks.

Mark and Terri stand side by side, in the posture of a couple; not colleagues from work. Mark, tall and attractive, presents himself as stoic and in control. Terri reminds Stella of a tiny bird. She hops from one foot to the other as she brushes Mark's arm every few seconds. "What brings you two out here today? I gather the bank is closed."

Circumstances seem odd, at least in Stella's estimation, when Terri takes the lead. "We needed to talk with a person who has information."

"There's nowhere for us to turn." Mark's voice is flat. Stella suspects he has decided their trip is a waste, and she will have no details to add to their limited understanding.

"I have little to share. Detective North and I are old friends from high school a hundred years ago." She grimaces as she makes a joke to exemplify the difference in their ages, "but he is only able to tell me what is, or has become, public knowledge." This is a slight lie, but she does not want to put up a wall between herself and the pair she is prepared to believe is responsible for Lorraine's death.

"Come into the kitchen and get a coffee. We'll go out to the veranda and review what is known about the investigation. Okay?"

They nod in unison and follow her like ducklings.

Coffees in hand, they settle into the comfortable furniture at the back of the house. A mower roars in the distance and there's the buzz of a saw nearby. She's sure Nick is after another dead tree. Paul might be working at the Black's trailer again today, or he might have stayed to help Nick. She isn't worried. Nick keeps everyone busy. Thoughts of the ragged bushes enter her mind again. She turns her attention to her visitors.

Mark begins. He holds his mug in both hands and leans his elbows on his knees. The space between himself and Stella is now minimal. "I was here when the body was discovered, but forensics and the cops sent the volunteers away before I even saw her. I'm aware they found Lorraine in a drainage ditch because Duke told the crew at the debriefing."

"What you say is true. The police took her car and scoured her trailer. She was seen by two different people when she came home a week ago Friday." Stella focuses on Terri as she says this. The teller's eyes are wide, and she doesn't blink.

"How did she get from the trailer to the ditch?" Terri's voice is breathless, as if she's engrossed in a movie and caught up in the action.

"We have no idea. Her trailer was locked from the inside; even the slide bolt on her screen door was engaged. This is public knowledge. She entered, but the police didn't discover any means by which she left." Stella watches them both to see who will react first.

"She wasn't very big. Is it possible she climbed out a roof vent?" Mark suggests a long-rejected option.

"A small child couldn't even squeeze out a roof vent, Mark."

"At work, she described the fancy new escape window she had installed. She told us how it was burglar-proof, and how she was able to raise the unit fast and get out if there was a fire. If the murderer followed her into her trailer and she left through the emergency window, then they caught up to her in the field."

"I guess your theory sounds plausible, but did Lorraine mention the one other major characteristic of her new window?"

"No. Why?" Mark responds while Terri continues to stare at Stella.

"The window releases with such a bang, it almost broke when they completed installation tests."

Neither Mark nor Terri visibly react to the information, so Stella moves on. "Since you're here, may I ask a couple of questions relating to Lorraine and her work?"

"Of course, Stella. We want to help." Mark drains his coffee and leans back into the floral cushions of the aged rattan. He's much more relaxed. Stella isn't sure why. Terri remains skittish and sits perched on the edge of her armchair.

"Was Lorraine a neat freak?"

They glance at one another as if for confirmation. Mark chooses to answer. His tone is instructional—a teacher who has repeated the same lesson a dozen times. "Banking demands a high level of organization. You can't be a slob. But, most employees of the bank can be messy at home. I've met guys from other branches who say they make mistakes when they balance their own cheque book, but they manage well at work."

Stella turns toward Terri. "And you?"

"Oh, I'm one of those messy types, but I keep my work organized. Right, Mark?"

"With my help." He pats her leg. Stella does not miss the intimacy of his touch. "On the other hand, Lorraine was a fanatic."

"Do you two favour a particular theory?"

"I've repeated this to both you and Detective North, a couple of times, but we're sure Lorraine uncovered proof regarding who embezzled from the bank. Did she report her discovery to the actual thief? She was scared most of the time. She confided in me. I can't help but feel responsible. I wish I had insisted she speak with the police."

"Why didn't you, Mark?"

"She was afraid she might accuse the wrong person. I suggested she at least talk to the area manager." By way of explanation, he added information regarding hierarchy over the managers from Shale Harbour and Port Ephron.

"But she never did?"

"Not to my knowledge. Did Detective North open a missing funds investigation? He told me he talked to the branches and Lorraine was correct, but the Savings and Loan never filed a police report. Banks prefer to keep investigations 'in house' most of the time." Stella detects a wink when he says this as if he belongs to a secret society of bank employees.

"Well, I imagine it's part of the investigation now. We all need patience."

Mark stands, and Terri immediately follows his lead. "Thanks for the coffee, Stella. I hope the police and your old friend, Detective North, figure out what happened soon."

"Me, too, Mark. Me, too."

****

"Sure. Love to see you." Stella gives Nick a quick glance. He's busy marinating chicken for the barbecue. "Come for supper. Simple fare. Barbecued chicken with a salad and baked potatoes. The park is quiet. I expect one more reservation to check in. Let's say we eat at six-thirty?"

She replaces the phone in its cradle. Nick has returned to the veranda to scrape the grill. "Aiden will be here in an hour, Nick," she shouts across the common room. "We bought enough food, right?"

The screen door creaks. "No problem. Did he mention the forensics report?"

Stella adds another potato to the three she placed in the oven not five minutes ago. She learned, back in her Home Economics classes in high school, how you always need an extra potato in case one turns out to be rotten inside. This particular rule has served her in good stead.

"He never spelled it out, but I assume he wants to discuss Lorraine, regardless of your fabulous barbecue skills."

Nick chortles as the screen door bangs again. With the salad made and the potatoes cooking, she opens a bottle of white wine and makes her way to the veranda.

No sooner has she managed to get wine into their glasses than a 1965 Winnebago Brave motor home rumbles into the lot. She motions to the driver to make him aware of the sign which indicates the direction of the office and then returns inside.

"Hi there. Welcome to Shale Cliffs RV Park. You must be Henry, from Ontario."

"I am. Henry Hastings. Pleased to meet you."

He extends his hand across the desk.

"Stella Kirk. Your site is ready for you, Henry. Here's a form for you to fill out if you don't mind. Cash or credit?"

After he passes his credit card to her, he proceeds to write down the pertinent information related to the number of people in his party, his home address and phone number, the plate number of the RV, and his expected date of departure. Henry Hastings is a tall man with a shock of thick white hair. His mop has a will of its own and flies out in multiple directions. His registration form declares a wife and two preschool children who Stella assumes are grandchildren, given his age. "Your site is straight along the main drive, turn right at the first intersection, and swing in to the third space, Henry. Your services are on your left side." She offers him the sheet of rules and a park map. "Do you need an escort? I am happy to take you to your spot."

"No thanks, Stella. We'll be fine. The old girl has a good sense of direction. She's covered lots of miles." Stella resists the urge to ask him if the reference is to his wife or his rig.

"Check-in go okay?" Nick, tall and handsome in his khaki shorts and T-shirt, leans against the door frame with two glasses of white wine, one in each hand.

She reaches for the wine. "You, sir, appear especially scrumptious tonight. It must be the hours of sun you soak up. You could be a beach bum from a Frankie Avalon movie."

His eyes are soft and filled with affection. He studies her for a moment. She's flushed and knows not to blame the temperature. "I'll set the table and fire up the grill. The chicken won't take long once it's on. What's the ETA on the potatoes?"

"Six-fifteen. We should be good with the timings."

"Come sit for a minute. The rig that came in—the old girl must be fifteen, do you think?"

Stella laughs out loud. "Now, I can guess you're talking about the RV. I wasn't so sure with Mr. Hastings." She curls up on a deck lounger, wine in hand. As they giggle about the 1965 motor home, Aiden's vehicle rolls across the crushed gravel of the parking lot and into a spot beside Stella's Jeep.

Her old friend's posture reflects a man who appears much older as he hoists his person out of the driver's seat. Rosemary's health must not be improving. "Welcome back to Shale Cliffs, Detective." She attempts an upbeat approach, but his expression, both sad and worried, does not change.

He waves with half-hearted enthusiasm as he makes his way toward the veranda stairs. "Hi. Beautiful evening. Thanks for the invite."

Stella stands up. "I see a man who needs a nice big glass of wine."

"Yes, a drink as well as an answer or two. I hope we can bang around a few ideas tonight. I picked up the report from forensics and it asks more questions than it answers." He drops into another side chair after Nick drags one from across the veranda. "Thanks Nick. How's business, Stella? Did you stay busy after the weekend?"

"We've wound down, now. There were several check-outs on Sunday, along with a pile of other chores. Yesterday was a catch-up day." She hoists her feet up onto a footstool. "I've finished with a new camper from Ontario." She takes a sip of her wine. "I don't expect anyone, but the office stays open until eight."

"Good. We will still enjoy an hour before sunset. I want to go to Lorraine's trailer again tonight and seriously study her window. We ended up doing interviews the other day instead. A measure of natural light is always helpful." He sighs. His gaze is focused on the grey painted floor boards.

"Ten minutes before we eat, Stella? I'm gonna check on the chicken." Nick turns his attention to Aiden. "Over supper, will you share what you can of the report?"

"Oh, I intend to tell you, Nick. I need help from you both."

At the table, they discuss little besides the case. Aiden provides Nick and Stella with a summary. "First off, there was not one scrap of evidence related to a precipitating event, or any indication of another person having been in her car. As for Lorraine, the cause of death was blunt force trauma. She incurred a severe skull fracture. The weapon was a heavy object with obvious edges. Forensics does not believe she was killed in the field where she was found because there are significant post-mortem abrasions on her back and side. The rain was ferocious, though, and washed any other potential clues away." He drains the last of his wine. Nick begins to clear dishes while Stella offers him a mug of tea.

"I want to go to her trailer. I'm sure whatever happened occurred there."

"But the window, Aiden. How does that emergency window play into her disappearance? Do you think the murderer climbed in through it and met her? Then the person took her body out the same way? Nick and I believe force is impossible. If we are correct, then did Lorraine enter one way and leave another way by choice?"

Nick reiterates his confidence in the security of his installation.

Stella starts to sense the pressure as her frustration builds. She runs water in the sink. She hears Nick call to her from the porch "We can do the dishes when we get back, Stella.". She folds the tea towel and makes her way toward the sound of his voice.

"Okay, let's go, you two, and find what we've missed."

Chapter 15

Reconsider the Facts

Lorraine's trailer is hot. Only a single roof vent has remained open since her disappearance. As luck would have it, the wind blew in the right direction and the vent didn't leak during the recent storm. There is a stale heaviness to the air, punctuated with the odours of warm plastics and panelling. The scene remains in the precise condition Stella found it a week ago.

Nick and Aiden sidle through the dining area, past the bathroom, and into the bedroom to re-examine the window which has garnered much of the attention throughout the investigation. "This water stain shouldn't be here, Aiden." She hears Nick express his frustration when he sees evidence of water infiltration.

Aiden is silent. Stella proceeds to the doorway. "Was I right? Is there a red rim around the stain, or was it my imagination, Nick?"

Always prepared, he uses his flashlight to accommodate for the dim light in the curtained trailer. "By God, there *is* a red rim, Stella."

"What does the red mean?" Aiden sounds annoyed. Stella notices the hint of exasperation in his voice.

"The discolouration is not from the damned rain. There was tap water on the sill."

"Really? I don't understand."

Stella provides the explanation. "Red stains happen because we have lots of iron in our water. We use a filtration system which needs to be updated. Nick replaced the filters…when?" She turns to Nick.

"A week ago, yesterday. Last Monday, remember?"

"What you mean is, however the water came in contact with the window sill, it was not the rain and the stain happened before you changed the filters, correct?" Aiden's expression has changed. He's no longer annoyed—more indifferent.

Anxious to move their investigation along, she takes a chance and adds, "might this relate to the condition of her freezer?"

Nick squints through the oppressive gloom of the trailer's interior. "What the hell is the problem with her freezer?"

"Lorraine Young was a neat freak and her freezer is a mess. The fridge looks normal, but I was surprised at how her freezer was jumbled. If an ice cube melted on the sill…."

Nick and Aiden eye one another with identical "this woman is crazy" expressions.

Stella narrows her eyes. "Is it possible an ice cube was used to prop the window and prevent a crash?"

"Let's experiment." Her theory generates enthusiasm on Nick's part.

Aiden raises his hand like a stop sign. "We have to let forensics do any experiments, you two…but I will order a test for tomorrow." He turns to Stella. "Good job. The question of why she came home to her own trailer, locked the doors, and climbed out the window remains."

Nick sticks to his first impression. "She wanted everyone to assume she was here. The ruse gave her lead time to get away with the stolen money from the bank."

"There's still the issue of her sneakers, you guys."

"Why are you sure her sneakers should be here, Stella?" Aiden peers across the bedroom. "People often throw out old ones when they plan to buy new."

"There's definitely a problem with the sneakers," Stella persists. "She was extremely picky. She was not the type to pitch the old ones before she bought new ones. Trying out the new ones to determine if they were suitable would be necessary for a personality like hers. There would be no space in her closet for shoes if none existed."

"Your conclusion is a leap and filled with assumptions."

Stella tries not to reveal how Aiden's remarks have offended her. She's trying to help.

"Nevertheless, let's schedule a team in here tomorrow to test the window." Aiden pulls out his notebook. "Nick, tell me the exact day you changed the water filters; days and times as best as you can remember."

As they walk back toward the house, Stella continues to wonder why Lorraine climbed out her own window. She could have waited until the early hours of the morning if she wanted to avoid Mildred Fox or another neighbour seeing her leave. If her objective was to create lead time, then ensuring her doors were locked from the inside made a significant difference. "Is it possible the person who drove her car was a look-alike?" Her words hang in the still spring air.

"A look-alike? What makes you consider the person wasn't Lorraine?" Aiden continues to trudge up the hill, head tilted to the side. As dusk begins to settle, his white hair is illuminated by the lights from various trailers along their way.

"I talked to Mildred again. She's bothered by how Lorraine's car was parked. If the driver wasn't Lorraine, then they were unaware of how precise Lorraine was with her car."

"From what Mark has reported, she was upset, Stella. We discussed her possible state of mind, especially if she embezzled from the Savings and Loan, or had a lead on who was the thief." Nick's voice has a hint of pacification.

She refuses to be pacified. "Dad made a funny remark, too."

Nick fails to muffle a snort. "Your father is demented, Stella. He's lucky when he remembers your name. Most of his remarks are funny. You understand this."

Stella chooses to ignore him. "He said, 'seeing is believing' and I wonder if the investigation is pinned on Mildred's incorrect observation. She watched someone drive Lorraine's car into the yard and go inside. It's conceivable she or he wasn't Lorraine."

"How do we explain the coat and purse? If what you say is true, and she was killed by the person who brought her car home, they wore her coat and carried her purse, so the neighbours would be certain Lorraine drove in. Could a man pull off the disguise?"

Encouraged by Aiden's use of the word "we", she contradicts him. "The person was female."

"Oh, no." Aiden is quick to dismiss her idea. "If the assailant killed her and dumped her body in the drainage ditch, it means her killer is male. A normal woman doesn't possess the upper body strength to accomplish the job."

"I agree with Aiden, Stella." Nick's voice is soft and not as dismissive as Aiden's.

Stella is annoyed with both men. She addresses her remarks straight at Aiden. "There is no clear idea of how or where Lorraine was killed, but a woman wore her coat and carried her purse, drove her car home, entered her trailer, and exited through the escape window. She wedged an ice cube, which she pulled out of the freezer, under the frame to brace the window once she was out. The ice melted, and the window shut gradually."

"Well." Aiden is thoughtful as they approach the house. "For you to be correct, there must be two people involved. The woman of the two-person team was tasked to drive the car and then set the scene. She took off through the field undetected." He sighs. "Your theory is possible, Stella."

"My theory even explains the missing sneakers." She tries not to sound smug.

"You and those damned sneakers." Nick climbs the stairs to the veranda, opens the screen door, and reaches inside to turn on the outside light. The porch is flooded with soft amber. They relax.

"Perhaps, whoever went into Lorraine's trailer had second thoughts. A trip across the field and back out to the main road in dress shoes is difficult. She grabbed the sneakers before she left."

"Do you want me to search every home in Shale Harbour for Lorraine's sneakers? If we find runners, then we've found the murderer?"

Stella remains serious despite what she understands is an element of factiousness stemming from Aiden's remark. "Whoever took her running shoes has thrown them in the garbage. By the way, Mark Bell and Terri Price were here at the house this morning. They're cozy, and anxious for information, although I didn't reveal what isn't public. It's possible the two of them are our culprits." There's a sadness in her tone. "I examine everyone with suspicion."

Aiden touches her arm. "At least now you understand what I go through every day." A grin accompanies his tease.

****

After Aiden's departure, Nick and Stella continue to sit together on the porch. She has turned off the outside light and made another pot of tea. They're stretched out in loungers. A glow created by a table lamp in the living room dribbles illumination.

"You weren't very supportive when I mentioned Dad." She knows her tone holds an accusation. Stella cannot let issues slide. If she avoids a necessary discussion, her emotions will boil over into another facet of her life—like the way she treats her staff or talks to campers. Deal with what's on your mind. This is her motto.

"Norbert can't help with a murder investigation, Stella. You understand this."

"I didn't say he helped me. His remark prompted me to reconsider the facts." She should keep her theories to herself, but she continues nonetheless. "The phrase 'seeing is believing' made me review Mildred's statement. When I spoke with her again yesterday, she said—with no prompts on my part— she wonders if the person she saw was even Lorraine. The car was parked crooked, and she didn't glance toward Mildred. Lorraine never failed to look over and wave."

"Okay. As crazy as it sounds, your idea makes a modicum of sense. Could she have sent a co-conspirator to the trailer to make it appear she was home—I mean, we assumed she was there on the weekend—to buy time to get away? Then the culprit who pretended to be her is the killer."

"You're wrong. I've changed my mind over the last couple of days. Lorraine was on to an embezzler. Mark Bell and Terri Price were up to no good and Lorraine caught them. Terri could have passed for Lorraine in front of Mildred." She takes a final swallow of her tea and checks her watch. "If the bank were open this week, I'd make a trip to visit Ruby and see what she knows, while I try to secure my loan."

"Remember what I said, Stella. I am happy to invest. I want to stay here and work with you; well, be here with you, too, but manage the place for sure." He stumbles over his emotions and blushes under the stubble of his cheeks.

"Let me get this straight. You want to invest in the park even if I don't come with the package? Is this your pitch?"

His voice becomes husky. Stella's heart thumps. "Stella, what I mean is, regardless of my investment, you would never be obligated to me because of money."

They stand at the same time. She hooks her arm in his. "You are a dear man, Nick Cochran. Let's see what happens, but at least you're in my corner no matter what, and despite my cockamamie theories," she adds with a chuckle. "News or bed? Your call." She knows the answer.

****

It's one of those overcast and cool mornings where the urge to stay cuddled in bed can override the work that waits to be accomplished. Stella and Nick sink into the covers for a few precious moments of privacy before practicality wins out.

Stella sips her coffee while Nick plows into a stack of toast and jam. "What's up for today, Nick? Shouldn't the septic pumper arrive soon?"

Nick smirks across the table at her. "Yup. My day to help pump tanks. I have a list of the seasonals who need service and, of course, our dump station needs to be pumped out. We've been busy for this time of the year."

She giggles. "You are to go back to your quarters after you're finished, and have your shower there, mister."

"I know. I know. I must run and change into my poop clothes in case we have a 'mishap'. Remember last week? The damned hose often gets a kink with no warning."

"This is the reason I have a staff," Stella giggles again. "Can't you envision Trixie and me pulling the honey wagon?"

"Right. Never happen. Anyway, Eve will start with bathrooms and then mow if the weather holds. If the rain starts, she'll vacuum plus do garbage detail here in the house. I told Paul I wanted him to stack the wood from the trees we cut. He can take the tractor to clean up any trash left at sites and dig out fire pits in vacant lots." He stands as he takes a final swig of his coffee. "Will you be in the office most of the morning?"

"I hope not. I intend to do a park tour—talk to folks and see if everyone is pleased with the service."

"You search for problems, Stella. Campers come up to reception if they're not happy."

People often express their dissatisfaction to their friends, but she chooses not to argue with Nick. "I want to give them the opportunity to have a conversation with the owner, Nick. Don't worry. I can manage our visitors."

She tilts her face toward him as he leans over to kiss her forehead. "I'll stop in when I get finished with the poop truck. The staff should be here anytime."

As he makes his way outside, Alice and Paul pile in past the open veranda screen door. Eve isn't far behind. Everyone knows their assigned jobs. Stella pours the last cup of coffee, brews a fresh pot, and cleans up the kitchen.

Sixty minutes in the office gets her to a point in her paperwork where she confirms, despite the healthy start to the season, her inability to upgrade her electrical and water systems without securing a loan or admitting to Nick help is required. *A financial alliance with Nick is a risk.* Stella is unsure of the idea, and practicality rears its ugly head. She wants their relationship to remain stable and fears the introduction of money might become a negative influence. The last year has made running the RV park bearable—more than bearable if she were honest. She heaves a sigh.

With these thoughts rattling around in her mind, she grabs a sweater off the back of her chair and walks into reception. Alice is busy on the phone. She motions she is off to drive the park and then trots out and down the steps toward the golf cart tucked in beside the house.

As she starts the electric motor, a sedan hums into her parking lot. Ruby Wilson alights from the vehicle. She's dolled up in pink capris and a coordinated sleeveless blouse with flowered appliqués on the collar. She has a dark rose cotton sweater tied around her shoulders. She wiggles her fingers in an attempted wave as she closes the car door. As usual, Stella examines her jeans and T-shirt. She is a rumpled mess in the presence of this pillar of fashion. Ruby puts Trixie to shame.

Stella turns off the motor. "Well, Ruby Wilson, to what do I owe the pleasure on this less than fair spring morning?"

Ruby is all business. "Hi, Stella. I haven't been out here in years. I wanted to take advantage of the opportunity, since the bank is closed for the week, to stop in and get a quick tour. Then we can have a word about the investigation as well." She smooths her pressed pants. "I'm nervous because no one has been arrested yet."

"There isn't much I'm able to tell you, Ruby. You want to hop on and we'll talk while we tour?" She indicates the golf cart.

"Drive around on this contraption?"

Stella examines Ruby's tiny heeled sandals. "The park is a big place."

"Okay, I guess." She removes her sweater from her shoulders and shoves her arms into the sleeves.

They climb onto the bench seat of the cart and purr along the main park road. Stella decides to give her the standard spiel. "This road goes straight to the cliff. There are three cross roads if you include the one at the final intersection. We have one hundred lots and forty-five of those are occupied by regulars—we call them seasonals because they are here and rent their lot for the summer. As an aside, their annual fee provides me with enough money to cover the basics and staff salaries. Twenty of the lots have no services and these are for tenters and overflow. The last thirty-five sites are booked for trailers and motor homes—travellers who park from a single night to an extended stay."

"Lorraine Young was a seasonal, as you call them?" Her voice is small and tossed by the wind.

"Yes. When we make the turn at the bottom of the road, you'll be able to see her unit at the end. Her lot is in a prime spot."

"What will happen to her trailer now?"

Slowing the cart to a crawl, she studies Ruby, who is staring off into the distance out over the cliff and across the water. "Not a clue. She's paid for the summer and has always left her rig here for the winter. If the unit isn't sold or moved by then, one of my staff will complete the winterization, and then we'll expect a decision come spring. I imagine the police are attempting to find relatives."

"I shouldn't tell you, but the person she listed in case of emergency is a lawyer at Stephens and Stephens. I told Sergeant Moyer the name when he came in and asked for her personnel records. I guess there are lots of us in this world who have no family." Her tone is wistful.

"You are alone in the world, Ruby?"

"Not in the strictest sense. My parents are dead. I have a brother, but he's been in trouble over the years. I don't maintain contact with him anymore. One day soon, we can split a bottle of wine and I'll tell you his pathetic story." Her expression is hard to read. The word forlorn comes to mind.

Stella completes the tour. She explains about the septic truck and how the park would benefit from an installed full septic service, but she expects a project on this scale will not be an option for the foreseeable future. They return to the parking lot after they roll past the pump house while Stella discusses the filter issue and the need for an upgraded system. Ruby seems satisfied with the information but preoccupied, as well.

"Come in for coffee, Ruby. I made a fresh pot right before you arrived."

Surprised she agrees, Stella abandons her initial idea of checking in with campers.

The weather is too overcast and windy to visit on the veranda. They curl up in leather armchairs placed face to face in the big living room. Stella assumes Ruby wants more details for her loan application, but instead Ruby mentions Lorraine's murder once again. "I must tell you, I am convinced Mark and Terri are behind her death. I'm sure Lorraine found out they were stealing."

"A few days ago, you were certain the embezzlers were Lorraine and Mark, Ruby."

"Understood, but since Lorraine died, the two of them have become an item. I saw them together yesterday. I can't prove they took money, but I have studied many of their interactions and I talked to the police and said I will do what I can to make a case."

Stella is incensed. "The police want evidence to lead them to suspects, Ruby. They follow leads. They don't choose a suspect and then try to find clues that point toward them."

"Oh, I understand. Sergeant Moyer told me they need hard evidence, but I said I bet I could find a trail leading to them. We'll see. Have you been inside Lorraine's trailer? Did the police find anything suspicious?"

In as much as she agrees Mark and Terri may be involved in Lorraine's murder, she prefers not to reveal details or working theories. "Forensics has combed the place. They've been here a couple of times. Detective North gets the reports. I guess their conclusions are with him."

Ruby sings her hello and slides off the leather chair to stand and greet Nick, who appears as she prepares to leave. "You must be Nick Cochran, Stella's manager. I'm Ruby Wilson and you caught me on my way out. Thanks for the coffee and the tour, Stella. Once we are open and I receive your application back from head office, I'll call to make an appointment for you and your sister."

"Great. We'll need notice, though. Trixie has full-time plus hours this time of year. It's hard for her to get away, especially last minute."

"No problem. It might be fun for you to come to my house for tea after supper and sign the papers there. Makes the ordeal much less stressful, right?"

Nick moves away from the door as Ruby's heels click across the wood floor. "See you both soon." Her sedan glides, Stella assumes, back toward Shale Harbour.

"Why did she visit?"

Stella frowns. "I'm not exactly sure. She said she wanted to see the park because of my loan request. We went on a tour. She didn't say much, and the cruise past Lorraine's place bothered her. Then she was anxious to discuss the murder, and now she insists Mark and Terri were involved in the bank theft together and Lorraine found out." She picks up the cups. "Coffee, Nick? You don't smell awful if one considers what you've been up to." The warmth of his expression caresses her as she turns toward the kitchen.

CHAPTER 16

Suspects Who Could Pull This Off

The police forensics cargo van rolls in the yard moments before Aiden's sedan turns up. The vehicle sits poised to continue down the main road of the park. Stella sees Aiden alight and approach the veranda as she dashes through the living room to meet him. The arrival of the unit the day after he requested they check out her ice cube theory is a pleasant surprise.

"Hi. On your way to Lorraine's, Aiden?" Stella yearns to tag along.

"Right, Stella. Are you free? Are you able to get away?" He stands on the threshold between inside and out, the screen door balanced against his tan brogue.

"Of course. Are you kidding? I want to verify my theory. Let me tell Alice." Aiden remains at the door while she rushes into reception to search for her assistant.

"Alice?"

"In the kitchen, Stella."

"I'm off to Lorraine's trailer with the police. If Nick comes back and has time, send him to her site."

The young woman, calm and organized as usual, turns from her task at the counter where she's filling a pitcher with fresh lemonade, and nods. "No problem, Stella. We're under control here. Do you know how long you might be in case there's a call for you?"

"No. At least an hour or more."

"Okay."

Stella arrives at the screen door in a few hurried strides. "Ready."

Aiden motions with an upraised arm for the truck to proceed, and the unit lumbers out of the lot and toward the trailers. "Let's walk, if it's alright with you, Stella."

"No problem." Her expression is amused. "I'll try not to get distracted with campers. People spot me in the area and they always want to ask me a question, obtain permission for their project, or report an issue. Nick says I should keep a low profile and not seek out trouble, but I encourage feedback." With a sudden realization that Aiden isn't interested in park politics, she adds, "Do we have a plan, Detective?"

"We need to attempt to duplicate your theory. First, they'll take pictures of the inside of Lorraine's freezer." He peers at her with hooded eyes. "You looked inside but didn't touch contents when you were in the first time, right?"

"I assessed for escape routes the first time and didn't look at her freezer until we went through her place together."

"Good."

"And the window?"

"They followed protocol in that case, but I want them to take close-up pictures of the iron stain, because this issue wasn't our focus earlier."

"After you get the necessary photos and possible prints, although I have my doubts there will be prints other than Lorraine's, what will forensics do then?" Stella can't prevent the hint of excitement as it bubbles out with her words.

"They will follow your instructions. The scene will become contaminated when they remove an additional ice cube and introduce more water to the window sill. We have released the trailer now, so we can experiment."

"Hey, Stella. Good morning! Can we talk for a minute?" Rob Black, Lorraine and Mildred's neighbour, resplendent in a blue Hawaiian shirt and camouflage pants a size or two too small, starts to approach them. He picks his way across the damp grass of his lot on tiptoe, arms flapping.

"Not now, Rob. I'll stop by later."

"Sure. Paul has helped us with the deck, but I want to dig out the sod to make the steps level, and Paul said I need permission first."

Stella gives Aiden a quick glance with a "see what I mean?" expression. "Do you need to dig now, or can the job wait until after I finish with the police?"

Rob wiggles his bulky shoulders and squints at Aiden. "Oh, the detective has priority. Sally and I are in no hurry. Paul is busy today and won't be able to help until tomorrow. Whatcha up to?"

Aiden is quick to respond. "Further investigation, Mr. Black."

He turns toward Stella with a look she interprets as a silent message. "Stella and I will stop by before we return to the office—in an hour?"

Rob's response is exuberant. "Sure, sure. I'll tell Sally to expect company. Always happy to cooperate with the police."

He retraces his steps across the grass to his trailer.

"I want to talk to him, Stella. After we finish here, you can inspect the place where he wants your opinion and I'll review a few questions?"

"You're not serious, Aiden. Rob Black is a genuine suspect?"

"Nope. Sally is, though." His response hangs in the air between them.

The van is parked in front of Lorraine's. Aiden climbs the stairs and unlocks the door. The familiar smell of panelling and plastic, along with a holding tank which has reached the point where it requires attention, assaults them as they enter. Stella remains near the entrance while the team follows Aiden's prearranged instructions.

They photograph the contents of the freezer, which reflect the status found when Stella first opened the door and noticed the ice cube tray was not placed to Lorraine's standards within its limited confines.

She watches the two forensic officers. Mutt and Jeff come to mind. Both men are quiet. One is tall and thin while the other is much shorter and round. They communicate through nods and grunts. As Aiden makes remarks, they nod and grunt at him as well. Despite their style, they are thorough.

When finished, they stand side by side and focus their attention on Aiden. "Okay. Stella is convinced Lorraine, or a person who resembles Lorraine, left the trailer through the escape window in the bedroom. Tell them your theory, Stella."

Although nervous in front of professional forensics officers, Stella does her best to explain her idea. "Lorraine was a neat freak to the point where people considered her compulsive. The freezer is messy, and the contents are cluttered. The window has a red stain on the sill. I am sure the stain is from the iron in our water immediately prior to the filter change." Both men are the picture of polite statues. She continues. "Whoever departed through the emergency exit expected the unit to slam shut. They put an ice cube between the window and the sill to avoid a bang when they left."

The tall one speaks. "You want us to remove another ice cube from the freezer, open the window, and wedge the ice between the frame and the sill to watch what happens?"

"Yes. The trick is, the procedure needs to take place from the outside."

Aiden addresses the men. "Whoever might have done this went out the window and wedged the ice cube between the bottom of the frame and the sill from the outside."

"The window isn't high off the ground. Mickey, here," he references his shorter partner, "can reach it as well as me. Not sure he won't get stuck though." He nudges Mickey with his elbow and smirks.

"Okay, you two. One of you grab an ice cube and go outside while the other holds the window."

Stella leans over toward Aiden. "I need to help. For this to represent what happened, a woman needs to climb out and then place the ice cube. I can try."

His expression is thoughtful. She isn't sure she should have interfered with his plan.

"Smart. Let's do it your way."

Mickey goes to the freezer and retrieves a cube. Stella holds the small square in her bare hand. The wet is so cold it burns. "Whoever did this wore gloves, but I'll work this way." She lifts the emergency window high enough to enable her to climb out, first one leg and then the other, like one would climb over a fence. She braces the raised window across the mid-line of her back. With her right foot almost on the ground, she eases her left leg out while she continues to support the window, until her movement requires her to use her left arm to replace her back as the support, while her right foot hits grass.

Thank God this window is out of sight. I hope I appear more athletic than I feel. Lorraine's trailer is the last in the line. Neighbours are unable to observe her actions, and she knows no one detected what happened the night Lorraine disappeared. Once both feet are on the ground and her elevated elbow remains as the window's sole support, she makes a minimal turn and holds the unit with both hands, while keeping a tenuous grip on the cube. In this way she can control the heavy glass as it moves. She guides it until she places the ice cube securely into the centre of the exposed track and lowers the window to rest on top of the ice. She then lowers the raised outside screen.

"There. I'm positive this is how the person exited." She looks up at Aiden, who has remained on the inside. "Now, we wait and find out if the window crashes and locks or if it slides into the locked position. Either way, if we consider the space between the window and the sill, the noise will not be loud enough for Mildred Fox to hear."

She wipes her damp and numb hand on her jeans and circles back around to the deck. By the time she returns to the bedroom, Conrad, the tall forensics officer, has started a stop watch. They wait.

The ice takes thirteen minutes to melt and the window drops and locks under its own weight. There is a thud; not a crash or bang, but a muffled thud.

Aiden stands up. "Conrad, you and Mickey write me up a report to go in the file. Let's get this scene locked up. Stella and I will stop at the Black's lot on the way to her place." His tone is flat; emotionless.

"Are you okay, Aiden?"

"Fine. Sorry. I need to organize my thoughts. Thanks to your keen eye, we can assume we have determined a way Lorraine, or a person who resembles Lorraine in stature, left the double-locked trailer. If we are correct, then certain lines of investigation are closed."

"You said you wanted to talk to Sally Black."

"Changed my mind. We'll go over, so you can check where they want to dig a space and damage your property." His tone is facetious. "We need to spend time reviewing each potential suspect again; to rule out anyone not able to pose as Lorraine, and anyone who did not have access to her vehicle."

"Supper later?"

"Let me invite you and Nick to the hotel. They have a couple of small dining rooms. We should be able to eat without the risk of stirring up village gossip."

"Sounds great. We can check with Nick when we get to the house. Let's go look at what Rob and Sally are doing."

****

"I can't remember the last time I've been in here, Nick." Stella gazes out the salt sprayed passenger window of the Jeep. The old Harbour Hotel anchors the end of the main street in the little town, with as much dignity as the saloon-style structure can manage. The three-story building is painted pale turquoise with bright yellow trim. A glassed-in sun porch stretches across the front. The lace curtains are not well suited. There is a worn deck to welcome travellers and diners alike. A dozen Adirondack chairs, painted a variety of shades which clash with the yellow and turquoise, are arranged with contrived disorder. The colours remind Stella of the buoys found tied in bunches near the fish shacks. If the aim of the owner was "Wild West meets a dory", they succeeded.

"We need to get out more often, Stella. Are they open for business in the winter? Easier for us to break loose once the park closes."

Alice agreed to work later tonight to make their meeting with Aiden possible. Stella tries hard not to ask the staff to stay extra hours. She saves those favours for emergencies. "I expect the customers they serve in the winter are Port Ephron residents stranded here during a snow storm. If I recall correctly, they are open for breakfast daily, but they only serve dinner on Friday and Saturday nights."

"Good. We have a date." He touches her elbow as they ascend the two steps to the deck.

The bells above the screen door announce their arrival. Stella squints into the gloom beyond the porch. The dining area is divided into a few small and intimate rooms—little retreats with one or two antique tables for four. *This is an ideal spot for secret lunches and illicit rendezvous.*

"Aiden decided supper here is okay because the three of us are not likely to attract any undue attention." She whispers this in a half giggle as she grabs Nick's arm and leans into his navy cotton sweater.

"Reservations?" The waitress is your typical college student who works for her tuition, the same as Stella's own staff. They often apply for positions at the park, so Stella knows most of the young people in town.

"Hi, Pepper. Busy start to the season? How are you?"

"I'm good, Stella. The hotel has been steady. Lots of bookings for the summer, too." Her blond ponytail swishes as she looks at the reservation book.

"Did Aiden North make a reservation?"

"Oh, yes. He's inside. I'll take you to the dining room at the back. He said you wanted to have privacy, but we have no other reservations tonight." She twirls around to meet Stella's eye. "It *is* Wednesday," she adds as an explanation.

Pepper leads them along a subdued corridor, past a couple of additional small rooms and into a space flanked by two big windows and anchored by a tacky gold light fixture meant to pass as a chandelier. Aiden stands as Pepper appears in the doorway.

Stella notes he has foregone the business suit and has instead opted for dress slacks and a green cashmere V-neck sweater. His hazel eyes flash with the green they reflect. "Good evening, you two. Pepper, here, has supper ready to go. They have made roasted chicken tonight."

Pepper, who has poured the water, stands beside the gate-leg table and waits to hear their drink orders. She appears to read Stella's mind. "One waitress and one dinner choice until June 15. After the middle of next month, I get help and the menu expands. I will tell you though, the meal is scrumptious, and dessert is rhubarb crumble. Save room." They order beer, and off she trots.

Supper arrives in no time. They eat in silent companionship and begin to discuss the case in earnest after their desserts are served. "Today changed the course of the investigation." Aiden looks at both Stella and Nick in turn.

"How can we help?" Stella knows they have been instrumental in moving the search for Lorraine's murderer out of the park and into the bank, but she isn't sure of the next step.

"Let's go through the people who are able to pose as Lorraine, get out the window in the way you demonstrated, and are also able to access her car and keys to drive the vehicle to the park."

"Okay." Stella glances over at Nick. He has finished his crumble. His elbows are on the table and he's ready to contribute. He beams at them both. "I have one fly to add to your ointment. If Lorraine drove her own car home, the assailant waited inside for her, forced her out through the window, and then they took off."

Stella speaks before Aiden has a chance. "The suspects with access to the trailer are Sally or Rob Black. They kept a key, as we know, but neither one of them could have over-powered Lorraine. There was no sign of a struggle."

"Neither one of them has the ability to exit through the window the way you did today, Stella. The perpetrator has to be a person in better physical shape."

Nick sits up straighter in his seat. "There's Paul, or Duke, or even Buddy, or her boyfriend, Kevin."

"None of them had access and Mildred Fox would have seen them if there was any attempt to overpower her at the door." Aiden sounds conclusive.

"I'm sure Lorraine was killed before she ever came home. Whoever was involved, and there may be a team of two people—one of them put on her coat and took her purse, parked her car, entered her trailer, locked both doors, and then exited though the window." Stella has never been as convinced in her life.

"Who are the suspects who could pull this off?" Nick acts as the chairman of their discussion group.

"Terri Price knew about the window and is the right size to pretend to be Lorraine," Aiden points out.

"She wasn't surprised when I told her the unit slammed if you let go of it."

Aiden gives Stella a quizzical look but continues following her interruption. "Ruby Wilson is capable, too." His expression is puzzled.

"Mark's involvement is necessary with either one of them, but I am more inclined to focus on Terri. On the other hand, the bank's regional manager's assessment is the embezzlement does not involve staff, but management. The finger then points in Ruby's direction."

"I have another idea." Stella is breathless as she tries to put into words what she has begun to formulate in her mind. "Have you interviewed her tenants, yet? I understand they are a couple who were desperate for a place to live and wanted to sublet Lorraine's apartment very much." She breathes slowly to maintain a reasonable tone. "Let's assume she visited them after work on May 16. They had access to her car if she stopped at the apartment. I've never met them. Have you, Nick?"

"They were in the park the day Lorraine moved back out—the tenth? They were anxious for her to stay at her trailer. They even brought a load of her linens and clothes in their station wagon. Their car is an old rattletrap and shouldn't be on the road."

"Did you find out any more, Nick?" Aiden's face hasn't changed expression, but his voice has a slight elevation in pitch.

"I was busy with Lorraine's services and Mildred was natterin' at me to redo hers. Her guy didn't set hers up right. I gathered the couple moving into Lorraine's flat both took jobs at the fish plant for the summer and were hopin' to get on for the winter, too. Permanent positions won't happen though. They're seasonal. He's a big man, sorta the same as Rob Black. She's small—smaller than Lorraine and more the size of Terri."

"Damn! I should have interviewed these two personally. Moyer visited the apartment, but I don't have much except their names." He rifles through his notebook. "Damn," he hisses again under his breath. "Here they are: Ken and Jewel Winslow—from Newfoundland but there's no specific address. Stella, motive seems weak. I can't fathom the murder of a woman for her apartment, although motives can be strange, sometimes. I'll run background checks, and will you accompany me when I go talk to them at the plant? I'll interview them individually."

Stella nods. Her old friend needs a real partner.

CHAPTER 17

Unbiased Assessment

Stella sits alone at a table near the window of Cocoa and Café. She holds a small white china mug filled to the brim with French vanilla coffee and waits for Aiden. She inhales the essence of the steam as the vapour rises around her face. She closes her eyes and lets the sun rest on her eyelids. The warm end-of-May weather promises her a long and busy summer.

Aiden notified the fish plant of their arrival this morning for interviews with Jewel and Ken Winslow. She offered to call Trixie, but he said his preference was to schedule their visit through the station. He emphasized he expects her to observe and not contribute. She continues to enjoy the sun on her closed eyelids as she ponders Aiden's motives. *Why me? Why not get Sergeant Moyer to assist? What's her old friend's point?*

"Are you asleep?"

She flinches when she hears Aiden's voice. Her eyes snap open and she instantly regrets the brightness of her chosen location. "Hi. I was ruminating." She tries not to appear startled. "Coffee before we truck over to the plant?"

"Sure. I told the manager ten o'clock. We have a few minutes. Did you call Trixie?"

"No. You specifically instructed me not to, Aiden." She's miffed he asked.

"Good, Stella. Your unbiased assessment of these two, after we interview them, is important to me. I did not want Trixie to express an opinion which might influence your observations."

"May I ask what the issue is?"

"Yes, but not until after our interviews."

It's difficult to perform a task as well as possible when I don't understand what my role is or what the expected outcome should be. She muffles a sigh.

The fish plant is a half kilometre down the road from the wharf. The parking lot requires the attention of a grader and a load or two of gravel. The area is predominantly dirt and full of ruts from the weight of big trucks which haul loads across the wide expanse. They park near the door. Stella recognizes Trixie's Volkswagen.

A giant warehouse, with a thousand square foot single-story addition tacked on to the front, perches on the gravel. The offices were once housed inside the plant. Office workers objected to the smells, the noise, and the exposure to tasks oftentimes unpleasant to watch.

Trixie jumps up from her desk as they appear around the corner from the covered entry. "Stella! Why are you here? We were told to expect Detective North!"

"Aiden asked me to tag along, Trixie. No big deal." She tries to sound casual since she possesses no firm answer as to the reason for her involvement.

"Stella is here to assist with the interviews, Trixie." He gazes around at the other two desks, one empty and one occupied by an older woman who continues to type without even a curious glance in their direction. "I hope we won't interfere too much with your day since you're shorthanded. Your manager told me there is a small meeting room at our disposal."

Trixie gives Stella a quick frown. "Yes. Yes. Right this way. There's fresh coffee."

"No, thanks." Aiden responds for them both.

"I can go get the Winslows off the line, Detective."

"We will interview them one at a time, and I want to meet Mr. Winslow first, Trixie."

North has become overly formal since they entered the plant.

Trixie shows them into a room without outside windows, but with a glass wall which provides a view straight out to the production line. Trixie points to the partition. "Workers can't see in. They won't be able to watch in case you're worried."

Aiden nods and indicates a chair at the far side of the oval table for Stella. "Thanks, Trixie."

They observe in silence as Trixie, in her stilettos and mini skirt, trots across the shop floor toward a big man with an unkempt beard tied in a hairnet. He unwraps his stained apron, removes his blue rubber gloves, and follows her back to the office. He waddles when he walks and glances at the mirrored window on his way past. Stella observes a woman, who looks years younger, wring her hands and visibly tremble as Ken Winslow leaves the work area. Stella assumes the waif-like creature must be Jewel.

The door opens and Ken Winslow lumbers through. Trixie peeks out from behind him. "Detective North, Stella Kirk, this is Ken Winslow."

"Good morning, Mr. Winslow. Please take a seat."

"What do you folks want with me today?"

Aiden folds his hands on the table and leans forward. "A description of your relationship with Lorraine Young, Mr. Winslow; how you met her and how often you came in contact with her."

"Oh. Okay. Are you still lookin' for who killed her?"

"Yes. This is part of the investigation."

"Well, Jewel and me came here from Newfoundland last month 'cause we was told the plant needed help. A note on the board said she was rentin' the place startin' as soon as she moved out to the RV park, the tenth or eleventh. I guess movin' depended on when her services were hooked in or whatever." He nods to each of them and continues. "Me and Jewel, we helped her move. She was nice. Terrible what happened to her. A fancy lawyer showed up to the plant and said he was gonna come to collect our rent the end of each month. We don't need to move in the fall. We're happy 'cause our baby's comin' by Halloween." He grins at each of them in turn. "I keep teasin' Jewel she's birthin' a punkin!" He tilts his face back and snorts. His beard, still within the confines of the hairnet, trembles with the effort.

"Mr. Winslow. Did Lorraine Young visit you and Jewel at the apartment on the evening of Friday, May 16 after work; perhaps to review your lease or get a deposit?"

"No, sir. We never seen her after we helped her move. We gave her first and last month's rent and signed papers on the same day. Didn't expect to see her again for a while. We's paid up for June."

Stella remains seated while Aiden accompanies Ken when he leaves. She nods with polite indifference, returning her attention to the plant floor. Jewel has attempted to focus on her work, but her eyes continue to slide toward the mirror on the end wall. Her nervousness is palatable. She has chewed her lip with a fierceness Stella imagines will result in blood-letting. With her soiled rubber gloves still on, she repeatedly scratches her dirty blond hair through her hairnet.

Trixie materializes in the frame of the one-way glass. Stella hears the muffled call for Jewel to come to the office. Aiden returns to the little room and remains on his feet. "This won't take long," he whispers to her.

"Jewel Winslow, this is Detective North and Stella Kirk. They want to ask you a few questions."

The asphalt tile corridor reverberates with the click of Trixie's heels. Stella is struck by the pitiful Jewel—frail and frightened—with her poor complexion and crooked teeth. Her pregnancy is not yet visible, even on her skinny frame. Both hands are raw and chafed. She wonders how an older Jewel might appear. The young woman looks middle-aged now. Stella expects she is no more than twenty-one.

When prompted by Aiden, Jewel repeats the story told by her husband, virtually verbatim; rehearsed. She reveals, without the question asked, how she is pregnant and thankful for a safe place to stay. She and Ken slept in the car when they arrived in Shale Harbour for work. They wanted to save what little money they brought with them for a place to live. They stayed at the hotel on one or two nights a week to shower.

"Lorraine Young visited you at the apartment on Friday night, May 16, Jewel?"

"No, Detective, sir. Not after we signed papers and paid her on the weekend before. She was excited to move out to the park. She was happy."

"Did you tell her you were pregnant with nowhere to live when she came back to town in September?"

Jewel focuses on her hands and the tissue she's destroyed. "Yeah, 'cause I've been scared ever since I found out."

"What did Lorraine say?"

"She promised to keep an eye out and help us find a new place. She said she met lots of people through the bank; folks who go away for the winter and might need a house sitter."

Aiden peers into her eyes as if they've known one another for years. "But circumstances improved. Right, Jewel? No worries now because you'll bring your baby home to Lorraine's old apartment."

Poor Jewel looks pleased to think they understand. "Yes, sir. When you're havin' a kid, you hafta keep it safe."

On their way out, Stella leans over toward Trixie. "Call me tonight after work. We can make a plan for Saturday."

****

Stella and North sit in his sedan in the fish plant parking lot for a few moments. He will drive her to the Jeep, parked near Cocoa and Café. "Tell me your thoughts, Stella. Did they murder Lorraine?"

"I don't think Jewel has the capacity. She's frail and skittish."

"You might be surprised when you hear their histories." He lets the words sit in the air between them.

"Did their background information play a role in why you didn't want me to let on to my sister about my presence at the interviews? Are there incriminating details?"

"Possibly, Stella. There are records on both. I expect Trixie is aware, if she's privy to personnel files."

"I doubt it. She works reception, not human resources. What did they do?"

"Ken Winslow did a deuce less a day for common assault and Jewel did six months for cheque fraud." He peers at her, his head positioned in the now familiar tilt. She can tell he wants a response.

"You think my theory has merit because of their records, Aiden?"

"Yes. When Moyer talked with them in the time prior to our search, he reported the basics. When we looked them up and added your speculations to the mix—a person other than Lorraine drove her car home and left via the escape window—the information started to fall into place."

Stella remains troubled. It's clear the couple wanted and needed a long-term residence. Nonetheless, after their interviews, suggesting they killed Lorraine and disposed of her body in the back field seems far-fetched. "Did anyone report Lorraine's car near her apartment or the Winslows' wreck of a station wagon out on the highway?"

"I want answers, too, Stella." He sounds annoyed and Stella suspects his questions needed to be asked a week ago if not sooner.

"Jewel is not physically able to walk to town from the park, without Ken to meet her in the car. Besides, she's a small person. She would slip right out of Lorraine's sneakers." The facts, though, continue to trouble her.

Aiden starts the motor and they creep through the little community starting to fill up with shoppers and tourists by this time of the day. "May I ask another favour, Stella?"

She sighs, frustrated at how she has talked Aiden into an acceptance of the Winslow couple as suspects. She is convinced this pair, previous crimes aside, did not murder Lorraine Young. "What can I do to help?"

He stops in front of her vehicle and puts the big car in park. "Rosemary is begging me to bring her to Shale Harbour for the weekend."

"Fabulous!" Stella brightens when she thinks how Aiden's wife's health must be improved and, therefore, she wants time away from home.

As he meets her gaze, his brow furrows. "Not really. Her sisters need a break. They convinced her she should be distracted for a few days. I guess the distraction is a trip over to Shale Harbour. I tried to explain how I am in the middle of a murder investigation, but, as usual, Rosemary will not recognize the gravity of what I do for a living." His gaze has reverted to his lap. "I hope, if it's not inconvenient, we could visit you for a couple of hours. The time at the park gives us an activity, at least. She can meet a few of the folks I work with."

Stella understands his dilemma. "Listen, Trixie and I already have a plan in the works for Saturday afternoon. You and Rosemary come. Nick will be there. My niece, Brigitte, and her granddaughter, Mia, as well as Trixie. You remember my dad?"

Aiden nods.

"He won't remember you." Her laugh is sad.

"Nick will fetch him from the manor. Times change, Aiden. Family isn't what it used to be. No matter. The day will be fun." Her touch on his arm is light.

"Thanks, Stella. I need all the help I can get."

"Well, Nick has to pick up my father because he refuses to climb into my vehicle, even though the Jeep once belonged to him. As a result, I appreciate the 'need all the help I can get' position, my friend." Her hand grips the door lever. "Before I go, what's the next step in the investigation?"

"A search warrant for the Winslows' apartment is the next step. After we execute the warrant, we'll see what turns up. I'll touch base with you tomorrow."

****

By the time Stella returns to the park, lunch is over. Eve is in the kitchen in clean-up mode. Alice can't manage to get off the phone. She spied Nick and Paul hard at work trimming the bushes. Never a dull moment.

Ensconced in her office, the afternoon flies by. There aren't many campsite changeovers, but the weekend is expected to be warm and the reservation line continues to hum. Alice emerges from reception at three o'clock.

"I think I can steal enough time to make tea. Would you like a cup?"

Stella brightens. "Sounds perfect, Alice. Blueberry, okay? Maybe you'll be able to take a break and sit out on the veranda with me."

Alice smiles with experienced resignation. "Let's work on the tea, Stella. The actual act of sitting to drink a whole cup might be a stretch."

She waves off the tease as Alice turns the corner and disappears. *She's a real gem. If the phone rings or a camper comes to the office while we have tea, I'll cover for her.* She can't fathom what she'll do when Alice graduates from university and decides to move along. Good workers, like she has this year, are hard to find.

Tea goes off without a hitch. Stella and Alice plan the barbecue on Saturday. If she or any staff wants to stay, they are always invited. They do, or they don't. The decision is theirs. The next call isn't until after four o'clock and turns out to be Trixie.

"Why didn't you tell me you were coming to the office with Aiden today?" She sounds cross; accusatory.

"Hi, Trixie. Off early? I wasn't expecting to hear from you before six."

"Yeah. Early. Right. I expect to be late, actually. There's an after-hours load on its way, so I've used my break to touch base. What's up with your investigation? Why were you here this morning?"

"Aiden asked me to sit in on the interviews. He said he wanted my impressions without any influence from outside forces. He was scared if I mentioned my inclusion to you, you might tell me details from the Winslow couple's personnel files."

"I have no information. I work reception, for God's sake!"

"Sorry, Trixie. I guess I was caught in the middle."

"Okay, okay. Did you make any progress?"

"Not for the most part." Stella is in no position to provide insights to her sister. Conversations are limited to Aiden and Nick.

"Well, they are over the moon because they get to stay in the apartment by default. They were in the lunch room and told staff they won't need to move in the fall. There will be no jobs, but they don't care. They'll be laid off with unemployment insurance the end of September, and they're happy as pigs in poop."

"You're sure about the lay-offs?"

"Absolutely. Only one part-time and no temporaries in the winter. The plant holds on to six permanents. I'm the one part-timer."

"Do you think you and Brigitte can come out to the park for a barbecue on Saturday? I've invited Aiden and Rosemary to join us." Stella is curious how her sister will react.

"Pardon? Did you say Aiden's wife will be at your place to eat on Saturday? Seriously?"

"Don't be catty, Trixie. You are a better person than your attitude indicates." She attempts to stifle a giggle. "I don't remember Rosemary from high school days. She lived in Port Ephron and I'm sure we met at basketball games or some other event, but I can't recall her. Aiden told me she wanted to come to Shale Harbour for the weekend, and I suggested they join us."

"Should be interesting. It's your funeral."

"What do you mean?"

"I suspect Rosemary North thinks you spend way too much time with her husband. You might have a fight on your hands, speaking of cats."

"Oh, for God's sake! You are ridiculous! Listen. I need potato salad and deviled eggs, plus a couple of bottles of white wine. You must contribute to your supper since you've been mean to me." She teases her sister.

Trixie is unfazed. "What are we grilling?"

"Nick has steaks to cook, and I will make buns and salad. He'll collect Dad."

"Great." Her tone is sullen.

"Be patient with the old guy, Trixie. I think Dad helped me with a lead on Lorraine's case; and no, I can't tell you. Once Aiden arrests the person or persons, then we can discuss what happened."

"Okay. I must run. Don't worry. Brigette will be around for Saturday, and I'll cobble together grub to bring. Wouldn't miss this for the world." Her chuckle replaces a goodbye.

Stella finishes her paperwork. She's anxious to talk with Nick. She senses a piece of the puzzle remains missing, and maybe he can help her sort out the details.

CHAPTER 18

Out of Options

The steps creak as he climbs her stairs. "Hungry?" There's an element of concern in his tone.

"Yes, but I decided to take a moment. I hoped you might find me, eventually." Her smile is contented as she indicates a second wine glass and the bottle on the table. She pats the chair beside her.

He pours a generous measure of her favourite white and takes up a position in the nearby chair. "Somethin' on your mind, Stella?"

She stares across the expanse of property and trailers out to the ocean and beyond. "Good day? We've been out of touch for hours."

His hand rests with possessive tenderness on her tanned, bare arm. "Very productive. We hope to be finished with the rest of the trees and bushes before the park ramps up next month. Lots more regular maintenance once the place is full. What's up?"

"After our interviews with Jewel and Ken Winslow, today, Aiden is convinced they killed Lorraine to keep her apartment. She's pregnant and they need housing for the winter."

"Sounds rash to me, but there's no accounting for behaviour. We both understand unreasonable acts by reasonable people, Stella. We live in a trailer park." He shrugs.

"But they're unsophisticated and uneducated—a sweet couple but they couldn't plan their way out of a wet paper bag." Stella has a sudden flash of clarity.

"Nick, I need to telephone Aiden."

"What?"

"I can explain why the Winslows did not do this."

"Okay. Okay." Nick grabs the bottle. "I'll make us an omelette. You call Aiden and then tell me your epiphany." He leans over to kiss her cheek before he clomps down the stairs to the big kitchen.

"Harbour Hotel. May I help you?"

"Hi. Is this Pepper?"

"Yes."

"Hi. I'm Stella Kirk. Is Detective North there? May I speak to him, please?"

"Hi, Stella. He's in the dining room. I'll run and get him, or shall he call you back?"

"No, this is important. Please ask him to the phone, Pepper."

The phone clunks a couple of times.

"Stella? What's the matter?"

"Aiden. I've raked my brain to try to figure out why the Winslow couple did not kill Lorraine, and now I can explain why."

"They fit the profile. She pretended to be Lorraine. He dumped the body and waited out on the road. There's a motive." His detective voice is calm, with a hint of indulgence which annoys Stella.

"The window, Aiden. I bet they didn't understand how it functions. And the one day they were in the park was when they helped Lorraine move. They never saw how or where she parked her car."

"Okay. Your window notion makes a good point, but Jewel didn't, in fact, park her car the way it was supposed to be parked...and she left the freezer in a mess. Ken may know the idiosyncrasies of trailer windows. Maybe Lorraine discussed her new window. I can investigate though."

"It wasn't them, Aiden. We need to explore options at the bank again."

"I'll talk with Ken after the warrant is executed. I'll ask him to tell me his history as it relates to trailers and try to determine if Lorraine discussed her renovations with them."

"Call me tomorrow. When do you go home to pick up Rosemary?"

"Friday night after work. We'll be back Saturday, stay here for the evening, and I'll take her home Sunday afternoon. She's excited to go to your barbecue on Saturday; says she remembers both you and Trixie."

Stella can't bear to tell him she is unable to return the favour. "I look forward to meeting her again, Aiden. Don't forget to call me tomorrow."

Nick's in the kitchen. A salad is tossed, cheese is shredded, and the eggs are mixed, ready to cook. "Did you get your issue settled?"

"Aiden wants to wait until after they search the Winslows', or should I say Lorraine's, to see if they discover additional information."

He slides the egg mixture into the frying pan as Stella pours another glass of wine and continues. "I'm still listening for the bell on the reception office door. I hope we'll be able to eat in peace. There aren't any reservations expected, at least."

She changes gears mid-stream. "Whoever pretended to be Lorraine and unlocked her trailer needed to be aware of how the damned window operated. It makes a fine escape route if you understand the need to accommodate for the noise. Jewel Winslow never, in a million years, figured out potential consequences once she was in the trailer. There is no evidence they heard renovation stories on the day they helped Lorraine move."

"I never saw them inside, except when they hauled her linens into the bedroom. Did Lorraine brag her new window up then?"

"Were they there long enough to learn details?"

"I'm doubtful, but Paul might have overheard more. He did a few jobs for Lorraine inside. I worked outside most of the time."

Still distracted by her anxiety, she begins to set the table. *Aiden is suspecting the wrong couple. Lorraine's murder must be related to the bank.* Stella is determined to focus on Terri Price, Mark Bell, and Ruby Wilson. She is convinced Aiden's search warrant will turn up no clues.

****

By seven, Stella and Nick are busy with breakfast as their staff begin to arrive. Alice and Paul are first in the door, dressed in neon green camp T-shirts. Before they ramp up for their day, Stella snags Paul. "May I talk to you in the office for a minute?"

"Sure, Stella. What's wrong? I'll clean fire pits today, if you're worried they won't get done. The bushes are trimmed the way you wanted."

"Work is fine, Paul. When you and Nick were at Lorraine's the day she moved out from town, were you there when the Winslow couple arrived with a load of stuff for her?"

"Yes. I ran the taps for Nick while he flushed the antifreeze out of her system. They came in and plopped a bunch of linens on her bed. There were towels, sheets, and a big comforter, a few pillows, and the bath mat. They didn't stay inside though; dropped the linen and took off.""

"Did they discuss her trailer?" Stella tries not to lead Paul in the direction of the window.

"No. As they left, she said she would see them the end of next month, to collect the rent. She didn't say much else, Stella."

"Thanks, Paul. You've been a big help. It was important for me to find out if she pointed out her new escape window to them."

"Oh! Well, she never mentioned another word. She thanked them and then they left. She was anxious to clean the inside and unload her car. We needed to get her water and power workin' first."

"Thanks for your help. I imagine Nick has a list for you as long as his arm."

As Paul leaves her office, he adds, "I hope they find who did this, Stella. She's been gone for two weeks. Whoever killed Lorraine has disappeared by now."

Stella is unconvinced the murderer left the community.

Back in the kitchen, she pours coffee and discusses the new day with Alice. Fifteen check-ins are reserved for the weekend. The weather holds promise. Nick has taken off with Paul and Eve. She expects to be assaulted by the sounds of the mowers and the loader running. Nick said there are three power connections to be replaced. He wants to accomplish the switch-outs before registrations start to arrive near eleven this morning. She decides to take a ride around to see if there are problems with any of her campers. She leaves the office in Alice's very capable hands.

Aiden calls after lunch. "The search warrant yielded very little, Stella. I remain convinced the Winslows will be implicated, although there's no connection between them and the murder right now, other than a weak motive."

"I talked to Paul this morning. He was in Lorraine's trailer when Ken and Jewel arrived with their station wagon packed full of her linens. He said there was never any discussion regarding the new window, her security procedures, or her rig in general. Lorraine mentioned a visit next month to collect rent." She sighs. "Her car wasn't parked in her usual spot, and the inside of her unit was chaotic, since she still needed to clean before most items could be moved. There was no clear indication of the real Lorraine. She wouldn't appear as fussy at that point on move-in day."

"Yes, Stella. I talked to Ken Winslow again. You're right. He has no trailer or window information, but he sure understood how obsessive she was." He pauses for a second to speak to someone nearby and then turns his attention to Stella. "Ken told me she locked the third bedroom with her personal items stored inside. Forensics has moved most of this room to their lab. She used this bedroom as her office, and there's a pile of paperwork. It might take a while for them to sift through her documents."

"Do you still consider Ken and Jewel prime suspects, Aiden?"

"Not sure. If her locked office reveals bank information, then my mind will be changed."

"See you tomorrow."

"Stella. I need to talk to you about Rosemary. I don't want you to be shocked when you meet her after so many years."

"What's wrong, Aiden? Is she not well?"

He sighs. She can sense the force of his resignation through the receiver. "During therapy, her psychiatrist asked her to describe the happiest period of her life and she told him it was when she was a senior in high school."

"Everyone remembers the 1950s with fondness, Aiden."

"You don't understand. She *lives inside* 1952 when she's anxious or upset. I can guarantee you she will be in full Annette Funicello mode tomorrow."

"Are you serious?" Her voice is soft. "Funicello's heyday was the early sixties, Aiden.".

"I know. You know. But when she walks into your home, you will realize Annette has dignified your party with her presence." He sounds grim.

"Never mind. With you and your beautiful wife as our guests, I expect a great afternoon." She attempts to sound upbeat and confident. "She is more than welcome to dress and act however she likes."

"Thanks, Stella. I appreciate your support. This is never easy for me."

****

Saturday begins with pleasant chaos as is often the case on weekends in the park. Unscheduled campers start to arrive before mid-morning, despite a posted check-in time of eleven. Alice has found spaces for six groups of tenters, three tent trailers, and a full-sized motor home with a speed boat in tow. The weather has improved each day, and Stella is thrilled with their summer prospects.

Trixie, Brigitte, and Mia roll in at two o'clock. Stella, from the big kitchen, hears them tramp up the veranda steps. The screen door slams as Trixie screams, "Anybody home?"

She never remembers there might be visitors in reception. "I'm back here. Come on in. Your help is required."

Her sister appears in the doorway. "You mean, if I had taken my time on the way out here, I could have avoided chores?"

"Not a chance. I've saved special jobs for you."

"But...I brought you vino." She holds up two big bottles of white wine. "Brigitte, do you need me?"

Brigitte, huffy in her high heels, replies with a whine. "Of course not. I can balance a hundred-pound bowl of potato salad, a plate of deviled eggs ready to slide to the floor, and a slippery toddler. Why would I want help?"

"Give me those eggs, Brigitte." Stella reaches for the platter. "Hi, Mia. You are such a good little girl. There, I'll take the bowl, too, and we're under control." She places Trixie's offerings on the counter and turns back to her niece. "I am very happy you came. Nick is on his way out to get your granddad. Aiden and his wife, Rosemary, will be here, too."

She meets Trixie's eyes. "I don't want any comments while she's here. Behave yourselves. She has mental problems and prefers to conduct her life, as Aiden phrases it, 'inside 1952'." Stella waves her finger. "Do not, and I repeat, do not make any remarks, okay? We are here to support Aiden today."

"Explain what you mean—she conducts her life inside 1952?" Brigitte is unable to disguise her curiosity.

"I'm not entirely sure. Aiden said I might wonder if Annette Funicello has walked into my living room. I assume she will be dressed like we did back in high school—your mother and I, that is."

Trixie grunts as she transfers the heavy bowl of potatoes into the refrigerator. She manoeuvres the glass dish holding the steaks covered in teriyaki marinade, and fumbles enough to make Stella nervous. "This ought to be a good show. Don't worry. We'll behave. By the way, if the bank calls about your loan, take Ruby Wilson up on her offer to sign the papers in the evening. Work is straight out this week."

Nick arrives at two-thirty. Norbert Kirk clings to his arm. The old man's eyes dart around the veranda. In total confusion, he clutches Nick's sleeve and asks, "Who are these folks, son? Is this the right house? You said we was goin' to a park."

Stella hears Nick respond with kind patience. "This is the Kirk family home, Norbert. Stella's your elder daughter. We brought you to the RV park for supper." Her heart swells as she watches Nick settle her father into an armchair.

She approaches the screen with a tumbler of ginger ale on ice. "Hi, Nick. Here's a drink for Dad."

He opens the door and reaches out to take the glass. She nods with a sad but appreciative expression, and he replies with a secretive wink. The afternoon will be fine. She has shared Aiden's concerns with Nick, so they are socially prepared. None of her staff plan to stay on for supper. Often, other weekend plans are their priority, but she always invites them to gatherings, regardless. They are scheduled until five o'clock and then she'll deal with any unexpected camper arrivals.

Returning to the kitchen, she finds Brigitte filling a small bottle with apple juice for Mia. She glances up and grins through strands of dyed red hair. "I found the juice, Aunt Stella. I didn't think you'd mind."

There are times she envies Trixie. "Of course not, Brigitte." She wiggles past her niece to the spot by the sink. She resumes her preparation of vegetables for the kabobs Nick will cook along with their steaks.

"Company!" Nick shouts from the veranda.

She takes a breath and moves across the living room. Trixie is well ahead of her. She's waiting at the foot of the stairs, with uncharacteristic patience, for Aiden to open Rosemary's door. *Please make Trixie keep her thoughts to herself.*

Stella stands beside her love. The sleeve of her light-weight knitted top barely touches Nick's tanned arm. Trixie skips toward the car. Rosemary alights with the allure of a movie star while Trixie bounces closer. Her hand is extended. She squeals her introduction. "Rosemary. Hi, I'm Trixie Kirk. I was a few years behind you and Stella in school. I don't imagine you remember me, but welcome to our little RV park."

Our little RV park? Stella squints into the sun-drenched parking lot. *Since when did Trixie consider this place ours?*

"Oh, my. Wherever did you get those shoes? I am in love!" Trixie can't stop gushing.

Rosemary examines her own feet as if they don't belong to her. She has chosen open-toed white canvas strap-backed platforms—styled with the fashion-forward but long-dead Dorothy Kirk in mind.

Her expression is vague, like she's assessing them from the other side of a glass wall. They are monkeys in a zoo she has come to visit. Aiden takes her arm. "Hi, Trixie. Nice to see you. May I present my wife, Rosemary? Say hi, dear."

"Hello, Trixie. Nice to meet you." She does not extend her hand to Trixie despite the initial offer.

"Hi, Stella." Aiden begins to guide Rosemary up the stairs to the veranda. "Rosemary, do you remember Stella? She was in high school with me here in Shale Harbour when you went to secondary in Port Ephron."

"I don't believe I do, Aiden, dear. I ran around with a different set."

Stella is well-versed in the hierarchy of sets—the pretty girls—but her recollection of Rosemary is dim, at best. With her polka dot halter dress and a pageboy hairdo, Stella has the odd impression Minnie Mouse has come to her home for dinner.

****

Later in the evening, Stella and Nick sit on the upstairs balcony and finish the second bottle of Trixie's wine. They decide the day turned out well. Norbert behaved and only asked Nick fifty times where he was and who were these people. Trixie and Brigitte were lots of help. They controlled themselves, so Rosemary and Aiden felt part of the group. They stayed sober…mostly. Mia wasn't sick. Rosemary was absurd.

"I heard her Aiden stories." Nick purses his lips and gazes out toward the ocean. "She said he was her 'big daddy' and he was the 'heat'—like she pulled old slang words from one of those game books—the ones where you're supposed to guess what year a phrase was popular?"

"She came to me to tell me they had to 'split'". Her laugh is soft. "I can't help but see the humour although I'm sad for Aiden. He was embarrassed. He wanted to get her back to Port Ephron and her sisters. I told him she was fine, and they are invited to come out anytime."

"You two were mumbling together at one point when Rosemary was outside with Brigitte and Mia. Any news related to Lorraine?"

"He hopes there's bank information in her paperwork. He said the single solid direction right now involves my ice cube theory, but they can't quite connect the dots." She reaches for her glass. "Aiden's had second thoughts about Ken and Jewel Winslow because they don't understand how trailer windows work. He's reluctant to imagine Mark Bell and Terri Price as perpetrators because they came across as honest and forthright during interviews. He continues to consider Ruby unreliable, but we've found no evidence she has an alliance with Mark."

She rests her hand on his. "We are out of options."

CHAPTER 19

Your Mission Is to Observe

"Ruby Wilson's on the phone, Stella. Can you pick up?"

Stella makes a beeline from the kitchen to her desk. *She'd better be calling about those loan documents.* "No problem," she bellows through to reception.

A press of the button and Line One stops blinking. "Good morning, Ruby. Nice to receive a call from you on such a glorious Monday. What's up?"

"I wanted to touch base the minute I received your application back." Her voice is smooth. It trickles along the telephone line and tumbles into Stella's ear. She finds the tenor of the bank manager's speech annoys her but she's unable to determine why.

Ruby pauses for a second.

Stella's heart beats faster. *What does this woman expect of me?*

"We received tentative approval for your loan, Stella." Ruby's laugh sounds condescending.

She understands in an instant how Ruby wants to be considered in control of the conversation. "Wonderful, Ruby." Stella adopts her business demeanor. Certain suspicions started to gel following her visit from Mark yesterday. "My sister and I need to impose on your generosity. Trixie can't meet until the end of her workday."

"No problem," the voice sings a response, "drop in at my house after supper tonight. Trixie can manage an after-seven appointment?"

"Oh, I'm sure. I'll call her and then confirm. You still live around the corner from the hotel, right?"

"Yes. Drive straight in and follow the flagstones to the deck. I spend most of my time in the great room and we will enjoy my view while we get the job done." She giggles. "Of course, my backyard overlooks the inland marshes, the flats, which can't compare to you and your direct line to the ocean."

Stella sighs. She imagines the few times she sneaks up to her balcony during the busy summer. "The view takes your breath away out here, Ruby, but I rarely manage the time to notice. I'll call you to confirm in a couple of minutes."

****

"Trixie? Stella here. If I buy you supper at Cocoa and Café, will you come with me to Ruby Wilson's so we can get my damned loan papers signed? We've tentative approval, but I need to ensure the terms are suitable."

"And you'll still clear enough money for me?" Her words fall dead between them.

Conversations where Trixie acts as if her primary concern is her joint-owner monthly pay cheque are stressful. "Don't worry. Meet me at the café around six and we can walk to Ruby's from there, okay? I need to call her to say we'll be there."

Trixie must sense her anxiety. "Fine, Stella. I was kidding, alright? This is a great opportunity. I want to get a peek inside Ruby's abode." She drags the word out, giving it three syllables. "The people who owned the place before her took this old, rundown New England colonial and put a two-story addition on the back. The structure is mostly windows." She takes a quick breath and continues. "Then they built a big deck. Ruby Wilson paid an arm and a leg for the house, but she can afford the price. Bank employees are given mortgages at cut-rate prices; at least that's what I heard."

"From one of your lawyer friends?"

"Don't be mean, but yes, one of my lawyer friends. Did you mention supper is your treat tonight?"

"Absolutely." Stella's voice is dry. "You'll be done work by six, right?"

"No problem. I'll be there."

"Good. We'll discuss strategy over a bite."

****

The day flies by as most do at the park. Duke spoke to both her and Nick because he sees a need for a better lock on the main gate. He caught a pair of non-campers when they attempted to gain access well after-hours. They turned and left, but he said he was sure they intended to force their way in.

This type of intruder cruises around late at night, searching for unsecured and empty units or unlocked cars. Even barbecues have been stolen in the past. He and Nick will work on improvements. Duke looked worn out but Kiki, typical for such a spoiled pup, sported a new sequin collar.

Eve stayed for a few minutes after lunch to arrange a day off. She needed time to take her Grandma Del to the doctor. Who could refuse such a request? Stella told Eve to leave the lawns in favour of other tasks. This way, Stella will mow if necessary. No big deal. She used to do most of the mowing when she was a kid.

Nick turns up in the office at tea time. She takes a much-needed break to rest her eyes on his handsome, tanned face. "Busy day." It's not a question.

"You're right," she replies, "and I need to tell you I'm meeting Trixie for supper and then we'll visit Ruby's house to sign the loan papers. I guess you're off the hook."

He grins, lopsided and understanding. "Okay, and I don't doubt you for a minute, but you might want my money in the end."

Their conversation is interrupted by the jangle of the phone. A quick glance at the buttons and Stella sees Alice is on Line One. She nods to Nick and picks up Line Two. "Shale Cliffs RV Park. How may I help you?"

Nick waves on his way out.

"Hi, Stella. Busy?"

"As usual, but work can wait, Aiden. Your trip home with Rosemary was uneventful?" She will not ask a direct question. She prefers to leave her remark open-ended, to allow him to choose to respond as he sees fit.

"She enjoyed her visit, but I need to wrestle this investigation to the ground and get back to sleeping in Port Ephron every night. For now, her sisters are supervising."

Stella, in a half-tease, offers Aiden an option. "You could always set up a trailer out here for the summer. When you're at work, there'd be lots of folks in the park to keep her busy."

"Who are you? Miss Fix-it? You do not need the burden of my wife in your RV park regardless of how tempting the idea might be for me to let your crew supervise her." His response is self-deprecating. "Careful what you wish for."

He pauses for a second and Stella understands not to push.

"The reason I called is I received a report from the investigative auditors who plowed through the paperwork we found in Lorraine's desk at her apartment. As I expected, the Savings and Loan in Port Ephron has been cooperative."

"What did they find—the investigators, I mean?" Her mind twists toward the information Mark gave her yesterday when he came to visit. The observations he shared with her amounted to pure speculation on his part. Her directions to Mark were clear. He needed to make a trip to see Detective North today. She will not repeat what he said unless she can connect the dots first.

"The report says she was comparing columns of numbers. They found a dozen or more parallel, but unmatched, sets of figures. Each was dated."

"Lorraine was well known and respected for her ability to remember lists of numbers. Do you recall our conversation with Mark? He said she was focused on figures and discrepancies. Did he contact you today?"

"No. Why?"

"I got the impression he wanted to talk to you. I told him you'd be back this morning. What do the numbers represent?"

"As far as we can tell, the dates for each column identifies the day a cash delivery arrived at the bank—most often, biweekly pay days. The protocol is for the manager and another staff member to document the cash by bundle. For example, three bundles of fifties, each containing one hundred individual bills. Lorraine kept other lists with different quantities. Specific lists match the bank's records and others don't. She was tracking an issue but there is no obvious answer to what or why. The Savings and Loan has decided to do a full audit of the branch here in Shale Harbour to determine exactly what she discovered. They are aware of an embezzlement scheme and hope this audit will point the investigation in a new direction."

During their numerous conversations with Mark Bell, he described how Lorraine reported she was attempting to find out if an employee was stealing from the bank. "Another conversation with Mark is in order." She wants Aiden to assess Mark's most recent observations and make his own opinion. "He knows Lorraine's concerns better than anyone, Aiden." She wonders why Mark did not follow her suggestion and contact the police.

"He could be our guy, Stella. I don't want to alert him without facts."

"Mark or Terri aren't murderers, Aiden. As far as I'm concerned, Ruby is our best suspect right now."

"Ruby could not have moved Lorraine's body—certainly not alone."

"Maybe she worked with a partner on the outside. The pieces don't fit together yet. When Trixie and I visit her place tonight, I'll be extra observant."

"Like the messy freezer in Lorraine's trailer?" His voice has an element of respect mixed with a veiled tease.

"Like the ice cubes, yes. Surprises happen."

"Coffee tomorrow," he suggests, "and we'll discuss your observations of Ruby and mine of Mark."

She begins to interrupt, and he stops her.

"I'm suspicious where Mark is concerned, but you're right. If he's not involved, then his recollections of Lorraine are more valuable now than ever before.

****

She responded to his soft knock on the screen door off her back veranda with a call of "come on in" when she realized who stood on the threshold. Mark Bell surprised her when he appeared yesterday afternoon. Casually dressed but wrinkle-free as usual, she couldn't help but be aware of how he always attempts to look his best. "Nice to see you, Mark. What has brought you out here today?" She felt a level of unease but searched in vain to put her finger on the reason.

"May I discuss an issue with you, Stella? On second thought, an observation and not an issue. I want to hear your opinion."

"Is this an impression you need to share with Detective North? Come in and sit." She directed him to the couches in front of the dark fireplace.

"Not sure." He hesitated before plunging into his speech. "Ruby Wilson has a boyfriend. I've seen her outside by the employee entrance with a strange guy. She tries to hustle him out of sight, but I've come upon them two different times."

"Can you describe this person?"

"Yes. He's average build and has dark features. He wears a ball cap pulled low over his eyes. He's clean shaven and not fat, but a good-size—not as tall as me, but big for his height, you understand." He sat on the edge of the sofa and faced Stella. His hands formed fists and dangled between his knees.

"You were able to get a decent view of him?" She tried not to encourage embellishment.

"Both times."

"Did you see a vehicle?"

"Not at the back. There are only spaces for four cars—Ruby's plus Terri's car and mine, as well as Lorraine's, when she was there." His eyes focused on the floor.

"Were they acting as if he was Ruby's boyfriend? Did she kiss him, or did he kiss her?"

"I never saw them kiss, but she laid her hand on his arm and left it there. If a woman acted the same way with me, I would feel she wanted to calm me down or make me stay."

"A reasonable assessment, I guess."

"Stella, if Ruby killed Lorraine, she needed help. Then this is the guy who helped her. Lorraine figured out Ruby stole money from the bank, and this boyfriend got rid of the body."

"You need to talk to Detective North tomorrow, Mark. The police will find this fellow."

****

"I'm off, Alice. Thanks for staying on. There's a stew on the back of the stove and buns in the bread box."

"No problem. Paul will stay too if you don't mind."

"Well, I don't expect you to hitchhike home once the office closes." Her tease is indulgent. "There's lots of food. Nick will be in, too. I'm off." She races down the veranda stairs and toward the Jeep. She hates to be late when she meets Trixie. Her sister is supposed to be the one who doesn't respect punctuality.

Cocoa and Café is not busy at supper hour. They don't serve full-fledged entrees but opt for a lunch menu from mid-morning until seven in the evening. By the time she pulls her vehicle into a spot near the café, she sees Trixie's Microbus turn the corner at the end of the street. Great. They will arrive together.

Stella has a plan. She wants to ask her sister to be a second set of eyes and ears as she observes Ruby's behaviour and environment. The prospect of an opportunity to walk around the bank manager's house in the same way she walked through Lorraine's trailer would be wonderful. She yearns for the chance to observe with due care, but this approach is the only option.

She waves while she stands on the stoop and waits for Trixie, who balances along the broken sidewalk in shoes Stella is amazed her sister wears all day at work. The stilettos are red with open toes. Stella knows the effect, for her, would be like she was balanced on little blocks of wood. She smirks as she observes her own tattered sandals, which certainly do not match her pale blue, wrinkled cotton pants and baggy navy sweater.

"Hi. I didn't make a reservation, but we're safe." Stella surveys the café, empty of patrons except for one couple snuggled into the corner.

Trixie wiggles into a chair on the side of the bistro table where she can peruse both the front steps and the entryway at the same time. Trixie does not relish being surprised by anyone who might see fit to show up while she's there. An opportunity could be missed. "This is your treat. Right?"

Stella sighs. "Yes, I'm buying because your first assignment is to sign the loan papers, and second, I need you to put your very powerful observation skills to good use while we are inside Ruby Wilson's house."

"Don't try to butter me up." Trixie glances toward the waitress as she approaches. "The seafood chowder and a biscuit for me, Julie. And you, Stella?"

"Oh, the same, I guess. And two glasses of iced tea?" She checks with Trixie for confirmation.

Once alone again, Stella reiterates her request. "I will need a report from you on every detail you see even if it appears unimportant."

"I can do that. What's your theory? Are you and Aiden in cahoots? Did you tell him what you're up to?"

"There's no particular plan. We will attend our evening business appointment with Ruby Wilson to get the documents for my loan signed by both of us. You work during the day. As a result, Ruby has offered to meet with us to complete the task tonight. Remember, our visit to her home is neither calculated nor for any other reason. Your mission is to observe, and we will discuss our mutual determinations after the papers are signed, and we take our leave."

"That whole speech sounded like a presentation designed to stand up in court, or an argument you hope to use with Aiden North." Trixie tilts her head to the side and winks.

Their suppers arrive. The chowder is rich and creamy as usual. The biscuits are big, but light and fluffy as expected. They eat in silence for a couple of minutes.

"We should walk over from here."

"Honest to God, Stella, these shoes are going to kill me for sure if I trot from here to Ruby's. Let's take your Jeep and then you can deliver me back to my van." Stella prefers the walk, but this option will suffice.

"Alright. Alright, but you need to pay close attention to the vehicles from the time we turn the corner at the hotel, go along the connector street, and then get to her house. If there's an odd car or truck, I want you to make a mental note. Can you handle the job?"

"Whatever. I don't understand exactly what you are concerned about, Stella, but I will keep an eye out for unusual details. If a truck needs tires, you will be the first to hear."

"Thanks, Sis." She pays the bill while Trixie stands on the front steps and gazes at the few cars trundling past.

Stella manoeuvres the Jeep out of her parking spot and they turn toward the hotel. At the T-intersection, she guides her vehicle to the right. Ruby's house is on the next street which runs parallel to Main Street and backs on to the flats. Ruby mentioned her view of the marshes.

With practised precision, she noses the truck into the driveway as instructed. She sees Ruby, resplendent in a green satin jumpsuit. She's standing at the top of the pale birch stained stairs of her impressive deck, and waiting with what appears to be a forced smile planted firmly on her bright pink lips.

Showtime.

CHAPTER 20

Message Received

Trixie's hand, unblemished by a myriad of park duties, reaches for the door handle. In that second, Stella questions the wisdom in not telling Aiden her thoughts and suspicions. He might well be annoyed if she reveals too much. *Remorse is a moot point now.* The fact remains, she is here to finish the application to secure funds for their business. As far as Ruby will see, she and Trixie are focused on a loan for Shale Cliffs RV Park. Her feet sense the gravel beneath her sandals as she slides out of the Jeep. She blinks an assurance to her sister before lifting her gaze to Ruby.

"Hi there. I appreciate you seeing us tonight, Ruby. This evening meeting is important to both Trixie and me."

"Happy to help. Come on up." Her green-shadowed eyes scan each woman in turn. "I imagine you're interested to see the inside of my house because of the extensive renovations." She turns toward the open centre set of garden doors.

Trixie's glance in Stella's direction is subtle. "This place was the subject of lots of gossip when the work was done. Everyone who contracted on the renovation said the space is an absolute transformation."

"Well, let me show you around. It's early. There's time." She waves pink tipped nails to include the entire expanse.

"Of course, Ruby. I am in awe." Stella's eyes drink in the cathedral ceilings, the three sets of identical garden doors across the back of the house, and the symmetrical windows positioned above. The view focuses over the massive deck and out to the inland waterway and flats where the tide ebbs and flows, dictated by nature's natural rhythm twice a day.

Ruby follows her gaze. "The landscape casts new images daily, Stella.

This view is the reason I bought the house although many people, my boss at the bank in Port Ephron included, considered I paid much too much for the property."

"Your furniture!" Trixie blurts; over-zealous in Stella's estimation. Trixie approaches the twin sofas upholstered in a bold shade of cognac. These aren't ordinary couches. These are matched L-shaped units facing one another to form a square of seating with small entry spaces at two corners. The coffee table, placed in the middle of the arrangement with strategic precision, is covered in a cream and cognac spotted hide.

Trixie trots toward the dining room. "Is this Lucite? Your suite is right out of a movie from the 1930s."

"As a matter of fact, the complete set originated in California, and *is* real Lucite. The dealer said Marlon Brando was once an owner, but there's no proof."

Stella pays little or no attention to furniture, or possessions in general, if the truth be known. She's satisfied if the pumps and vehicles operate, and if the roof doesn't leak.

"May I hang your jacket up, Trixie?"

"Yes, thank you. There was a chill in the air when I left the house early this morning, but the weather always warms up by late afternoon."

Ruby breezes through the shiny white kitchen with the pink composite stone countertops and disappears around a corner toward what Stella presumes is the coat closet situated nearer to the front door. When she's out of sight, Trixie turns to Stella and opens her mouth wide. She draws a dollar sign in the air to communicate her notion of how much money Ruby has invested in her décor.

"There! Shall we get down to business? Your documents are over here on the island. You can hop up on the stools and review the paperwork. It appears orderly to me, but you need to read through each individual section."

They don't jump, in the strictest sense, but lift their middle-aged bottoms onto high-backed Lucite bar stools placed under the overhang of Ruby's kitchen island. The Corian countertop soothes, in its coolness, on such a warm and muggy night. The sisters wade through each document and sign where the bank has indicated their signatures and the date are required. Ruby sits, legs and arms crossed, in a petite antique lady's parlour chair near the window. The delicate piece is upholstered in a pale pink fabric which matches the countertop to perfection.

"Done!" Trixie leaves her perch, returning to the living room and the big leather couches.

Stella follows her and notices how her sister is drawn to the cream wool shag carpet. She kicks off her platform heels and then stands in the middle of the conversation space.

Ruby is out of her chair and over beside Trixie in an instant. "Sit. Relax. Time for a word before you leave?"

This opportunity to gauge Ruby's reaction to progress in the investigation cannot slip away. Ruby will ask. "Sure. The paperwork's out of the way. We're in no hurry, are we, Trix?"

Stella and Trixie created a secret code of communication years ago. Since they were children, they never shortened their names unless required to alert the other of danger, or to be on guard. For Stella to address her sister as Trix, she expects Trixie to remember her role is to observe. If Stella heard Trixie call her Stell, it would elicit a similar reaction.

A twitch of her sister's lip is barely discernable. Message received.

"Any updates in the investigation, Stella?" Ruby snuggles into the corner of one of her sofas as she indicates for the other two women to sit. "Whatever you're permitted to share, of course." Her expression holds challenge as if she expects Stella to reveal confidential information in exchange for the after-hours appointment.

"I guess the biggest news relates to my ice cube theory, Ruby." *Be coy. Let her dig for information. Make her dig.*

Ruby's eyes darken. "What kind of theory involves ice cubes, Stella? Your role as assistant investigator has swelled your head." Her giggle doesn't hold any tinkling effect. It sounds forced and hollow.

Trixie's eyes dart around. Worried Ruby will notice, she interjects, "Trixie, I know you want to peruse Ruby's fancy kitchen." She turns to Ruby. "Trixie adores modern kitchens. May she admire your cabinets from a closer vantage point?" She leans in toward Ruby to create the image of co-conspirators. "Trixie has no interest in police investigations."

Although, historically, Trixie's preferences always led more to boudoirs than kitchens, she plays her role with a movie star's flair and emphasizes Stella's description of her. "I'd love to wander around. The space is gorgeous."

Ruby waves her hand as if she's indulging a child. "Away you go. The counters aren't too cluttered." There is not one item out of place as far as Stella can ascertain. Trixie trots barefoot into the kitchen.

"Now, what's your ice cube theory?"

"Well, we assume Lorraine did not return home the Friday night she died. Another person *pretended* to be her, drove the car into the park, and entered the trailer. Since the doors were both locked from the inside, whoever *pretended* to be Lorraine climbed out her brand-new escape window."

Ruby uncrosses and then crosses her legs. She rolls and unrolls the waist tie of her jumpsuit. "Why wasn't it Lorraine who came home and then climbed out the window? If she embezzled money from the bank, she wanted to disappear."

"Because, Ruby, her freezer was a mess." Ruby's choice of green for her outfit tonight was clearly a mistake. The colour serves to reflect her eyes and her pupils are dilated. Stella sees fear.

"What does a messy freezer have to do with her disappearance? Freezers can be messy. Mine is a mess as we speak." Her tone elevates with each sentence.

Stella keeps her voice low. Ruby leans in to listen because the high ceilings tend to swallow the sound. Trixie stands in the kitchen behind the island. Ruby's back is toward her.

"Describe Lorraine as an employee, Ruby. People say she was particular."

Ruby squirms. "Lorraine was extremely fussy, even compulsive."

In Stella's imagination, a cartoon light bulb suddenly appears over Ruby's perfect hairdo. Stella allows the freezer revelation to sink in before she adds with quiet authority, "Lorraine was not a person who accepted disorder."

Ruby waves her hands in front of her as if she needs to swat away the words. "None of your theorizing makes sense to me, Stella. I'm sure Mark Bell killed Lorraine. They worked together. One of them double-crossed the other, and the result ended in Lorraine's death. The chain of events works."

Calmness envelopes her. Stella indicates, with a barely perceptible nod, for Trixie to join them. "Mark is a tall fellow, Ruby. The idea he pretended to be Lorraine is unreasonable. Even old Mildred Fox understands a man his size was not Lorraine Young."

"Then he was partnered with Terri Price. What a calculating little witch. Did the police investigate her?" Ruby's voice has developed a weak tremor.

"Yes, but she's credible enough. They don't think Terri was involved."

Ruby shifts in her seat. The leather against her satin jumpsuit causes problems if she doesn't sit still. She slides into the folds of the big sofa like it's eating her alive. She readjusts again. "What about this? Lorraine fought with her boyfriend. They planned to run away together. Then he lost his temper and killed her." She huffs with satisfaction. "There you go—a reasonable option." Her expression is self-satisfied.

"Indeed, although Kevin Flores has proved to be helpful, and not the least bit suspicious throughout the investigation." Stella maintains an even tone in her voice. "He's a nice guy. Lorraine planned to marry him."

"Men are good actors. He could have pulled the wool over Detective North's eyes, Stella."

"Indeed," Stella repeats, while she continues to stare at Ruby. "Well, Trixie, I suppose we should be going so I can deliver you back to your van."

Trixie jumps in her effort to scramble off the sofa. "I'll run out to the hall closet and retrieve my coat, Ruby. Don't get up." She waves her hand toward Ruby, still enveloped in cognac leather.

"Your efforts to assist me with this loan application are appreciated, Ruby. To see us after-hours has enabled the process to move forward." Her formality is not an accident. She focuses on Ruby's face. "Nick, my manager, is anxious to get a new filtration system. It's necessary to change filters often, now. Campers complain because of iron stains on their fixtures."

A soft pink blush begins to spread up her neck. By the time Trixie returns with her denim jacket, the pink has reached her cheeks and clashes with the green satin.

****

"Quiet until we're out of the yard, Trixie." Her sister's short breaths indicate her need to reveal observations. "I don't want Ruby to peek out a window and see us in the truck with our heads together. Let's go over to your place for tea. I want you to fill me in on every detail."

Trixie lives at the opposite end of the little town, in a two bedroom, dilapidated rental house. "You need to insist your landlord do repairs around here, Trixie. What if Mia fell off these steps?"

"Oh, don't be such a worry-wart. Brigitte and I will borrow Nick for a day and get a few odd jobs done. We'll find lots for him to do." She glances at Stella and winks as they wriggle into the front porch.

Broken stairs and ripped Lino aside, her home is cozy enough. Trixie and Brigitte do the best they can to keep the place clean and presentable. She sighs. "Ask Paul if he wants to make a couple of bucks on a Sunday. He'll welcome the work."

"He's as cute as Nick," Trixie giggles. "Brigitte will be interested, for sure. Brigitte! Are you here?"

"For God's sake, Ma, Mia is asleep. She's been as cranky as a bear today." Stella is always amazed when her sister and niece are together in a room. They are older and younger versions of the same person. Truth be told, their resemblance puts her off balance, but over the years, she's learned to live with their mirror reflections. It must feel odd to face a younger copy of yourself daily—an experience unavailable to her.

"Will you make tea, Brigitte, while I sit and chat with your Aunt Stella?" Her voice softens. "It's important, although I don't understand why, yet."

They relax at her scarred and wobbly kitchen table. Stella remembers when this table was in the family house. Trixie said she needed it after Stella moved home and her own furniture was delivered. Trixie was in dire need of many household effects. Every time she broke up a relationship, she walked away from her possessions. As long as she had Brigitte with her, she didn't care. Her circumstances improved over the years, but she has never owned much.

"Do you want my report, Stella?" Trixie leans across the table.

"Tell me your observations, Trixie. I'm ready when you are."

"She has expensive stuff for a person who works in a bank. She's not a doctor or a lawyer. Did she inherit money? Those sofas are worth ten thousand dollars each."

Stella's breath catches in her throat. "Are you sure? How do you know their value?"

"Let's say I get around, and Brigitte and I window shop. Besides, if the dining room set and bar stools are what she says, and they're antique, I bet their value is well over twenty."

"Thousand?"

Trixie sighs. "Yes, thousand. Lucite is real collectible. You don't understand squat when it comes to this sort of stuff, do you, Stella?" She chuckles, but her eyes are soft.

Stella understands the tease. Her focus has been lawn mowers and water filters. She barely takes the time to buy new shoes. "The reason I rely on you, my dear. What else did you happen to notice?"

"The front of the house—you know the two original parlours on either side of the door—they're empty. I sneaked in to each of them when I left to retrieve my coat as you successfully kept her occupied. I noticed a big green duffel bag on the floor. There's a powder room off the kitchen, and I didn't get upstairs, but I assume there's a couple of bedrooms, and a bathroom carved out, up there."

"She spent her money on furniture for the great room."

"Did Ruby Wilson murder Lorraine Young, Stella? By herself?"

"With help. I have a theory, but I don't want to show my hand yet. She squirmed when I mentioned the ice cube and the messy freezer." She sighs, knowing her nervousness shows. "I imagine Aiden will be annoyed with me for revealing those facts. If she didn't kill Lorraine, I am sure she pretended to be Lorraine on the night of the murder."

They sip their tea in silence for a moment. "What else, Trixie?"

"Well, I know shoes aren't important to you, but there were two pairs of sneakers in the front closet."

"Lots of people own more than a single pair. What's the big deal?"

"One pair was the fashion type; not walkers or exercise sneakers. The other pair was at least two sizes bigger and they were real; the kind you'd buy if you wanted to walk a few miles every day."

Stella stomach knots as she listens to her sister describe Ruby's footwear. *Did Ruby take Lorraine's sneakers to trek across the field and meet her accomplice at the highway? She had a limp the day I went to the bank after Lorraine disappeared. Ill-fitting shoes can give you blisters. Why, in God's name, did she hang on to them if they're Lorraine's?*

"Gotta go, Trixie." She stands but bends to hug her sister before she turns to Brigitte and does the same. "Thanks for the tea as well as your signature and your help. Gotta go," she repeats as she turns toward the porch. "Kiss Mia for me. I'll call tomorrow."

****

On the way into the park, she steers the Jeep past Nick's little cottage, but he isn't there. The screen door slams. She strides across the living room and finds him in the kitchen, drying dishes and listening to CBC radio. She can't contain her excitement. "I am sure Ruby Wilson killed Lorraine," she pants. "Trixie found sneakers too big for her in her front hall closet. Her eyes widened when I mentioned iron in our water and my ice cube theory."

Nick's expression is soft and indulgent. "I'll be finished in a minute. Pour us some wine. We can talk."

She recognizes his attempt to calm her. She takes a deep breath as she reaches for the glasses. "Okay, but I need to review this with you."

They sit on the couch in front of the darkened fire place. She relates the visit. In her mind, the pieces start to fall together.

"Was it wise to reveal so much to her?" Nick plays devil's advocate. "Dilated pupils do not necessarily indicate guilt, Stella."

His arm is around her and her head rests in the crook of his elbow. "Aiden will only be pissed off if I'm wrong, and I'm right. There was no hiding her guilty expression, Nick."

"Because Ruby has two pairs of tennis shoes in two different sizes, and expensive furniture?"

She peers up at him and tries her best not to be annoyed. "You make our conclusions sound ridiculous, but Ruby Wilson, with help from another person, killed Lorraine Young."

CHAPTER 21

Believe Me, I Understand

Early morning fog rolls in with the tide. Her bedside clock reads two. Stella listens to Nick's even breaths while she sits in the chintz-covered wingback positioned to the side of the balcony door, open for the cool June mist to join her. Thoughts swirl—troubled and weighty. She realizes what to expect if Aiden were to discover her suspicions. She understands she should call him, discuss her theory, and let the police do their job.

However, Nick's reaction to her observations, which included the results of Trixie's keen eyes, has undermined her confidence. Two pairs of sneakers in different sizes does not make you a murderer. Showing physical signs of discomfort and unease throughout a conversation is not necessarily suspicious.

Nick does not know what she knows. She has told no one; at least not the details. She's positive Ruby has embezzled money from the Shale Harbour Savings and Loan, and equally sure Lorraine was investigating. Either Lorraine showed her hand, or Ruby came upon her on one of the occasions when she snooped.

The opportunity to assess Ruby's possessions at her home tonight served to verify what she questioned when the big sedan rolled into her parking lot last Wednesday morning. Ruby has more money than any bank employee in her position. There is no indication she received an inheritance. The source of the woman's finances remains a mystery.

Stella chooses not to make use of the tiny yet efficient kitchenette in her apartment and pads downstairs to the big kitchen on the main floor. She needs tea. The yard is illuminated by a series of low intensity lights. She stands at the sink in her cotton dressing gown and stares as the fog thickens. There is little visible past the bushes and road to the camp sites. Silence envelopes her.

A mug of chamomile tea in hand, she trots into the big living room and curls up on the overstuffed sofa near the cold fireplace. The evenings aren't cool enough to justify a fire as much as dying embers might cozy up the space right now. Over the years, she has seen chilly June days where a fire was needed long before twilight drifted to darkness. She expects this summer to be muggy and warm, instead.

She sips her tea in comfort, wrapped in quiet shadows. A plan gradually reveals itself. She will go to the bank and chat with Ruby again. Dorothy Kirk resorted to a trick, of sorts, to get honest answers out of her daughters. If one of them was supposed to be at a friend's after school, but she heard how they were at the local diner, she asked a question to the effect of, "Were you at the diner or were you cruising around?" The automatic response was to answer the question even though both options led to trouble. Anxiety prevented the safe rebuttal of, "Neither," despite the fact that the simple one-word lie might extricate you from the glue in which you were most certainly stuck.

Her decision is made. She will confront Ruby at the bank tomorrow morning and ask an "either/or" question. Her plan is that Ruby's uneasiness, which bubbled up regularly this past evening, will prevent her from determining she has a third option, where she can lie and escape from the corner Stella expects to construct.

Although full of anticipation, Stella suddenly becomes aware of her fatigue. The day was long and tomorrow promises to be the same if not worse. She rinses her cup and returns up the worn stairs to her small apartment. She removes her cotton robe and crawls into her warm bed beside Nick. She isn't sure he's awake when he wraps tanned arms around her and she nestles her cheek on his shoulder. The wind, and sound of the waves as the tide reaches its high-water mark, will lull her to sleep. Her own personal lullaby will help her to drift off, wrapped in the scent of him; the strength of his naked body next to hers.

****

By six-thirty, she's in her downstairs kitchen with coffee ready to serve. She paces the floor. She stops to gaze out the windows and admire the bushes, trimmed and perky as the sun rise shows promise of another glorious morning. Nick is still asleep. He's a man who could sleep through a war. She imagines his fury if he knew her plans. She is convinced he would accompany her to the bank if asked, but she hopes to entrap Ruby and she doesn't want to take the chance he might inadvertently interfere.

She sits at the big table and sips her coffee. She makes toast. She uses the brown bread Alice brought from home and jam Eve's mother contributed to their community pantry. She reminds herself how lucky she is to employ reliable staff. She starts to pace again. She wipes the counters and pours more coffee. There's a possibility she's drunk too much, and the caffeine is jangling her nerves, as well as her determination. A call to Aiden is in order. *No.* She will postpone his inclusion right now. She could be wrong. This could be a huge mistake—but her sense of purpose remains.

Nick rumbles down the stairs. He gives her a peck on the cheek and frowns as he pours his coffee. "You're up before the birds. Were you Ruby Wilson obsessed the whole night?" He meanders toward the table. "Call Aiden. Discuss your suspicions with him."

Indifference is her option. She will not lie to Nick, but her resolve will be threatened if her theories are discounted. "The dots aren't connected yet, Nick. I'll include Aiden when I think I can put the puzzle together. Toast?"

Alice and Paul appear before Nick and Stella finish breakfast. They're early for work every day. Paul pulls up a chair to the table and Nick begins to review the day's plans. "We need to mow lawns and weed flower beds, Paul. Mow or weed? Those are the choices." Nick munches on his third piece of toast as he talks. The air is heavy with the molasses scent of toasted brown bread and the sweet fragrance of the first summer flowers wafting through the open windows.

"I'd prefer to mow, but you know Eve. She'll want to be on her machine for the day."

Nick is conciliatory. "You two do the mowing. I'll weed." He casts a teasing glance toward Stella. "Maybe the boss can help out."

Stella attempts a stern response. "The boss has to make a trip to town. One of us needs to run this place."

As she stands to take her dishes to the sink, Alice pops into the kitchen. "The reservation line was busy last night, Stella. I think we'll be fully booked for the next two weeks. I hate to turn people away, but I expect five units from Virginia who want to stay for ten days."

"Do what you can, Alice. Accept until we're full. Recommend Port Ephron RV to campers we can't accommodate, okay? They've sent customers our way more than once."

"Hi, you all. What's shakin' this fabulous morning? Thought I might scare up a cup of coffee." Duke strolls into the kitchen with Kiki tucked, like a five-pound sack of potatoes, under his arm. He bends to put her on the floor. She speeds, toenails clicking, into the front office and straight to Alice. Miss Kiki has her own preferences.

"Good morning, Duke. Help yourself." She's thankful for the distractions. No one will pay much attention when she leaves for town. "I gather we were quiet last night. I was up a couple of times, but lights were off everywhere."

"No problems. I did my final round at eleven o'clock. Fog was on the roll. There was one idiot with a fire, or a smoke pit. I felt sorry for the rig beside him. There was breeze enough to push the smell into the other guy's vents."

He pulls up a chair near Paul as Eve arrives. Everyone talks at once.

"Yes, you can mow today."

"The place needs attention."

"Well, the damned fog waters the grass every night."

"You can weed flower beds, Nick, but I want to do the planters."

"Let's get the bathrooms done and then mow."

Conversations drift away as Stella wanders into her office. She knows she must regroup and focus on the task at hand. The bank doesn't open for another two hours. She forces herself to complete a stack of filing which has sat on her desk for a week. She reviews the list of current campers over and above her seasonals. She putters. She checks the clock.

****

The staff disperse except for Alice, who continues to work the phones. Her priority is to confirm reservations and respond to messages left the night before, so Stella decides she can leave without causing any disruption. She stands for a moment on the veranda, hearing a mower in the distance and catching a whiff of damp earth turned over in the planters. Her sandals crunch on the gravel as she makes her way to her Jeep. Her stomach is in knots and second thoughts bombard her brain.

Her drive to town is as stunning as always. The ocean twinkles in the sun. Distant fishing boats bob. Still early in the day for tourist traffic to pick up, she enjoys the solace, despite her nerves and their battle to get the best of her.

She parks in front of the local library and bookshop, not far from the bank.

The yellow Gothic Revival farmhouse belongs to an American woman who often spends winters in the south although her summers are reserved for Shale Harbour. She welcomes people into her home to buy books, to borrow books, or to sit and enjoy a cup of tea with her while they read or discuss a book. She has morning readings for children a couple of times a week. Although there is no formal business name, folks refer to her place as the Yellow House.

Stella surveys the bank. Her watch says ten to ten. She will time her arrival for the moment the door is unlocked. There are a few customers standing at the entrance. She hopes one of them is not booked for an appointment with Ruby.

There's Terri. She's come to open the plate glass entry doors. She acknowledges the group queued up to be first to complete their bank business this Tuesday morning. Stella swallows hard and unlatches the Jeep door. There has never been a need to secure a vehicle in Shale Harbour. She wonders, with random absentmindedness, if residents started to lock their doors once Lorraine was murdered.

The trip across and along the street takes longer than she expected. Other customers entered before her—additional to those who waited at the door. She walks through the entry and into the open space of the bank. Terri and Mark regard her in unison. She tilts her head toward Ruby's office. Mark gives her a subtle nod and returns his attention to the elderly man at his wicket.

Ruby Wilson is visible through the glass partition which separates her from the customers.

"Knock, knock." She attempts to insert an upbeat tone into her voice as she makes her presence known.

The manager's sudden reactive expression of annoyance disappears from her heavily made-up face in an instant. "Well, I didn't expect you today, Stella. Do you want to ask me a question regarding your application?"

Stella does not miss Ruby's initial response, or her reluctance to invite her into her space. "There are a couple of issues we need to discuss. May I come in?" She enters the room before Ruby can respond. She assesses her surroundings. She takes in the office without moving her eyes—desk, chair, credenza, two guest chairs, and a wide filing cabinet. The uncluttered desk supports a phone, a notepad, a pen, and one open file folder. There's a plant on the file cabinet and a crystal object on the credenza. If she sits in one of the guest chairs, she'll be close enough to the prism-shaped item to read the engraved inscription.

Ruby stands. "Your loan has been, as I am given to understand, approved, Stella. With your signatures gone to Port Ephron, I expect the money to be deposited into your account by week's end. I can't imagine any issues. Your terms are satisfactory. The money is secured."

"Thanks, Ruby. May I take a seat? I was up before dawn. I should eat a bigger breakfast."

Ruby nods and returns to her chair behind the desk. Stella sits and stalls for time. Those second thoughts are impeding her judgment. She reaches for the award, but instead, leans over to read what's written on the side. "Wow, Ruby. Manager of the Year 1979! What an honour. You must be very proud."

"I was. I was." Her voice is impatient. "What can I do for you, Stella? I am scheduled for appointments later this morning."

Stella hopes her impatience will keep her off balance. She continues to lean toward the award, and is turned away from Ruby by half, although able to see her peripherally. She keeps her tone soft. "How long has your brother been in town?"

Ruby wriggles in her chair when Stella turns to face her full on. "A few weeks. Why?"

Round one complete. Ruby did not take the opportunity to deny because she boxed the woman in. Stella is sure if she had asked the direct question: "Is your brother in town?" Ruby would have responded with an emphatic, "No."

"No reason. An acquaintance said they thought they saw you with a boyfriend and I wondered if your brother was released from jail." Without a missed beat, she changes the subject with a sharpness she's convinced Ruby will not anticipate. "I bet Lorraine bored you people to tears when she prattled on and on describing the fancy escape window my staff installed in her trailer, eh?"

Not as cautious in her response as Stella expected, Ruby spouts, "My God, the woman never shut up. She repeated, I don't know how many times, about how a break-in was impossible; how the unit lock mechanism had a hair trigger and if you let go, the damned thing crashed on the sill. She said your staff almost broke it and the glass wasn't even up very high. I think the more she talked security, the more she was convinced of her safety."

"Yes. Remember, I shared my ice cube theory with you?" Stella's voice holds soft authority, as she attempts to maintain Ruby's focus directly on her. "Whoever hurt Lorraine understood how the window works. They used the window to leave the locked trailer but needed a way to make sure the glass didn't fall, break, and alert the neighbours."

"Well!" She shakes her curls and adjusts her suit jacket. "Mark, Terri, and I each heard her blab non-stop. Therefore, I guess we all could be suspects, right? I said last night it's possible Mark killed her, and Terri returned her car." She stands. "Was this the reason you wanted to see me, Stella? My schedule is packed."

Stella doesn't stand immediately. She recalls the duffel bag Trixie mentioned she saw in one of Ruby's unfurnished front rooms. "Your brother is staying with you." This statement confuses Ruby.

"No. Yes." Her voice is tense; abrupt.

"I'm sorry we missed him yesterday."

"He was busy. Besides, Stella, you and Trixie weren't on a social call. We did business. There are confidentiality issues. My relatives hanging around while you sign documents is inappropriate."

"I guess you're right." She stands. "Nonetheless, I want to meet him. You and he must come out to the park. I imagine there will be challenges as he gets accustomed to life back in society."

Ruby's reaction is sullen; her tone impatient. "Sure, Stella. I'll drag my jailbird brother out to your place for tea. He has always been a burden. This visit is no exception."

"How long has he been here? You mentioned your brother last week when we talked, but you never even let on he was in town."

"It's been a difficult couple of months, and I don't discuss him, Stella. Let's finish up, shall we?"

"No problem. I appreciate your time this morning, Ruby. I hope you and your brother—what did you say his name was?"

"I never said, but his name is Carmen."

"Well, I hope you and Carmen are able to work through his issues. I imagine the present circumstances must be trying." She leans over and taps Ruby on the arm. "I've lived my whole life with Trixie for a sister." She rolls her eyes and giggles for exaggerated effect. "Believe me, I understand." She reaches out to shake Ruby's hand and senses the fury vibrating within the bank manager's touch.

CHAPTER 22

What the Hell Were You Thinking?

Stella gallops to Cocoa and Café. She needs a phone.

She tears up the steps to the restaurant and throws her sweaty person, breathless now, toward the counter. "Hi. Can I use your telephone? A local call. I'll only be a minute." Her breath comes in spurts. Beads of perspiration tingle her upper lip.

The young woman serving has a familiar face, but Stella can't remember who she is. She has jet black hair and wears bright red lipstick. She has a disco vibe. She withdraws her attention from the coffee she's poured, to focus her eyes on the phone at the end of the counter. "Help yourself, Stella. No problem."

What's her name? Crap! "Thanks. Excuse me." She acknowledges the elderly couple, whom she has interrupted, and grabs the receiver. In a burst of anxiety, she realizes she can't remember the number for the police station. "Phone book?"

Black hair tilts toward the back counter.

"Thanks." Stella curls her lips at the couple. She hopes she doesn't seem crazed.

She thumbs through the pages, locates the number, and punches the key pad.

"Shale Harbour RCMP. Sergeant Moyer. How can I help you?"

"Sergeant. Stella Kirk. I need to contact Detective North. It's urgent."

"Detective North is on his way back from Port Ephron. He should be here in less than thirty minutes. May I assist?"

Cupping her hand around the receiver, she tries to whisper. "I'm sure Ruby Wilson killed Lorraine Young. She's at the bank right now, but she might try to get away with her brother. His name is Carmen. He might be at her house. I'm not sure." She sounds unravelled. She is unravelled.

"I could come over and have a talk with Miss Wilson. Where are you?"

"The Cocoa and Café. Listen, Sergeant Moyer, I'm concerned she'll leave. Once they cross the causeway, they could be God knows where before you go after them."

"What makes the bank manager a suspect, Stella?"

A hint of pacification coats his tone. She tries hard not to let his attitude impact her next remarks. "I am going back to the Savings and Loan. Please come over or send Detective North when he returns. I hope her brother doesn't take off on his own. Thanks for your help."

"Hold on there. Stella. I'm on my way. I'll leave a message for North."

"Okay. Okay." She plunks the receiver in the cradle, casts a quick glance around and determines she has attracted no attention. She decides to call Nick.

"Shale Cliffs RV Park, Alice speaking. How may I…?"

"Alice." She interrupts before the end of the spiel. "Alice, is Nick nearby? I need to talk to him."

"He's in the flower beds over by the back veranda, Stella. I'll get him right now. Are you okay?"

"I need to talk to him, Alice. Hurry, please." She shifts her weight from one foot to the other. Her breath comes in short puffs.

"Hi, Stella. Alice says you sound panicky. What's the trouble? Where are you?"

"In town. I went to see Ruby Wilson. I confronted her about her brother."

"Her brother? What brother?"

"I can't go through the whole story right now." She sighs. "Sergeant Moyer is on his way to meet me at the bank. Aiden is coming from Port Ephron and isn't aware of the whole story. Will you help me keep her at the bank? I need to be able to ask the sergeant to block the causeway or Carmen will take off."

"Carmen? The brother?"

"Can you come?"

"On my way. The old yard truck might blow smoke and burn oil like a bitch, but I'll get there. Don't go into the bank again without Moyer."

Stella ignores his last remark and hangs up. The waitress looks her way, so

Stella nods her thanks. She retraces her steps. Sergeant Moyer pulls up beside her in the squad car. "Lift?"

She jumps in the front seat and the old Caprice lumbers along. "Tell me what's happening, Stella. I don't want to offend the manager of the Savings and Loan by going in their guns blazin', pardon the expression." He looks sheepish, like a kid you've asked to do something they know is wrong. "To be clear, the use of an officer's weapon is only if the situation proves life threatening."

Right now, she could use his gun with little or no provocation. "In the simplest of terms, Sergeant, Ruby Wilson has been stealing from the bank and Lorraine suspected. She was gathering evidence. Ruby's jailbird brother, Carmen, has been out of prison for a couple of months. He turned up here and helped her. Who killed Lorraine is still up in the air, but I am positive Ruby Wilson pretended to be her the night Mildred Fox thought she saw Lorraine come home. If they manage to get across the isthmus, you may never catch them."

The big car shudders to a halt. Stella sighs with relief. The radio crackles. "Moyer, are you there?"

"Yes, Detective North." The cop turns to Stella with confidence. "I told you he was on his way. Sir, I am in front of the bank with Stella Kirk in my vehicle. She says we might have to close the causeway."

"What? Stella? Don't enter the bank until I get there. Moyer, call for back-up and park at the causeway. Give me two minutes, Stella."

Nick barrels around the corner in the park work truck—an old and tattered, yellow Ford F150—as she climbs out of the police car. Moyer puts the Caprice in gear, but the expression on his face illustrates his unhappiness with the departure. "I'll do as I'm told, Stella, but stay out of the bank. North will be here in a minute."

She leans into the lowered window on the passenger side of Moyer's vehicle. "If you don't close the causeway, Ruby's brother disappears, Sergeant." She tosses a conspiratorial glance at Nick. "I'll explain to Nick what's happened."

"I wish you'd explain to me. This is against every rule in the book." Moyer backs the car away from the bank and drives at what Stella considers less than adequate speed, toward the entry to the isthmus.

"Are we instructed to wait for Aiden, Stella, or do you have other ideas?"

He watches the patrol car make the turn. "I gather we're supposed to wait."

"Ruby will bolt. I can sense it. I want you to keep an eye on her Lincoln. If she tries to leave through the back door which is her best option, the exit will be secured."

"Your instructions are for me to cover the back? Are we in the middle of an episode of *Columbo*? Seriously, Stella. Shouldn't we wait for Aiden?"

"He's on his way. I'll occupy Ruby until the cops show up." Her words are expelled in puffs of anxiety. "His two minutes are gone. He should be here."

She rushes up the steps to intercept a woman with a little girl in a stroller. "Could you return later this afternoon?" The woman assesses her with a patience reserved for the elderly and infirmed.

"What? I need to deposit a cheque."

"I understand, but could you go for coffee now?" She scrounges her brain for a reason. "There's been a medical issue and the ambulance is arriving. I'm a nurse. I came to help."

The woman, tanned and fit, leans around the hood of the stroller to adjust her toddler's coverlet. "Okay. I have other errands. I hope whoever is sick will be alright."

"Thanks." Stella gently taps the young mother's shoulder before she grabs the door handle. A quick scan of the bank alerts her to three customers. She can see Ruby through the glass wall partition. She's absorbed, shoving personal items into a box—coming to the realization her world is imploding.

Stella walks up to an elderly couple at Terri's wicket. She leans toward them both, slight in stature as they are, and whispers so only they and Terri can hear. "Please finish your business later today. Miss Price will escort you out. The bank is closing in a few moments." The anxious teller runs around the divider and guides the couple toward the exit. She catches Stella's eye but doesn't utter a word.

Mark has caught on, but Stella approaches him anyway. He has completed a deposit for the gentleman who owns the print shop. Stella knows his name but has never met him. She overhears Mark. "Here is your receipt, sir. I will escort you to the door. I'm afraid the bank must close for a couple of hours. There has been an emergency."

"What kind of emergency?" His voice is elevated to a pitch where Stella checks across the open area to see if Ruby has noticed. Oblivious to outside influences, Ruby is preoccupied with the immediate needs of Ruby.

"Mr. Gorman? Yes. Nice to meet you. Please follow Mark. If you have additional business with the Savings and Loan, I'm sure Mark and Terri will be available later today."

His expression is quizzical but not alarmed. "Who are you?"

"Stella Kirk. Mark, please escort Mr. Gorman out and lock the front door. Thank you."

She assesses. Mark and Terri are statues on either side of the entry. Nick is posted at the back. Ruby is in her office and Aiden is still not here. Ruby glances up and Stella sees from her expression she has begun to figure out she will not be given the opportunity to depart the bank of her own volition.

Her heart pounds. Talking takes effort. *Deep breaths.* "Good morning once again, Ruby. Are you packing up your office?" She's surprised at how calm her voice sounds.

"Get out of my way, Stella. I'm leaving Shale Harbour. I have a family emergency. I need to go."

"Family emergency? Your circumstances are much more troubling than any family emergency. Has Carmen left with the money you stole? Is he headed across the isthmus with the cash?"

Ruby's head snaps up as she turns her attention from the box in front of her to the issue at hand. "You don't have a clue. You have no idea what I've been through."

"You're correct. I am not aware of your story, Ruby, but I'm clear Lorraine figured out how you skimmed money from the deliveries." Ruby snatches a notebook off the desk. "You might as well leave your records there because the police are on the way. They found Lorraine's documentation in a locked room in her apartment. You are implicated. She cornered you, didn't she?"

Now, Mark has adopted a position outside the manager's door. Terri remains by the entry to let Aiden in if, and when, he ever arrives. Stella is happy to see Mark. If Ruby reveals any details while they talk, another set of ears is important.

"Lorraine Young was a goddamned snoop. Every time I turned around, she was watching me. I caught her in my office twice."

"Did you threaten her, Ruby?"

"No, Stella." Ruby heaves a sigh. She may be ready to admit her role. "I have a brother who threatens people. Carmen went to her apartment and put the fear of God into her. I pretended the incident never happened. It made her crazy."

Ruby sits in her chair because she realizes there's no way out. She'll try to blame both the embezzlement and the murder on her brother. Maybe she has a plan.

Leaning her elbows on the desk, Ruby peers at Stella with eyes turned to slits. "She focused on her stupid window to convince me to call Carmen off." Her voice becomes low and quiet. "Carmen cannot be called off."

Stella hears the bank door rattle as Terri turns the bolt.

Mark steps aside as Aiden North enters Ruby's office. Two uniformed RCMP stand immediately outside. "Mark, please go to the back entrance and inform Nick that Detective North has arrived."

She turns her attention to Aiden. "Detective North, Ruby Wilson has a story to tell you. It involves embezzlement, Lorraine Young, and her brother Carmen." She makes her way past him to the door. "I'll wait in case you want to talk with me."

Aiden, head tilted in his usual quizzical demeanour, blinks once to acknowledge her plan before she departs. She overhears him suggest Ruby might be more comfortable at the Port Ephron detachment. He expects they will be there for a considerable amount of time.

Positioned near Terri's wicket, she waits. Nick has come inside, and although he rests his hand on her shoulder, they have not exchanged words. Mark has telephoned the bank in Port Ephron and an assistant manager is on his way to support them for the remainder of the day. She watches the two officers walk out to their cruiser and guide Ruby into the back seat.

"What happens now, Aiden? Did you get Carmen, too? I wondered, because I didn't have a last name."

"Oh, we detained Mr. Wilson. Moyer was smart. He radioed Port Ephron for patrol cars to wait on the other end of the causeway. They stopped each vehicle on the Port Ephron side until they found him. Carmen is cooling his heels in cells, now. Ruby is on her way. There was cash in the car."

"Her beloved brother was absconding with the money." Stella's voice is flat.

Aiden changes his focus back to the matter at hand. "Stella, come over to the local office. I want a full statement and every detail as to how you worked this out. You may have managed to fit the puzzle together, but I need a few more pieces." If he's angry, his face holds no clue. "And, as an aside, what the hell were you thinking?"

Stella tries to appear contrite. "Nick and I will be along once the support for Mark and Terri arrives. We'll keep them company until then." Their expressions reflect how traumatized they are.

"Another observation, Aiden." She grimaces when she sees the hint of frustration on his face. "I never touched the item, but you might want to throw Ruby's Manager of the Year award in a bag. The crystal has soap residue on one side. It could be the murder weapon."

"Manager of the Year award? You can't be serious!" He barks his incredulity. "Forensics is on the way. I'll alert them. What made you focus on the award?"

"The shape and the fact it appeared to have had a sloppy wash not too long ago. She turned away when I noticed it on the credenza and made a remark." As an afterthought, she adds in an ironic tone, "I wonder if my loan is still approved."

Forensics and the assistant manager arrive. Aiden leaves. She and Nick plan to follow in due course. First, they need to have a discussion. Nick is a rocket ready to blow. She knows he's upset. She might as well listen to what he has to say.

"You said you planned to go inside the bank but then wait for Aiden. Tell me what happened."

She is behind the wheel of her Jeep and he's in the passenger seat. She reaches for his hand. "I convinced the customers to complete their business and leave. I instructed Terri and Mark to lock the door and stay by the entry. By then, she noticed me." She sighs. "I couldn't let her leave."

"What if she had produced a weapon, Stella? She could have had a knife, or a gun, for God's sake!"

"I'm sure her weapon was the crystal award on the credenza. My guess is that the murder of Lorraine Young was an act of anger and she made use of the object closest at hand. Carmen is the dangerous one, and I felt protected from him by you as well as the locked front door."

"You were reckless. You could have been hurt." His voice sounds petulant now. They both understand he won't win this round.

"I scared you and I'm sorry. I was afraid they would get away. I needed to keep her inside."

"Aiden will want to hear every minute detail, from sneakers in two sizes to 'weird' emotions when you talked to her last night. He knows none of this, correct?"

"Nope. The man has taken my suspicions on blind faith. On the other hand, his office and the bank in Port Ephron have dredged through the figures for days since they found Lorraine's lists at the apartment. I imagine he's confident they have the right perpetrator." She smirks across at him. "Although the existence of the jailbird brother was a surprise."

He moves to exit the Jeep. "Okay, I'll follow you to the detachment in the truck."

"No need, my dear. I suspect Aiden will want to come out to the park to talk to everyone. You don't have to wait around for me."

His voice is firm. "I'm right behind you."

Stella suspects he wants to sound stern.

CHAPTER 23

Works Every Time

Aiden is at the front desk with Sergeant Moyer when Nick and Stella walk in. He motions for them to follow him to a nondescript cubical lodged at the centre of the minuscule detachment office. The oval table supports one manila file folder and three glasses of water. Aiden carries a clipboard which holds blank lined paper. Stella decides to settle in. She expects a long afternoon. Weariness overwhelms her. Hunger nags at her belly. *When did I eat last?*

"Take a seat, you two. Stella, honest to God, I should put you in cells, as well as Ruby and her brother. Whatever possessed you to confront Ruby this morning? Why didn't you call me? A turn for the worst was a distinct possibility."

"I understand, Aiden. Nick even said I should talk to you, but I needed to be sure." As much as Stella wants to act contrite, she isn't. She satisfied her own suspicions first, to avoid the chance that she might lead Aiden and the police along a fruitless bunny trail of unrelated information.

The detective leans back and begins to relax. His obvious need to get the necessary rebuke off his chest before proceeding has been accomplished. "Okay. Ruby and Carmen Wilson are both enjoying our hospitality in Port Ephron. Before I question them, I want to review each detail with you, from the beginning. There's information I know but pieces you haven't shared." He furrows his eyebrows as he peers across the table.

"You two can manage without me," Nick interrupts.

Aiden gives a cursory nod.

Nick touches Stella's forearm. "I'll leave for home and check on the staff." His gaze is directed at Stella.

"Good idea, Nick. Tell them we'll meet tomorrow morning." She focuses her attention toward Aiden. "Will we be able to provide basic information to people involved from the beginning?"

"As long as you don't delve into any details, yes. Until we obtain confessions, and we may well not get confessions, we can't reveal much. You understand."

"Of course."

Nick has pushed back his chair and stands, ready to depart. "Arrests were made. Police continue to investigate. Blah, blah." He leans over and touches her forehead with his lips. "See you at home. Man, I'm happy this is behind us."

Stella knows the overt homage to their relationship has not gone unnoticed by Aiden.

"Alright, Stella, let's start from the beginning."

"The first issue was with Mildred Fox. Lorraine parked her car crooked and never acknowledged her neighbour out by the fire. Mildred insisted the woman was Lorraine, but the poor parking and personal affront became difficult to justify. Then, my father's innocuous little remark, when he reminded me how 'seeing is believing', made me reconsider. We assumed Lorraine came home because that's who Mildred assumed she saw. Then Mildred started to have seconds thoughts if the person was, in fact, Lorraine."

Aiden nods. "In addition, you understood Lorraine's compulsiveness was prevalent, but I didn't consider the scene especially abnormal. We, the police, rationalized away small clues as a result."

"Doors locked from the inside, and her coat and purse left in the kitchen, bothered me, Stella continues. "No matter how preoccupied, the Lorraine I knew would not leave them lying around. But, other issues ate at me, Aiden. Her damned security window grew into the biggest question. It was such a huge deal for her. She talked about the unit at work and with us at the park. The red-rimmed water stain on the sill annoyed me, and Nick was apoplectic. Rain doesn't leave red-rimmed residue." She smirks.

Aiden's look is one of surrender. "Yes, the freezer moved the focus in the direction of a theory other than Lorraine disappeared on her own."

"The freezer was in a mess. My ice cube theory, as you often referred to it, grew from the condition of the appliance and what turned out to be an iron stain on the sill. The murderer needed to be aware of the challenges and therefore used an ice cube to prevent a sudden and loud slam."

"Until this point, our perpetrator fit many scenarios."

"Whoever impersonated Lorraine wore the victim's sneakers to walk across the field and out to the highway. Ruby had a slight limp on the Tuesday after the long weekend when I met her at the bank. The observation meant little until I discovered two pairs of runners in her front hall closet—one fancy pair and one larger pair of walkers, not a designer brand."

"You managed to get a peek into Ruby's closet?"

"No. Trixie poked around when we visited her home to sign my loan agreement papers. The idea was Ruby's, by the way, to invite us because of Trixie's impossible work schedule this time of year. Eagle-eye Trixie also spied a green duffel bag in one of the otherwise empty front rooms. It appeared Ruby had company."

"How did you discover the existence of Carmen? Did Ruby tell you?"

"Not in so many words. When the bank closed after Lorraine's body was discovered, Ruby came out to the park for a visit. Her goal was to pump me for information. I steered the conversation toward family and she mentioned a brother often in trouble."

"When did you find out he was out of jail?"

"I didn't, Aiden. Mark visited me on Sunday and said he wondered if Ruby had a boyfriend. He convinced himself Lorraine stumbled on suspicious behaviour which involved Ruby. This unknown man provided the link to how Ruby hurt Lorraine. She needed help to dispose of the body."

"Carmen Wilson left prison two months ago. You asked Ruby if her brother was out of jail?"

"Not in those words. I had no way to confirm if he ever served time, although I suspected, because of her expression when she mentioned him— sort of sad and done in. She said he was always in trouble over the years."

"Why didn't speak to me, Stella? If a situation such as this happens again, check with me." Aiden's tone is stern. "Okay. How did you ask?"

"I asked her how long he had been in town. The question surprised her, and she told the truth before she thought her response through." Stella leans back in the uncomfortable metal chair. "Works every time."

"You were foolhardy when you went to the bank this morning."

Stella remains steadfast in defence of her decisions despite Aiden's annoyance. "There were other people around. I wasn't afraid. Besides, Aiden, I ran to the coffee shop and called. With you in Port Ephron, Moyer came. Nick, too." She does not want to sound defiant, but what did he expect? Was she to sip coffee and let the Wilsons take off?

"Well, I'll share some information with you, now, before we drive to Port Ephron and interview Ruby."

"Interview Ruby? You want me to tag along?"

"You apply a certain approach when you ask questions, Stella; and you interpret answers in a particular way. Your style is unique." His demeanour is self-deprecating. "You can teach me a trick or two."

Stella is flattered beyond words but refuses to be charmed. "I'm happy to assist in questioning Ruby, but I wouldn't be much help with the brother. I don't know him well enough."

"I agree, but the interview with Ruby will proceed better with you there."

"What did you want to tell me?"

"Oh. Yes. The Port Ephron Savings and Loan conducted a nice long meeting with our forensic accountant and Ruby did, in fact, manipulate records. She skimmed money off the transferred cash each week and substituted her own lists for the ones Lorraine compiled with her at the time of delivery. Although it's necessary to make a few assumptions, Lorraine found a duplicate list on Ruby's desk and made a copy. This is how she discovered Ruby rewrote the transfers."

"Did she steal a bundle?"

"One hundred thousand dollars over a two-year period. We'll find out the details when we talk with her, but I assume Carmen wanted her to cash out, and she got sloppy."

"I can ask her to describe the pressure from her brother. You may not agree, Aiden, but knowing her history and why she felt compelled to do what Carmen demanded is important; understanding why she told him what she was up to. There must be a strong bond between the two. There's information still not uncovered."

****

Stella follows Aiden across the causeway and into Port Ephron. She hasn't taken the drive over this way in weeks and wishes for Nick's company. They could visit one of the classy local restaurants for dinner. She glances at her wrinkled cotton drawstring capris and changes her mind. Home for a burger on the grill if she's lucky.

She trots along behind Aiden North through the RCMP detachment to a room not dissimilar to the one they used in Shale Harbour. Aiden settles at the side of the table and motions to Stella to take the seat nearest him.

"Where's Ruby expected to sit?" She has a plan, and position is pivotal.

"Across. Standard protocol." He's patient but curious. "Another option in mind?"

"I'll anchor the end, if it's okay. She'll be forced to turn toward me when she talks. I want her to presume she's the primary focus, and the two of us are here together to chat. Are you good with the idea?"

"No problem. I hoped, when I brought you here, you might get more out of her than me. Here we go."

He stands as Ruby Wilson is accompanied into the room. She is not handcuffed. This surprises Stella, but she supposes she's read too many detective novels and watched too much television. Nick and his murder mysteries.

Ruby attempts to straighten her rumbled pin striped suit. The crimson ties of her silk blouse, designed to be formed into a stunning bow at her throat, hang limp and useless. Her expression indicates surprise when she sees Stella. "I didn't expect you." Her tone is flat; defeatist.

"Hi, Ruby. Detective North asked me to tag along. He thought you might be more comfortable with someone familiar in the room." Stella plasters kindness across her face, despite the urge to wring the woman's neck.

"Whatever," she mutters as the uniformed officer leads her by the elbow to the chair directly opposite Aiden.

Stella takes her seat at the end of the table. "This has been a long day, Ruby. We're here for one simple reason. We want to hear your story." Although Aiden is not aware, Stella suspects Ruby struggled most of her life. Her remarks, when she referred to her parents as dead and her brother as a pathetic part of her history, are the basis by which Stella decides to begin the conversation.

"You want me to tell you what happened to Lorraine?"

"No. Not right this minute. There's lots of time." Stella does not miss the consternation on Aiden's face. "I want you to describe your childhood and how you grew up; about how you travelled through your life and ended up in the prestigious position as the bank manager at the Shale Harbour Savings and Loan."

Ruby's eyes light up for a moment when Stella flatters her with the word prestigious, but her voice is subdued. "First off, Stella, I told you my parents are dead—not the exact truth—although who knows? Carmen is my half-brother. Different fathers; use our mother's last name. Unless Carmen possesses information he's never shared, neither of us has contact with, nor even knowledge of, our fathers. I say my parents are dead because they might as well be."

Aiden jots notes while Stella leans closer to Ruby and follows up with a question. "And your mother?"

"No one ever chooses to admit to being unwanted, and it's no excuse, but Carmen and I were abandoned. My mother and her latest boyfriend left us in the front yard of our Great Aunt Millie's in the middle of the night. She told us not to move and her Aunt Millie would find us in the morning. She called us presents left on the doorstep." Ruby glares at Stella. "We sat on the front stoop for the whole night. In the morning, I knocked on the door and Aunt Millie let us in." She rubs her hand across the front of her blouse. "I remember my dress—wet through from the dew. I was certain I would never get warm again."

"I gather she raised you."

"Sort of. I give her credit. She inherited two kids. She never had children. Her husband worked on the railroad and after he died, she collected a paltry little widow's pension to go with their savings. With no other help, the poor woman was forced to bring up two kids. She never gave us up to some government office, at least."

"Did she try to find your mother?"

"I was only ten, but I imagine she did. We never heard from that woman again."

"Millie took care of you, then?"

"Yup. She was seventy when we landed on her doorstep, literally. She died." Ruby drags her eyes away from where her fingers are tangled in her crimson tie. "Eight years later, she dropped dead while she stood at the kitchen sink. I found her on the floor when I came home from school. My graduation was in a month."

"Oh Ruby, my condolences." Stella reaches out her hand, but Ruby drops both of hers back into her lap.

"Don't pity me. I graduated. I took care of Carmen and I got accepted into commercial college. I did well." Her gaze travels from one of them to the other. "Carmen did not. He was thirteen when Millie died and by the time he turned sixteen, he had been in juvenile detention twice."

"What happened?" Stella is shocked to hear Aiden's voice. She had forgotten he was in the room.

"Who knows? A teenager stuck raising another teenager doesn't analyze much. Carmen takes what he wants and hurts without any regard for the person or the consequences. Over the years, I've tried to figure him out. I read an article in a magazine once where they said people who act like him are morally bankrupt, with no empathy. We experienced the same challenges in life, but he was the one who caused problems all the time."

"Describe the differences between you and Carmen, Ruby." Stella attempts to keep her questions open-ended.

Ruby sits up straighter in her chair and squares her shoulders. "Stella. Detective North. I am a productive member of society. I worked hard and advanced in the bank because of merit. I never, to the best of my knowledge, hurt anyone. Do you realize they released my brother from prison two months ago? He served three years because he hit a man and then took his wallet. When the judge asked him why he committed the crime, he said for the money." Her eyes, smudged with mascara, dart between them. "When the judge asked if he realized the man almost died, Carmen said the guy should have given him the wallet in the first place, so it was the victim's fault."

She heaves a satisfied sigh and leans back in the chair. She continues to look from one to the other as if for confirmation. "You see what I mean? Not an ounce of compassion for anyone but himself. You'll understand when you talk to him."

"What made you decide to embezzle from the Savings and Loan?" Aiden does not lift his focus from his notebook when he asks the question.

"The idea fell into my lap. Every time I visited Carmen, or talked to him on the phone, he asked me why I didn't help myself to the money. In his eyes, the bank owned millions and a few bucks here and there isn't important. When I first examined the cash delivery process, I realized he was right. I started to *revise* the confirmation slips more than two years ago."

"A few dollars disappearing was of no consequence." Stella accepts Ruby's information with a nonjudgmental tone, to give the impression she understands the woman's logic and behaviour.

"Well, they didn't discover any irregularities. Head office never audited, but then little miss 'won't mind her own business' started to snoop around." She leans forward again. "Her actions had to be stopped."

Stella keeps her eyes focused on Ruby. "How did Carmen react when Lorraine interfered?"

"Oh, my God! If not for me, Carmen would have killed her six months ago. He wanted to go over to her apartment and beat her to a pulp, but I convinced him to scare her and then I expected her to back off."

"You tried to help Lorraine, didn't you?"

"Of course, I did. If not for me…I'm not a bad person, Stella. Carmen is the bad one. Always has been. Lorraine refused to listen. She figured out I took the money. The last time we received a cash delivery—the Friday before the long weekend—she hung around after everyone left. I expected her to call the police if we didn't talk."

"Do you want to tell us what happened? It isn't necessary, Ruby. We will assign you a lawyer."

"Oh no. I'll tell you." She giggles. The sound unnerves Stella for a moment. "I'll need a lawyer, for sure, but I'll talk. You'll soon realize her death wasn't my fault."

"Take us step by step." Aiden tries to stay calm, but Stella knows from his posture he's anxious to finish the interview with a confession.

"You won't believe what she did." Ruby puts her elbows on the table as if she might relate a story regarding how an employee turned up late for work or made a mistake when they balanced their cash. "She came into my office and confronted me! Confronted *me*! She presumed, after saying she discovered evidence I took the money that I would reply: 'Why yes, as a matter of fact, I did'. She expected the whole mess to be over." Ruby purses her lips.

"What did you do, Ruby?" Stella makes her voice sound conspiratorial, as if she's interested in the conclusion, although she knows what happened.

"I was in a rage. She thought I came around my desk to cozy up beside her in the other chair and talk. I grabbed my crystal award and slammed the edge into her skull. Lorraine Young was a stupid, nosy woman who needed to be silenced."

The interview, delving into the complications of cash transfers and the intricacies of debits and credits, dragged out another hour before Stella, mercifully, climbed back into her Jeep and drove toward the safety and security of the Shale Cliffs RV Park. The police will do their work. She cannot imagine a trial of any sort. Aiden will interrogate Carmen. Her involvement is over for now.

By seven o'clock Tuesday evening, Stella is stretched out in a chaise on the veranda, wine in hand, watching Nick grill a burger for her. He hasn't asked her any questions. She loves this quality in Nick. He waits for her to organize her thoughts. Aiden has told her she can report to her staff, as well as those campers involved, that arrests were made and the identity of the suspects. He's confident the details will be wrapped up in due course.

CHAPTER 24

Can't Eat Shrimp Without Beer

She accepts the cup of tea offered to her by Nick after their quiet supper and idle conversation. Exhaustion overwhelms her with a fierce surge she knows he sees in her eyes. She wants to relieve the pressure; to weep.

"We can discuss your meeting any time you're ready…or not, Stella. The choice is yours."

"Aiden allowed me to ask her whatever I wanted. Ruby Wilson and her brother were dropped off at an elderly aunt's home when she was ten and Carmen was five. How do you ever recover from such an experience?" She doesn't need an answer.

Nick sits across from her on the upstairs deck and sips his tea. "Lots of people live through lousy childhoods, Stella. You don't get a pass because of how you were treated when you were a kid."

"Understood. Ruby says Carmen is morally bankrupt whereas she is a good person. She saw Lorraine as a stumbling block requiring removal. Lorraine deserved to be hurt." She stares out at the distance views of park and ocean. The wind rustles the bushes below with a gentle steadiness. Clouds drift in for what promises to be an overcast and rainy day tomorrow. "She has no idea her behaviour is parallel to her brother's. She sees herself as better because she never ended up in detention when she was a teenager. She has no self-awareness. She maintains she has a conscience, Nick. She said Carmen is the bad one. I am overwhelmed by her lack of personal insight."

"What happens now?"

"Besides the fact I could sleep for a week? Aiden will interview Carmen. The lawyers will get involved, and I expect both Ruby and her brother will be charged tomorrow morning. Ruby confessed to the actual murder, but

Carmen helped her."

"Is Aiden coming out to the park to meet with everyone?"

"No. He gave me permission to report the basics to staff, and those people aware from the start—no details regarding my interview with Ruby. I want to call Trixie and invite her, along with Aiden, to supper tomorrow night." He nods. "The staff can assemble in the kitchen before work, and we can talk to them then. I'll do one of my park runs mid-morning and visit with the residents."

She sighs. "I imagine Aiden, or Sergeant Moyer, will meet with Kevin, Mark and Terri, as well as her tenants, the Winslows, and her estate lawyer. I'll contact the others if he asks, but I assume I'm out of the picture as of dinner tomorrow night."

Nick purses his lips. His expression is indulgent. "Your input has only just begun, Stella. Aiden wants a reliable support person who understands the community and has the lay of the land."

Her eyes are closed. Her feet are propped on a footstool. Her mug of tea has cooled in her hands. "I'm doubtful, but would my occasional consultation with Aiden bother you?"

"Bother me how?"

"You understand what I mean." She blushes despite herself.

"Be more explicit."

"Okay. Okay." She swallows. "Does my periodic involvement with a former high school sweetheart give you any cause for concern?"

"Concern?"

She could slap him or kiss him but is uncertain regarding the more effective option. "Does the possibility of me working with Aiden make you jealous, Nick?"

His voice is tender. He's not teasing her anymore. "Not in the least." He reaches for her hand. "I've met Rosemary. She is Aiden's dearest love, regardless of her challenges." He leers at her when she opens her eyes. "Rosemary is not his *first* love, but she's his number one now. I'm not threatened." His grip tightens. "Besides, the time to upgrade the water system has arrived, no matter what happens with the bank. We'll be partners. You'll never be rid of me. What do you say?"

She reaches out to run her fingers across the stubble on his face. His long-term commitment has not escaped her notice, but she chooses to focus on her sister. The topic is less emotional. "Trixie must get a vote, but she won't give a rat's ass as long as her cheques arrive every month." Stella will accept his declaration, no matter how reluctant she is to believe he wants to commit to an involvement with a cranky old broad like her. "Okay. If you're sure. Let's call it a night. Big day tomorrow."

****

The early morning light is dim through rain-splattered windows as Stella makes her way to the big kitchen on the main floor. Sleep did not come easy, and she has left Nick to purr with rhythmic steadiness while she lights a fire in the living room and puts coffee on to perk. There won't be much to be done in the yard today although the weather is expected to improve by noon. Eve can clean bathrooms and showers while Paul completes high priority equipment maintenance with Nick.

Within the hour, Nick rumbles down the stairs. He sits at the table, sips his coffee from a mug large enough to hold two cups, and gawks at her over the rim. "You appear mighty fine this morning. Good sleep?"

She replies to his expression with the best argument she can dig up at a moment's notice. "I look crappy, and no, I barely slept a wink. You, on the other hand, rumbled through the night—a sound resembling the water pump we *should* install." She is attired in grey sweat pants and a sweat shirt emblazoned with the logo for Acadia University, in Nova Scotia's Annapolis Valley. Both pieces are grubby. She needs to shower.

"We will be the proud owners of a new pump before the week is over. The plumbing contractor told me the parts arrive today and installation is Friday. He has the proper filters and will be finished by the weekend."

Spinning around from the toaster, she bursts out, "You sneak! You were bound and determined to fix the water no matter what happened. You never said a word."

"No." His voice mocks her response. "I asked if I could invest and you insisted you wanted to get the money from the bank. You caught a murderer for your efforts, but not much cash. Correct?"

She sighs. Despite her instinct to rebuke his advances as they relate to the business, she is grateful for both his input and his involvement. She knows she couldn't run the place without him. Their arrangement is a healthy one, but she's taking a chance. If their personal relationship falls apart, he will still be invested in the park.

"You are a good man, Nick Cochran." She swallows her pride—hard—and trundles across the kitchen in her flip flops and baggy clothes. Her kiss grazes his hairline as she plunks a piece of cooled toast on his plate and turns toward her apartment. "I'm off to jump in the shower before the worker bees arrive. Try to keep them busy with breakfast until I get back."

She lets the hot water wash away any fragments of doubt clinging to her. The park is poised for a successful season. She has great staff. Nick is a fine man. Trixie is cooperative, at least. She can ask for little more.

Patted dry and with her unruly short hair still wet, she drags on a pair of clean jeans and an oversized pink cotton shirt before she pads downstairs to the kitchen. When she rounds the corner, she's greeted by Eve and Paul in unison. "Good morning, Stella."

Paul adds, "Slept in, did you?"

"Listen, mister, I was up well before dawn. You never mind."

"Great day for a staff meeting, what with the rain." Eve butters her toast and sips her tea.

"Alice, are you here?"

"Are you serious? Alice would never go home, given the opportunity." Paul munches as he talks.

As Stella prepares to respond, Alice scoots into the office, a sheaf of messages in her hand. "Hi everyone. I'll return for the staff meeting, Stella, but we need to review these reservation requests."

"What's up?" Stella moves toward a kitchen chair and sits.

"There are five units who want to stay for two weeks. They asked to be together, but I can't find five sites connected for the whole fourteen days. I want you to assess moving a rig or two. At least one camper needs some persuasion to make the arrangement work."

"We'll figure out the logistics, Alice. Don't worry. I need to take a run around the park after lunch, to meet with a few of our seasonals who were involved in the Lorraine Young investigation. If we need to move a camper, I'll talk with them."

"Good morning! Good morning! How are the troops today?" Duke Powell appears beside Alice in the doorway to the kitchen. He and Kiki are decked out in coordinated clear rain coats with multi-coloured polka dots. Kiki's hood is still up. Her nose is her one exposed feature.

"Nice to see you, Duke. Get out of those wet coats, you two. Don't drip on the floor."

Eve responds to Stella's remark. She reaches for Kiki, disgruntled when Eve grabs her instead of Alice. Duke peels off his rain jacket and unfastens Kiki's as well.

The dog squirms and whimpers until Alice drops the papers on the end of the table and removes her from Eve's grasp. "Kiki and I will go tidy the office. Yell when the meeting starts. Come on, little one. I bet there's a treat for you in my purse."

"I'll bring your messages." Eve tags along behind.

"Pour yourself a cup of coffee, Duke. Toast is still warm in the oven. Once everybody's settled, we'll get the staff back in here." Nick leans forward and meets Stella's eyes.

He's starting to act like an owner, and the behaviour is fine with her. But today, the meeting doesn't involve the park. She wants to close the chapter on Lorraine's murder. The whole ordeal has been unbearably difficult and unsettling, but her staff has come together. She is grateful.

"Okay? Is everyone here? Good." She gazes around the table. Nick, Eve, and Paul are attired in park T-shirts. Nick's is neon green. Paul and Eve happened to choose orange today. If the fog doesn't lift soon, at least they'll be easy to find. Alice holds Kiki, who chews on a piece of rawhide with unbridled enthusiasm. Her little paws clutch Alice's fingers. The initial silence enhances the tick of the kitchen clock and the smack of Kiki's lips. Five expectant faces watch her.

"Yesterday, Ruby Wilson, the manager of the Savings and Loan, was arrested for the murder of Lorraine. Her brother, Carmen Wilson, was also arrested. I took part in Ruby's interview with Aiden. The details aren't public, but I expect there will be charges."

"What the hell did Lorraine ever do to Ruby?" Duke is the first to comment.

"That's part of the investigation." She gazes around the table. "You folks understand. I want to express my appreciation though. Whether it was the numerous times Alice and Eve covered for me, or how you, Duke, and you, Paul, worked on the search to find our friend. We were a team and I am forever grateful."

Alice continues to hold Kiki's chew stick as she comments. "This could happen again, Stella, where Detective North needs your help."

"Let's hope this was an isolated incident, Alice. One murder in a town the size of Shale Harbour is enough." She studies each member of her crew in turn. "Our discussions are confidential. The story will be in the papers in a couple of days. Your confidence is appreciated until then." She stands. "Alice, you wanted to reorganize those reservations. Off to work, everyone. The rain has begun to let up, and the fog has lifted."

"Yes, Stella. I can book five trailers into adjoining sites, as they requested, if we ask one camper to move three lots south of where she's currently set up. I'm worried because this lady is here alone. Her husband brought the trailer out, but he won't be back for another week."

Stella glances across the room toward Nick who has rinsed his cup and retrieved his work boots. She knows he heard Alice's request. "You talk to her. We can move her unit with the old truck. Tell me where and when."

"I guess I need to make a visit to which lot, Alice?"

"She's right in the middle of Level Two, on the left—forty-five."

"Alright. A couple of phone calls and then I'll take a run around the park."

As Alice enters the office with Kiki under her arm, Stella turns to Nick once more. "I'll call Trixie and Aiden. We can visit and put this whole business behind us. I noticed someone went to Lorraine's trailer yesterday. Paul said he saw a For Sale sign. I assume her estate lawyer wants the unit sold before next year's rental deposit is due, or they'll need to move it into storage somewhere."

"Supper with Aiden and Trixie sounds fine. We should be able to relocate the rig from lot forty-five, too."

"Okay. See you at lunch time." His hand brushes her shoulder as he leaves.

****

"Trixie, please. It's her sister, Stella." Stella is caught off guard when she does not hear Trixie's voice at the end of the line.

"Good morning. Trixie Kirk here. How may I help you?"

"Didn't the other woman tell you your sister was on the phone?"

"Hi, Stella. Nope. She won't cover for me, even when I take a trip to the can. Leaves the line open and the receiver on my desk. What's up?"

"A dinner invitation. The arrests are processed in the Lorraine Young case and I hoped we could get together and debrief. I'll call Aiden as well."

"Yes, there's been two arrests."

"How did you find out?"

"Moyer turned up here bright and early to confer with Ken and Jewel. They were relieved when he left. They couldn't wait to blab." She continues without so much as a breath. "The plant has fresh shrimp. Came right off the boat at dawn. I'll get a mess cleaned and we can grill them. Okay?"

"Fabulous. Come over when you're done work. I'll make biscuits and coleslaw. We'll cook a good old-fashioned feed."

Next on her list is Aiden. She hopes he plans to spend another night in Shale Harbour but expects he's soon to move back to Port Ephron. She calls the local detachment first and is pleased to discover he is, in fact, still in town. "Detective North, please. Stella Kirk here."

"Hi, Stella. I expected to call you before day's end. I wanted to buy you a cup of coffee and debrief. I need two hours to finish paperwork here and then back to the port."

Stella tries not to sound disappointed. "I called to invite you for a feed of fresh barbecued shrimp tonight. I asked Trixie and hoped the four of us could go over the case one last time. Any chance you might stay?"

"Sounds wonderful, although I can't be late, since I promised Rosemary today is my final day here. She expects me to sleep in my own bed tonight."

"Well, thank God for the long days. You will come?"

"You don't expect me to refuse fresh shrimp, do you? I'll be there."

****

The afternoon turns out to be gorgeous in the way a June day right after a good rain can be. Blossoms, flowers, leaves, and even the grass, seem to be clean and fresh. Earthy salt smells fill her nostrils. Stella speeds around the park on the little golf cart. Her first stop is at Marnie Firth's place. She booked her lot for a month. Stella hopes she's flexible with her exact location. If so, Nick will move her to a different spot for the next week or two.

Marnie sits beside her trailer, a glass of cola on a plastic side table. Her lounge chair is positioned to take full advantage of the sun. A detective novel is open in her hands. "Why, Stella Kirk, to what do I owe the pleasure on such a gorgeous afternoon?"

Stella climbs off the golf cart and makes her pitch. For a moment, as she assesses the annoyed expression that crosses Marnie's face, she worries she'll be forced to leave well enough alone.

Thankfully, the frown disappears as the camper nods. "I guess my exact location doesn't matter in the long run. My husband will find me when he returns from the job he took. The sun will shine on the new spot the same as this one. Nick and Paul will help, right?"

Success. In the end, the move is arranged for the next morning. Alice will be able to reserve the five lots in a row for a Friday start date.

As usual, Mildred is installed on her rattletrap deck. Her lemonade, as she refers to her concoction, sits close at hand. "Time for a drink, Stella? I made fresh."

Stella perches on the edge of the rickety contraption. "It must be five o'clock somewhere, eh Mildred? Thanks, but no thanks." She nods toward the golf cart. "I'm driving."

"What's on your mind, Stella? No more dead bodies, I hope."

"Nope. I came to give you information though. Detective North asked me to tell you arrests were made and any relevant details will no doubt be in the paper in a couple of days."

Mildred doesn't mince her words. "Who hurt her, Stella? Who killed the poor girl?"

Tears well in Mildred's eyes. She misjudged the old lady's capacity to empathize. "They arrested Ruby Wilson and her brother, Carmen. Detective North says additional details will be available in due course."

Mildred takes a quick sip of her drink while she regains her composure. "Are you a letter from the government? Don't be so formal. What happened? Did you figure it out by yourself, or did the cop help?"

"I won't say any more, my friend. I still must drop in and see Rob and Sally as well as Buddy McGarvey. On top of the notifications, I expect company for supper. I'll tell you the details when I'm given the go ahead, Mildred. You take care, now."

In a sudden show of affection, Mildred pats Stella on the arm. "Thanks for tellin' me."

Stella nods before jumping back on her cart to continue her rounds.

The Blacks' responses are the same as Mildred's. Buddy is no different. They are each pleased the arrests were made but want Stella to provide more information. Not today.

****

Trixie arrives at six, lugging a bucket of shrimp on crushed ice, cleaned and ready to hit the grill. "Anybody home?"

The screen door to the veranda slaps shut and her sister's heels click their way through the great room, into the big kitchen. Stella peers into the bucket as the smell of the sea rises to meet her face. "Man alive, those are beauties. Nick has the barbeque fired up. Aiden called a minute ago. He's on his way." She stops in her gush of enthusiasm and kisses Trixie on the cheek. "Thanks, kid."

"For the shrimp?"

"No, you idiot. For your help over at Ruby's the other night."

"Did we ever get the money, or what?"

"Not yet. The paperwork might catch up to us one of these days, but Nick has arranged for the new pump and filtration system. He will be our partner if we decide to forego the loan and not pay him back."

"Do I still get my cheque every month?"

"Yes, of course." Stella crows. Trixie's predictability shines through. "Nick becomes a ten percent shareholder and we'll each own forty-five. Can you live with those arrangements?"

"Tell me where to sign, Stella. Hi, Aiden. When did you sneak in?"

"While you two discussed park finances. Where's Nick? I brought beer. Can't eat shrimp without beer."

The evening roared with success. Aiden gave them as many details as he could ethically share. Trixie re-told the story about their visit to Ruby's and exaggerated as only Trixie could do. They raised a glass in salute to Lorraine, whose death served to teach them how seeing is not necessarily believing.

"Somebody put a For Sale sign on her trailer. I don't imagine the place will last long." Nick nurses his second beer.

"I should arrange a meeting with the estate lawyer and find out the asking price."

"Aiden! What a great idea." Stella raises her glass again, this time to Aiden. "To old friends."

"Speaking of old friends, Trixie, did you get an invitation to Jacob Painter's wedding?"

"Didn't check the mail today, but I'm expecting one." She sips her wine.

"I told Cavelle, when we were out for coffee, how I can't imagine the three of them letting Baby Brother tie the knot."

"Who are these people?" When it comes to the locals, Aiden always wants more details.

"You must remember the Painter sisters—not to be confused with the Pointer Sisters, who are much more famous." The comparison strikes her funny every time. "The oldest, Opal, went to school with us." She directs her attention toward Trixie. "And you and the middle sister, Cavelle, are close, right?"

Trixie nods.

"There's a third sister, Hester, who never went to school. Their mother died when she gave birth to Jacob," Stella continues. "And the girls raised him. Then their father died when the boy was eight. I cannot believe those three women will step aside and allow him to marry."

About the Author

L. P. Suzanne Atkinson was born in New Brunswick, Canada and lived in both Alberta and Quebec before settling in Nova Scotia in 1991. She has degrees from Mount Allison, Acadia, and McGill universities. Suzanne spent her professional career in the fields of mental health and home care. She also owned and operated, with her husband, both an antique business and a construction business for more than twenty-five years.

Suzanne writes about the unavoidable consequences of relationships. She uses her life and work experiences to weave stories that cross many boundaries.

She and her husband, David Weintraub, make Bedford, Nova Scotia their home.

Email – lpsa.books@eastlink.ca
Website – http://lpsabooks.wix.com/lpsabooks#
Facebook – L. P. Suzanne Atkinson – Author

Watch for:

Didn't Stand a Chance: A Stella Kirk Mystery #2

The second in a series of cozy mysteries, set in Shale Cliffs RV Park
Coming in the spring / summer of 2020

CPSIA information can be obtained
at www.ICGtesting.com
Printed in the USA
BVHW082007250319
543613BV00004B/924/P

9 780995 869646